To Sleep,
Perchance to
Scream

To Sleep, Perchance to

Scream

"The Rebirth of Adamm"

by Stone Wallace

BearManor Media

2021

To Sleep, Perchance to Scream: "The Rebirth of Adamm"

© 2021 by Stone Wallace

All rights reserved.

Published in the United States of America by:

BearManor Media
1317 Edgewater Dr #110
Orlando FL 32804

bearmanormedia.com

Printed in the United States.

Typesetting and layout by John Teehan

ISBN—978-1-62933-680-0

*With Love to My Wife and
Soul Mate Cindy who has remained
my strength and inspiration throughout
my various creative journeys.*

And Special Thanks to a man whose passion,
generosity and personal kindness has allowed
many authors to achieve their dreams, and
with whom I have enjoyed a long professional
association—but more importantly a person
I am privileged to call a friend:
Mr. Ben Ohmart.

"And when, finally, I sank into slumber, it was only to rush at once into a world of phantasms…"

– "The Premature Burial"
Edgar Allen Poe

"And the three insurgents were banished from the land by the sea/Forever separated from their forms/To be consumed wholly by the Great Cloud that descended from the Heavens/And He Who Rules All forbade them ever to return."

– "Origin of the Alpha Traveler"
Sir Ronald Hyatt

"But in my dreams you always come around."

– "Dreamin'"
Cliff Richard

Prologue

Descent Into Nightmare

THROUGH THE DARK

Conscious only of the total being. Singular.

You are propelled, effortlessly, through the abyss of black.

Deep and all-consuming.

Seemingly infinite.

So very cold.

You are aware of rapid movement yet experience no real sense of advancement.

There is silence. Complete.

Your senses are numb.

Your mind gradually becomes devoid of all thought.

Oblivion defined.

Travel on through the endless black tunnel of eternity.

Progression…

Minutes?

Hours?

Merely a millisecond.

A blink in the fabric of time.

You continue onward.

Slowly, renewed awareness dawns.

Individuality takes on a bold new meaning as the significance of your being amplifies.

Not embracing the confines of ego but the freedom of existence.

You are one.

You have become the most important element in this strange universe.

And as one you must face destiny—

Alone.

Travel on.

Hardly have you begun to adapt when there is a rumbling—ever so slight—that succeeds in stimulating your higher consciousness.

Your senses have returned.

Each sense is greatly enhanced.

Acceptance is forgotten.

You now feel relief.

Because—

You are enveloped in a blanket of comforting warmth.

A broken glow of shifting multi-colored light filters through the black, filling your eyes and encasing the spirit.

You, alone, are being thrust through the void.

Escape from infinity?

The melodious rumbling increases to a thundering crescendo.

Awareness plateaus.

You have broken through.

INTO THE LIGHT

And a new world unfolds before you.

A strange, abstract world illuminated by bright, blinding, pulsating colors and majestic trees boasting the most magnificent foliage.

A world of... silent sounds.

You stand before it, awed.

But gradually you realize it must be faced—

Alone.

You are hesitant.

Brilliant hues of every color in the spectrum—and colors beyond the imagination—stream upward from the milky mist that blankets this surreal landscape.

Your eyes feast upon this wondrous vista:

And you take your first step forward.

A step that touches no surface but lifts you above the swirling mist.

Advancement.

THE JOURNEY

You are the explorer.

Traveling *alone* through a land where the sky blossoms in a colorful canvas.

Then—almost immediately the landscape inexplicably shifts... transforms. You now find yourself in an environment where the trees are no longer trees... but rather bent and twisted shadows. Where the hills that stand in the distance are not hills... only black, ill-formed protrusions. Blemishes.

Where an entirely new definition has been given to nature.

You find that you are unsure to go on…

Until a strange new awareness embraces you. Encourages you.

Comforting in its absurdity.

You belong.

This world is of your own making.

Yet do you master?

OF MASTERS AND SLAVES

Present dread:

Dominated in your own kingdom.

Neither Heaven nor Hell.

Purgatory?

Where no man rules.

Where no man serves.

A mere existence. Nothing more.

Bizarre, questioning thoughts surge through your brain as you continue your journey.

Unsure of your ultimate destination.

Unsure of distance already made.

Floating footsteps transport you—

To where?

A wall of pinkish fog suddenly rises before you.

Undulating, like the restless tide.

You stop.

Wait with a blending of anticipation and apprehension.

…The rolling pink fog opens, parting like some ethereal gate.

And it beckons you forward.

Yet you remain motionless for the moment that quickly passes into time.

Until…

You advance.

THE ENCOUNTER

Disappointment.

The answers to your questions have not been revealed.

Because…

What lies beyond is just emptiness.

Lost… frightened… angry, you open your mouth to cry out your fear and frustration…

When "they" rise up from the swirling ground mist.

Misshapen, shadowy forms.

Ill-defined, faceless beings that slowly claw away the thick clouds of mist that cling to their emerging bodies like cobwebs.

They face you, mouthing silent sounds—but do not move toward you.

For that must be up to you.

But you sense danger and resist.

…Until—an urging beyond your control begins to propel you forward.

They wait. Motionlessly.

Silently.

You attempt to halt your progress as your eyes squint into the mist to determine what precisely these figures are…

And the gnarled hands reach forward to claim you.

The salivating mouths widen into gaping maws and howl horrid sounds.

Creatures too hideous for any sane mind to comprehend leap forward, their motions slow and oddly graceful.

In your panic you find your own strength and break away from the influence that compels you toward them, a desperate scream lodged in your throat.

More of the shadowy beings rise up from the mist.

They are intent on preventing your escape.

But overwhelmed with the instinct of survival, you maneuver and manage to keep free of their grasp.

You are uncertain of reaching safety, but realize that your only chance comes with returning to where you first arrived.

If only you can find your way!

Still more of the creatures appear.

You are desperate.

But so are they!

They will not permit you to get away.

You glide hurriedly through the mist.

Confusion sets in as you are unsure of where you are meant to go.

And there is a powerful tug at your leg.

You twist.

Pull!

But the clawed, clammy hand grasping you is too strong.

The creatures, arms outstretched, surround you.

You close your eyes, tightly, and wait for the inevitable.

Fast becoming mercifully numb to your fate.

All vestiges of fear are gone.

And...

All is still.

ESCAPE

Glorious silence and a deep feeling of peace overcome you.

Slowly, ever so slowly, you venture to open your eyes.

Once again you are traveling through the tunnel, surrounded by black emptiness.

Only this time you seem to be descending.

You are aware of the speed.

Again, you remain oblivious of the time…

As you plummet deeper into the pit.

Deeper!

Faster!

There is a powerful body rush as you feel yourself being sucked into the funnel of—

Reality?

More darkness.

Motion ceases.

You quickly open your eyes to greet whatever now awaits you…

Seven-year-old Krissie Carver shot bolt upright in bed, screaming… screaming…

Part One

A City Somewhere In Western Canada

1978

1 Night Call

THE DROP-LEAF DIGITS on his alarm clock had just flipped to 3:06 a.m. when the telephone on the bedside table sounded its first ring. Lawrence Carver, resplendent in his expensive tuxedo, a glass of expensive French champagne raised to his lips, had just been ceremoniously handed the vice-presidency in his public relations firm when the vision dissolved into stardust and he regrettably found himself back to a hazy sort of reality, snuggled in bed with one of his two pillows lying folded over on the floor.

His co-workers' smiling faces. Their sincere applause, congratulatory slaps on the back and hearty handshakes. The overwhelming feeling of achievement, not to mention relief and acceptance, associated with long sought-after success.

And damn it, it had all been a dream.

The phone rang a second time. But Lawrence remained stiffly in his position under the sheets, quietly defiant, disappointed that his beautiful fantasy had come to such an abrupt, unsatisfying conclusion.

On the third ring, after muttering a few choice expletives, Lawrence rotated his pajama-clad body and fumbled for the phone. Clearing a layer of phlegm from his throat, he snapped up the receiver.

"Yeah, hello," he rasped.

"Lawrence, this is Maureen." The caller was his ex-wife, and she sounded frantic.

Maureen… as if it was necessary for her to identify herself. Even at this ungodly hour the shrillness in her voice was instantly recognizable.

Lawrence's acknowledgement was a dry cough. He propped himself up on an elbow, and, after flicking on the bedside lamp, reached for his pack of cigarettes and lighted one.

"Lawrence, are you there?"

"Yeah Maureen," he breathed, succeeding in his effort to sound annoyed by this unwelcome intrusion. "I haven't hung up yet."

Maureen ignored his sarcasm and spoke to the point. "Lawrence, it's Krissie. She's had another one of her nightmares."

Lawrence didn't respond. He drew heavily on his smoke and exhaled slowly.

"Did you hear what I said?" Maureen said impatiently.

Lawrence's tone remained flat. "I heard. How is she?"

"How do you think she is?" Maureen's voice dropped to just above a whisper. "She's absolutely petrified."

"Well," Lawrence said, unable to stifle a yawn, "you tell her that you spoke to Daddy and that he said everything's all right and there's nothing to be afraid of."

"Lawrence," Maureen was getting that patented irritated tone in her voice, "I really think she needs you here."

Lawrence hesitated; then he spoke slowly, and deliberately. The thoughts that coursed through his brain were much harsher than his measured words. "Maureen, it's after three in the morning and in five hours I'm supposed to be at a breakfast meeting with Tom Wittmeyer…an account that Sanborn has promised to all but demote me over if I screw up." He took a breath before he continued. "Hell, be reasonable. I can't run over every time Krissie has a little nightmare."

"Little nightmare?" Maureen sounded almost incredulous. "Lawrence, it's the fourth night in a row where she's gotten up like this! I think this has gone beyond being just a 'bad dream.'"

"So, what am I supposed to do?"

"Just you being here—for Krissie. Please."

Lawrence sighed; then he forcefully stubbed his cigarette in the ashtray. "Okay, dammit, okay. I'll be over as soon as I can."

He was just about to slam the receiver back into the cradle when he heard Maureen murmur, "Thanks."

Lawrence could usually complete the drive from his downtown apartment to the fashionable duplex at the other end of town in about thirty minutes. This early morning, though, with virtually no traffic to compete with, it took somewhat longer. Lawrence couldn't fool himself that it wasn't deliberate. After all, it wasn't necessary for him to steer his Volvo into the 24-7 self-serve gas bar and pump a few gallons into the tank when the fuel indicator told him he wasn't even half empty. He also would have made much better time had he followed his usual route rather than avoiding the detour that would have saved him a good quarter hour. To aid in settling his mood Lawrence switched on the radio and pumped down on the selector buttons to pick up some classical music, or better yet, early jazz, settling on a Bert Kaempfert instrumental. He acknowledged the song with an ironic smile: *That Happy Feeling.*

It was a just past four a.m. when Lawrence pulled in front of the front-lighted two-story duplex, now outwardly asking himself what the hell was he doing here? He flicked off the ignition but remained seated in the car, indulging himself to another cigarette. He remembered something about a recent city ordinance that prohibited motor vehicles from being parked on residential streets after a certain hour. Was that law still in effect, he wondered; then, in the next instant, realized it didn't matter a damn either way. He wasn't planning to stay that long. Just long enough for him to be the concerned, comforting Daddy; perhaps to exchange a few barbed words with Maureen (since the break-up cynicisms had become an integral part of their conversational pattern).

Lawrence finally pulled himself from the car, closing the door behind him with just a bit more force than was necessary. He tossed aside his cigarette after drawing a long, final puff and paused, taking a slow, wandering look along this residential street. Because of the early hour Lawrence found himself briefly caught up in the prevailing atmosphere. The neighborhood was quiet, peaceful, and particularly picturesque at this time of day. A thin blanket of dew covered the neatly-manicured lawns, glistening in the deep blue darkness like a billion tiny light bulbs illuminating a miniature city. The air was fresh and crisp, too, unlike the steady diet of crud and car exhaust Lawrence fed his lungs by living in the heart of the city. As he inflated his chest with a generous breath of the clean, moist morning air, Lawrence once again experienced those familiar twinges of resentment: Resentment at having to give all this up.

Sure, maybe he did the pressing for the divorce, but Maureen drove him to it, what with her endless nagging and parade of neuroses. By God, he had no other choice but to leave her, to hold onto what was left of his sanity. What's more, he could never remember Maureen putting up much of an argument when he told her of his decision. Oh, she shed the few customary tears, and there was some discussion—not a hell of a lot, though. But damn it, if the marriage ever meant anything at all to her, she could have at least put some honest effort into saving it.

Yet on reflection none of this should have come as a surprise to him. Maureen's family was a strong argument for those who claim mental dysfunction is hereditary. The family album stood as verifiable proof. The old man, "Buckskin" Frank Hanover, was, to put it generously, a case study in eccentricity; perhaps more accurately: an example of early senility. Lawrence never rightly knew his age but figured "Buckskin" must be somewhere in his early to mid-60s. Always with his mouth in motion but with nothing of value ever expressed. In all the years Lawrence had been acquainted with the family (too damn many) he was sure he'd never once heard the old man utter a sentence that was even remotely intelligent. There was Flora, the old lady, who shriveled up and died in 1976. He remembered her as a mousy personality who, in contrast to her loudmouthed husband, barely squeaked out a complete sentence at any urging. Brother Franklin, an irresponsible overage juvenile, forever in debt and always just a few steps ahead of the law with his gambling and other vices. And yet there was a wife and God knows how many kids (legitimate and otherwise) in the picture. Lastly there was Maureen, who had developed and nurtured her own unique set of odd and neurotic traits, most of which took only a couple years of married life for Lawrence to discover.

Lawrence's back teeth clamped together. The feeling had intensified. The same feeling he'd had those long months before the divorce. The vice grip that tightened around his gut whenever he was guilt-trapped into seeing his ex-wife.

Slowly, but with deliberate steps, he started up the walkway, yanking another cigarette from his pack and thrusting it between his lips, though not lighting it.

The porch light switched on. When Lawrence was halfway up the walk, the front door swung open and a pathetically slim, blue-clad figure stepped outside. His ex-wife, Maureen, her body wrapped snugly in the fluffy periwinkle housecoat Lawrence had given her either their second or third Christmas together... the housecoat Lawrence was positive he had never seen her wear before.

Maureen stood slightly hunched over, her broomstick arms (which perfectly matched her spindly legs) folded tightly across her no-chest.

"Oh Lawrence, thank God you're here!" As usual, she was stretching it in the near-hysteria department.

Lawrence came up next to her, but he remained silent, his features locked in a frown. His heavy-lidded eyes briefly took in the faintly tremulous form standing before him and he once again was reminded of just how unattractive Maureen had become. The jaundiced coloring produced by the muted glow of the overhead porch light did nothing to improve her appearance.

Maureen said, "I finally got Krissie to calm down, but she's terrified of going back to sleep."

Lawrence scratched the stubble on his chin and glanced up at two moths that were fluttering around the circular light fixture.

"Did you give her some warm milk?" he asked blandly.

"Hot chocolate, but she wouldn't drink it." She spoke abruptly. "Lawrence, she really wants to see you. As a matter of fact, knowing that you were coming over is the one thing that's cheered her up a little."

Lawrence nodded absently.

He blew out a breath and said, "It might be after four in the a.m., but I sure could use a drink."

Maureen eyed him—with a knowing look.

"But I put on a pot of coffee."

Lawrence flashed a quick, sardonic smile. "Keeps me awake." He brushed past his ex-wife and stepped inside the house, slipping off his shoes, then taking off of his university-crested jacket and hanging it on the doorknob.

Maureen, still standing outside, experienced a shiver, frightening in its familiarity. She could remember Lawrence doing the same thing the last time he was over, just about a month ago. He wouldn't see his daughter until he first downed a straight scotch.

No, it's nothing, Maureen reassured herself, quickly becoming embarrassed at her thought. *Nothing at all.* I brought him all the way over here. He's entitled to a drink.

She ignored the fact that once more she was attempting to justify her ex-husband's behavior.

Lawrence entered the living room and took a slow look around. He was hoping to be critical—but the place was immaculate! The green shag carpeting freshly shampooed, the pile feathery soft and slightly moist under his feet. The furniture was almost geometrically positioned and the wood and chrome pieces polished to perfection. Perhaps it was just his present mood but Lawrence could never remember the house looking this neat and orderly when he was around. As a matter of fact, while they were still "blissfully" wed his only real complaint against Maureen was that she was never much of a housekeeper.

He tightened his jaw to keep his resentment in check.

Now he wanted that drink more than ever.

He crossed over to the sectional bar at the corner of the room, sitting down on a stool and hooking his feet around the tubular legs.

Maureen came inside the house and walked behind the bar. Her arms were still folded, only now a cigarette hung loosely between her fingers. To Lawrence that dangling smoke really completed the picture of a middle-aged neurotic.

As Maureen took out two highball glasses and placed them on the bar, Lawrence eyed her curiously. Maureen—the old Maureen he was once married to—never drank. Hardly ever. Maybe a glass of wine at a social gathering that she would nurse throughout the evening. She claimed to have an aversion to alcohol. Of course, Lawrence had a pretty good idea why she was tipping the bottle now: to try, in her own Maureen Hanover way, to make him feel guilty; to remind him once again of the difficult time she was having, with a young daughter to raise— and a nightmare prone one at that! Lawrence's hands tightened into fists. His back straightened like a rod and he could feel a pounding pressure start to build at his temples. Well, goddamn it, it was not going to work. She sure as hell wasn't going to get to him that way. She drove him to the divorce. She never gave a damn about the marriage.

"Lawrence," Maureen said quietly, pouring the scotch into a shot glass and emptying it into her tumbler, repeating the action for her ex, "Krissie's waiting to see you."

Lawrence pretended not to hear and instead removed two coasters from their piano-shaped holder. He placed one coaster in front of himself and slid the other across to Maureen.

"Lawrence?"

"Look, I'm here, aren't I? Just let me have my drink first, please." He pushed a hand into his trousers pocket, closing his fingers around the key ring, and squeezed, almost relishing the quick surge of pain.

"Well, you *do* plan on seeing her?"

Lawrence squeezed his hand harder.

"Naw," his tone was brutally sarcastic. "I just drove all the way across town at four in the morning 'cause I was thirsty and the bars were closed."

Now it was Maureen's turn to react, though her emotion was kept inward. She'd made a vow earlier not to let Lawrence upset her. She reminded herself that Krissie was her main concern.

"Lawrence," she said, her voice subdued, "can't we call some kind of a truce, just for now?"

Lawrence took down his drink in one swallow and slid the glass back over to her (a dismissive movement with which Maureen was all-too-familiar). He eyed her drearily for a moment, then swung off the bar stool and headed for the stairs.

Krissie lay still on her back in the middle of the bed, the goose down comforter pulled up to her chin. She looked unusually small, younger than her seven years. Her skin was pallid and slight semi-circles had formed under her eyes. She may have looked asleep, but she was not. She had been fighting sleep for the last two hours; every time she felt she was going to doze off she would shake herself awake.

She never wanted to go to sleep again.

Lawrence stood as a framed silhouette in the doorway, the corners of his mouth pulled up in a strained attempt at a smile.

"Hi sweetheart," he said.

Krissie's eyes popped open at recognition of her father's voice. Her unsettled expression immediately gave way to an ear-to-ear smile.

"Daddy!" she exulted, scrambling to her knees and extending her arms to welcome his hug.

Lawrence walked slowly over, embraced his daughter almost tentatively, and sat down on the edge of the bed. Maureen, nearing the top of the stairs when she heard her daughter's excited whoop, had rushed over to the bedroom and stood quietly, smiling, outside the open door. She'd watched an ecstatic Krissie practically leap at her daddy, grabbing him and hugging him tightly around the waist. But Maureen's smile faded as she saw Lawrence hesitate for just a moment too long. He seemed unsure of how to respond to his daughter's affection.

Lawrence turned in Maureen's direction, his face registering no expression.

Maureen grimaced, turned away and went back downstairs.

* * *

"Damn it, she's your daughter!"

Maureen was finding it increasingly difficult to keep both her voice and her temper in check.

Lawrence was back on the stool. The fingers of his right hand were rubbing the padded arm rest on the bar. "I know," he said miserably, "I know."

Maureen poured herself another drink, a double. Lawrence knew he was in no position to pass judgment this time.

Maureen said, "Be honest, Lawrence. Is it because of *us?* Because of *me?* A reminder that you'd rather not have? She loves you, y'know."

"I love her," Lawrence said, but the words were halted and the tone not altogether convincing. He took a fast swallow of his drink; then mumbled, "Why'd you have to be standing there?" He finished his scotch but his hand continued to tightly grip the glass. "And no, dammit, it isn't because of—you."

"Then tell me what it is," Maureen pleaded. "It *is* something."

Lawrence spit out a quick breath. He was sure Maureen knew the reason. She had to. The only problem was that it was so difficult for either of them to acknowledge, let alone accept.

He pulled away from the bar. "You told me to be honest," he blurted. "Maybe you should be the one who's honest."

Maureen's eyes took on an intense, questioning look.

"What are you talking about?" she said, her words coming slowly.

Lawrence eyed her hard, as if trying to penetrate her brain with words he was unable to articulate.

Suddenly the color looked to drain from Maureen's face.

"You don't mean…" The words felt heavy in her mouth and she, too, was unable to speak them.

Lawrence turned his head away.

"Oh God, it—it can't be," Maureen mumbled through the open fingers of her hand. "Lawrence, what happened… that was *two years ago.*"

"Just under two," he corrected for really no good reason.

Maureen reached for her pack of cigarettes on the bar and with a slight tremor in her fingers, she pulled one out. She jammed it into her mouth, fumbling to light it.

"I don't know what to say," she said, her voice unsteady. "I can't believe that you…"

"I'm sorry," Lawrence replied with a deliberate shrug.

"But—your own daughter?"

"Look," Lawrence said as he rubbed his fingers roughly alongside his temples, "don't think I'm proud of the way I feel. But I…" He couldn't finish.

"But Lawrence, just tell me why? Especially after all this time?"

Lawrence understood there could be no sensible explanation he could offer Maureen, and certainly not one that she would accept. He had to end this discussion—and fast. He had to put up some form of defense, however obvious it might be.

He coughed self-consciously and looked along the bar for the pack of matches with which to light his cigarette.

"Well, Krissie's nightmares," he said gently, trying to avoid the now-penetrating stare of his ex-wife and hoping to change the direction of the conversation. "What are we gonna do about them?"

Maureen could see only too well what Lawrence was trying to do. And in a way it pleased her… Hell, it really pleased her! But what's the use, she thought. She didn't share his vindictiveness. Why push it? Lawrence's stubbornness had always proved an impenetrable barrier.

"I think it would be a good idea if we took her to see Dr. LaFreniere," she suggested.

Lawrence lit his cigarette and drew deeply on it. It tasted good. In need, a friend indeed.

"You really think she needs a doctor?" he asked, breathing easier now that the outcome of where their talk had been headed had been sidelined.

"I don't know what to think," Maureen said tiredly. "But something's gotta be done. I can't figure it—apparently the exact same dream, four nights in a row."

"Yeah, well that is—strange," was about all that Lawrence could offer.

They shared a silence. However brief, they had actually conversed in a relatively civilized manner, no thrusts and parries. Of course, the reason wasn't difficult to understand—at least not to Lawrence: Maureen had uncovered a disturbing truth (perhaps one she'd already suspected), and if necessary could use that truth to her own advantage.

"Then we agree?" she said.

Lawrence merely nodded. He checked his wristwatch and decided it was time to go. He was tired and admittedly a little drunk. He still had that drive back into the city and had to somehow prepare himself for his important breakfast meeting.

Maureen spoke abruptly. "Can I count on your being there?"

Lawrence clenched a fist that he thrust into his trousers pocket. Bitch! Not only does she have him over a barrel, she's rolling it perilously close to the edge.

He rose from his stool. "Listen, I'll try." He paused, dragged quickly on the last of his smoke. "No, I'll—be there." He butted the cigarette into the ashtray.

* * *

Krissie was sitting up in her bed, rocking gently back and forth, staring blankly at the many kindergarten and school drawings that peppered the opposite wall of her room. A multi-colored display: there were pictures of fairy tale characters, of flowers, animals; there were a few that were her view of trips the family had taken when they were still a family. But on each end, set a fair distance apart from the rest, almost like big, comical ears sticking out of a head, there was a drawing of Mommy and a drawing of Daddy, each with cherry red, exaggerated smiles.

But Krissie wasn't concentrating on any of her pictures. She really wasn't focusing on anything in particular. She had started to hum, softly, and was rocking more vigorously.

The small (black?) object scurried across the top of the Cinderella comforter. Krissie's humming and rocking both ceased abruptly.

Her eyes scanned the bed carefully.

It was a spider. Not very large or threatening, but an icky eight-legged crawler nonetheless.

Krissie felt herself tensing as she watched it.

The spider stopped midway across the blanket, changed its direction, and scurried toward Krissie.

(*Go away, spider*)

Krissie's eyes contracted; they were focused directly on her tiny aggressor. The rest of her face tightened.

(*I don't like you*)

The spider kept coming, scurrying faster over the rises, almost as if in defiance of Krissie's thoughts.

The little girl's body had become unnaturally stiff. Her face was livid and slight beads of moisture glistened on her brow.

(*Go away*)

Krissie's eyes closed, and when she next opened her eyes they were like luminous gems, alive with a transcending energy.

(*Go away*)

And the spider stopped, dead. Its body crumpled, collapsing in on itself.

(*Go away*)

And it began to bubble…

…swell…

(*I SAID GO AWAY!*)

And the spider popped, spreading a small stain of jelly across her blanket.

Krissie loosened, relaxed. She again closed her eyes, and this time when she reopened them they had returned to their usual soft blue. She looked down to where the spider had been and gasped in surprise. She started to giggle, not understanding what had just happened, but it was comical nonetheless.

"Goodbye, spider."

2 The Think Tank

MAUREEN WAS BOTH PHYSICALLY and emotionally exhausted but she knew that sleep wouldn't come easily to her. Building anxieties were gnawing away at her mental state, which by this point had become as worn and frail as her thirty-eight-year-old body.

She was no stranger to dealing with acute anxiety. Her first experience had come when she was still in high school. She was sitting in biology class, not wholly attentive to the lecture being delivered, when, with no warning, she suddenly felt her head go light. Fear developed out of nowhere, enveloping her completely, causing her heart to take on a wild life of its own. She didn't know what was happening to her, but she had to get up... move around. "I'm going crazy," she mumbled aloud, and the terror that accompanied this thought was like nothing she had ever experienced before. The lecture continued, the attention of everyone in the class focused on Mr. Pomeranski, and Maureen had a frightening image of herself flipping out right there in the classroom and no one even noticing. She remembered fighting to gain control of her thoughts, which were not only becoming incoherent but were coming at her faster than she could process. This struggle, however, was the thread which attached itself to reality and provided her with something to hold onto. Let go, girl, and you'll slip over the edge. It seemed longer, but not a minute had passed before Lorna Hanks turned to her to ask her something, only to realize that Maureen was in some sort of distress. Lorna got the attention of Mr. Pomeranski, who could see that Maureen was not well and gave his permission for both girls to leave the class. Once outside the building, on the steps, after several good breaths of air, Maureen felt herself easing out of the attack, though she determined not to return to class to face the embarrassment she was sure to encounter. Lorna walked home with her, amusing herself by giving Maureen a detailed description of her colorless and panic-stricken appearance, which Maureen did not find humorous.

Maureen had almost managed to cast this incident from her mind—until another attack exactly one week later convinced her that she was indeed going crazy.

Private consultation with the family doctor revealed that Maureen was in no danger of losing her mind. Anxiety attacks were frightening but essentially harmless experiences, according to the doctor. The best cure, he explained, was simply to acknowledge what you were up against. Maureen was to learn from experience that understanding anxiety attacks neither lessened their frequency nor their severity.

Up until the divorce Maureen had found that she could combat the attacks without relying on any kind of crutch. Alone, and with the added responsibility of a child, she discovered that she could no longer depend on mere inner strength and found alcohol to be a most effective panacea. Although she could barely tolerate the taste, its benefits could not be denied.

At times it seemed that anxiety was always with her, as if melded into her being. But it remained beneath the surface, and alcohol helped to keep it there.

This was why Maureen found herself back at the bar, pouring another glass of scotch. She could feel her anxieties priming for a massive assault, and she was readying her defenses.

She felt herself starting to calm after only a couple of sips. To heighten the effect, to reach a state of total relaxation, she decided to take a bath.

Glass firmly in hand, she climbed up the stairs and first checked in on Krissie. She was grateful to find her asleep, but the slight twitching of her young body indicated to Maureen that it was not a sound sleep.

Maureen frowned. "My poor darling," she muttered.

She then went down the hallway to the bathroom, quietly closing the door behind her. She placed her drink on the vanity and turned on both the hot and cold faucets, carefully adjusting the temperature. She kept the pressure low so that it wouldn't disturb Krissie. Surface sleep or not, she needed her rest.

Maureen went over to the cupboard under the sink and removed a bath oil bead from its plastic container. She chose the Forest Pine scent, her favorite, but her pick was random. She dropped it into the tub and stood for just a moment, watching it dissolve.

As she disrobed before the mirror, she eyed her reflection critically. How was it possible for a close-to-forty-year-old woman, bone-thin, to still look flabby? Maureen pulled at the flesh that had loosened around her belly and thought about how far she'd fallen. Not that she was ever a pin-up queen, but at least her body had been toned, giving her spare figure a firm appearance. Now her skeletal frame remained unchanged but the tautness had long since gone, giving her, in her eyes, the shape of a sideshow freak.

Turning quickly away from the mirror, she turned off the faucets and took a tentative step into the bathwater. As usual, she had just missed the perfect temperature. This time the water was a trifle too hot. But it would soon cool sufficiently.

She reached for her drink and carefully lowered herself into the tub. Once her body was completely submerged beneath the scented surface, she settled into a kind of repose. The effects of the scotch, the warm water, and pleasant fragrance made for an incomparable soothing combination.

Regarding her glass of scotch with slightly blurred eyes, Maureen's thoughts once again focused on her ex. Before tonight she'd kept her drinking from him. Whenever he had come over, he'd go straight to the bar while she pretended to be the perfect little non-imbiber and sipped coffee, the whole time suffering great pangs of conscience—as if she should feel guilty about deceiving Lawrence. *Why?* she often found herself questioning. Was she obligated to him? Did she still owe him something?

But there had to be something there, some kind of dependence that maybe even she tried not to recognize. Why else did she race to the phone earlier to get him over for Krissie?

Was it for Krissie?

Maureen never pretended to be one of those liberated types who paraded for independence. Like her mother, her purpose in life was to be a housewife, raising children and providing a good home for her husband. Her present situation was certainly not of her choosing. It was Lawrence's decision. And what could she do?

Maureen took a deep swallow of her drink.

And what was she doing for Krissie? Or was it what was she doing *to* Krissie? Why was her daughter having these awful nightmares? Was it something that she—her mother—was responsible for? Maybe her own fears and frustrations had somehow been passed on to her daughter, making her a victim through no fault of her own.

Maybe... *Oh God*! Maybe she could even be held responsible for that terrible incident two years ago. Although Krissie, mercifully, had no recollection of *that* day, for Maureen it remained the most vivid and traumatic period of her life. A day she couldn't cope with then and wasn't handling much better now.

No one, including Lawrence, held her to blame for what happened, but maybe she was more responsible than anyone realized. She just fell apart, feebly trying to comfort Krissie with words that made little sense to *her*, let alone a near catatonic five-year-old.

She couldn't even rely on Lawrence to take some of the burden because he was struggling with his own anger and complex emotions. Besides, all advice was directed at *her*.

There was no question the constant pressure that resulted from that day contributed to the divorce. Lawrence, however, never would—or could—admit to this. Maureen was sure that he'd so often thrust all blame on her for their domestic situation that he finally had himself convinced there was no other reason for them not staying together.

And it wasn't just Lawrence. Family, friends, even neighbors... Oh, they weren't direct with their askance looks and questioning whispers, but there wasn't much that Maureen's suspicious eye didn't detect.

Well, maybe they were all right. Maybe everything *was* her fault.

The tears that cascaded down Maureen's cheeks and plinked into the bathwater were not so much tears of self-sympathy, but of desperation. She was feeling the alcohol, true, but she now had determined to find some way to rectify this situation, this mess that she had made of three lives!

3 Ernest

ERNEST SLAPPED A FIVER down on the beer-sticky table and calculated the amount of change he should be receiving. He grinned through tobacco-stained teeth when his mental mathematics informed him that he should still have enough for another round.

The waitress—a pimply girl both short and wide (she did have big knockers that blasted like torpedoes out of her tight-fitting tee shirt)—waddled over with his two draft beers. Ernest rolled the crumpled, well-worn bill around his middle three fingers, stretched it, and watched as the waitress first gave his table a fast wipe, then replaced the two empty glasses with the two filled ones. Still grinning, he handed her the money.

"Yeh, an' keep a quarter for yerself," he said gutturally, taking a generous swallow of his beer.

The waitress pulled the silver out of a can on her tray. A quarter? she thought miserably. Hell, she'd only been serving this joker for the better part of the afternoon.

Ernest wiped around his mouth with the sleeve of his checked flannel shirt. He sloppily chugged down the rest of his beer and went to work on the second glass.

He stifled an acid belch. "Might as well bring me another couple," he said to the stony-faced waitress, playfully throwing her one of his more devilish winks.

And how many was that? About eight glasses? He hadn't counted the two straight shots of rye he'd also consumed. Yet he still wasn't nearly as drunk as he wanted to be. Ernest paused from his drinking marathon just long enough to peer into the half-filled glass of draft sitting before him. He watched with a subdued fascination as the tiny golden gas bubbles floated to the surface to evolve into foam. The physics of beer, he considered. But who cares? Ernest tossed back his drink and slid the two glasses over to the opposite end of the table.

The hotel pub had an atmosphere that was decidedly downbeat, with lighting that was too somber, almost funereal; a decor that was drab and colorless. And today, as was usual at this time, the place was virtually empty. It was just getting on for four in the afternoon and Ernest counted, beside himself, eight other customers, all male. Two men were off in the corner intensely battling it out at the shuffleboard table. At a rectangular table by the men's washroom, under the old black and white portable with the rolling picture and the volume never on, sat three employees of the nearby meat packing plant. Ernest wasn't positive that was where they were from, but he had a pretty good idea. Every time one of them walked by his table for a bag of chips or a pickled egg or some other "delicacy" from the bar—the accompanying smell almost knocked him out of his chair. Off at another corner table sat a solitary drinker: fiftyish, balding, dressed conservatively, looking morosely into his drink. A guy with something troubling his mind, Ernest presumed. Just getting up to go to the toilet was a definite under-ager, replete with long oily hair and a face ravaged by adolescent pustules—and likely carrying a fake I.D. And finally there was "Joe," a pot-bellied nobody, drinking to excess and clearly not giving a damn.

Join the club, pal, Ernest thought grimly.

The waitress came over with Ernest's two drinks balanced on her tray. He absently handed her the money. He snapped back to himself and gave the girl a smile. She didn't return it.

"Oh honey," he snapped, "could ya gimme change for the smoke dispenser? I'm a buck short an' all I got's a bill." He handed her the dollar; now he was almost completely broke. And he would remain broke until his next welfare check arrived.

She fished around in her little can for four quarters. One quarter short.

"I'll have to go to the bar," she said tonelessly.

Ernest nodded. "That's fine."

The waitress really couldn't have cared less if it was *fine* with him or not. She was still insulted by his "generous gratuity."

Ernest had to take a leak, and bad! Damn, he thought, it always hits so fast when you're drinking beer. One minute you're fine, and the next it's a damn urgent kidney call—*bang!*

Maybe he should wait for the girl to bring him back his quarter first. He couldn't afford to be free with whatever money he had left over.

What was that Bible verse he used to know: "The spirit is willing but the flesh is weak"?

"Shit-damn," Ernest muttered under his breath. He pried himself loose from his chair and headed for the door marked GENTS at the back of the pub (where the smelly meat workers were). He must have been sitting longer than he thought, his legs were stiff; he felt as if he'd just climbed off a horse.

"Who's winning?" he asked the two shuffleboard combatants as he walked by them.

Neither man responded. They merely regarded him with an icy silence, and resumed their game.

Ernest didn't care. His priority was to get himself into a stall before he springs a leak.

As soon as he passed through the washroom door—almost running head-on into the under-ager who clearly had indulged in a few inhales of something more potent and pungent than cigarette tobacco—he hurried into the closest stall and stood over the toilet, legs spread wide apart, and released the contents from his bladder.

As soon as the stream hit the bowl Ernest grinned and exhaled a deep sigh.

And in the next moment, suddenly, inexplicably, a memory was triggered.

That memory.

A persistent and haunting remembrance from which he could never be free.

He had been drinking, hoping to get drunk enough to numb his brain against this relentless assault that threatened whatever sanity he still possessed.

But now it was too late. The thought, like a rank weed, had again burst through into his consciousness. Once more he was fated to relive the tortured events of that day... of that hour...

Was it two years ago?

Why was that wire mesh fence so prominent in his thoughts? Was it because he first saw the little white-haired girl while peering through the links? Or was it more like a symbol, a reminder that he was forever to be a prisoner... to an influence that he couldn't understand? Ernest wasn't sure of the answer. He doubted that he would ever know...

It was hot and muggy that spring day in mid-May. But from what Ernest could remember it had been hot that entire week. Hellishly hot. The sun was a large and blinding ball in the sky, enveloped in a haze. Even the sporadic drifts of wind that coasted in from the east failed to provide much relief from the oppressive heat.

Not only the five- and six-year-old kindergarteners, but all the children were shouting and laughing, skipping and playing, stampeding out of the schoolyard. They seemed oblivious to the heat generated by the scorching sun. Ernest watched. He couldn't help but smile at their youthful innocence. Perhaps it even served as a vague reminder of the simple freedom he'd long ago enjoyed.

But no, that couldn't be. His own youth was forgotten. And at that moment, it could only serve as a blessing.

A *blessing*? he silently mocked. He couldn't know that the "black mark" had already been stamped upon his soul.

He scanned the schoolyard and instantly knew which of the children she was. But it wasn't because he recognized her; he'd never seen her before.

"It" told him who she was...

He stood outside the fence and tried in vain to block his brain against the dark inroads of its manipulation.

The voice: The whispered voice that spoke to him through his thoughts.

—and it commanded—

It drew him toward her.

She was so young. Ernest knew it wouldn't be difficult.

But no! He mustn't!

His protest was met with a sudden, lightning-like pain that flashed within his skull, a momentary blinding agony.

Ernest remembered pleading, silently mouthing his objection, until the tears squeezed out the corners of his eyes. But the pain flared again, this time even more intense. Ernest grabbed the sides of his head. He pushed his palms against his skull, as if attempting to physically force out its influence. He tried to resist. But his suffering was more than any man could endure. Finally, his will was spent and he was forced to surrender.

—the voice commanded—

The little girl left the schoolyard alone. Ernest waited, and then he followed after her, keeping a careful distance behind. Two blocks, then she was away from the masses of children, walking slowly down a quiet residential side street. Ernest stepped up his pace, the sweat pouring out of him in torrents. He was sure he could hear her humming to herself—a sad, simple tune. He came alongside her. The little girl stopped and looked up at him with squinty eyes. "Hello," she said with her youthful naivety.

(*Weren't you taught never to talk to strangers...?*)

Ernest again attempted to fight against its control. Once more the flaming psychic knife sliced through the inside of his skull, slashing across his brain. He started to double over.

The little girl looked at him with uncomprehending concern. "Are you all right, mister?" she asked.

Ernest didn't answer. He knew he had to go through with what was expected of him. With words that left his lips hesitantly, he introduced himself as a friend of her daddy's. Her mommy was sick and he was asked by her daddy to get her home quickly. No questions. As expected, the trusting little girl accepted his story. Ernest took her by the hand and swiftly guided her away...

...Ernest hitched a breath as the memory came to an abrupt end, the final frames of film running free of the projector, cutting the climactic act. He instantly broke out in a cold sweat.

Why did it have to be him? Why was he the one chosen to hear and obey... *the voice?*

In his rage and resentment, Ernest slammed a heavy fist into the wall in back of the toilet stall, skinning his knuckles on the chipped tiles.

The truth could neither be denied nor hidden.

He could drink himself into a stupor—numb his brain all he wanted. But he knew it was impossible for him ever to forget.

Until he could be freed by the mercy of death he'd be forced to live with a devastating memory—one that tainted a proud if forgotten past and painted a bleak and likely tragic future.

4 With Dr. LaFreniere

DR. ROLAND LAFRENIERE (Dr. "Friendly," as Krissie referred to him) had been the family physician since before Krissie was born. He was a humorless professional who took his work as a man of medicine seriously. Perhaps too seriously, in Lawrence's view. His stolid demeanor made Lawrence uneasy, especially since the "incident" with his daughter. Not that Lawrence expected levity in his personality, but he couldn't help but feel that LaFreniere was subtly probing him each time he came into the doctor's office. It was often a struggle for Lawrence to conceal his discomfort around the man.

Today, both Lawrence and his ex-wife sat across from the doctor as LaFreniere reviewed a chart containing Krissie's test results.

After a few minutes, LaFreniere pushed the chart to the side of his desk.

He spoke to the point. "My examination shows there is nothing wrong with Krissie—physically."

A few concerned lines creased Maureen's forehead. "Doctor, why did you pause before saying *physically?*"

"Because," LaFreniere replied, "I believe Krissie's problem is psychological."

Maureen pushed forward in her chair, stiffly, her fingers tightly gripping the sides of her purse. "Dr. LaFreniere," she said impatiently, "are you saying that there's something—mentally wrong with our daughter?"

LaFreniere waved his hand briskly. "No, no, of course not," he said in his most reassuring tone. "It's just that *something* is causing these recurring nightmares, and since I can't find any physical reason for Krissie to be experiencing them, I think the next logical step is to start looking for possible psychological reasons. But I certainly don't believe your daughter is—abnormal, if that's what worries you. Absolutely not. On the contrary, I find Krissie to be a pleasant and extremely bright child."

Maureen eased back into her chair. "I'm sorry." A slight embarrassment was evident in her voice. "I guess I just got a little excited."

LaFreniere smiled understandingly. He pulled some tissue from his shirt pocket and began wiping his spectacles.

"You mentioned earlier that Krissie tends to keep to herself. Rather introverted," he said.

Maureen nodded and cleared her throat. "Yes, well what I meant was that she didn't have many friends. But there's nothing wrong with her. I think she's just shy."

LaFreniere gave a slight nod of his head. "Perhaps. But it may be a good place for us to start."

Maureen glanced over at Lawrence, who was half slouched in his chair, appearing bored and disinterested.

"I'm afraid I don't quite know what you mean," Maureen said to the doctor.

LaFreniere crumpled the tissue and dropped it into the wastepaper basket at the side of his desk. Adjusting his spectacles before fitting them back over his face, he said, "To put it simply, introverted individuals are almost always sensitive types, and it's usually these children of a sensitive nature who have the most active imaginations."

Finally Lawrence spoke up. "Okay, fine. I can understand that. But a seven-year-old girl dreaming of fog and monsters—and damn near every night?"

"Something has to trigger that negative imagination," LaFreniere offered.

"Something...like her parents splitting up?" Maureen queried sotto voce.

Lawrence found himself suddenly craving a smoke.

"Yes, that could be a possible catalyst," LaFreniere said.

Lawrence said, "Well, naturally Krissie was upset when she learned her mommy and daddy weren't going to be living together anymore. But I really can't see it being that traumatic. She was too young to really understand the situation."

A pained look pierced Maureen's expression and for a moment it looked to both Lawrence and the doctor as if she might say something. But she resisted.

LaFreniere smiled. "Ah, I don't quite agree, Mr. Carver. We all too often underestimate our young."

"How do you mean?"

"Sometimes I think that children—younger children in particular—come equipped with a type of... let's say radar system that picks up tensions, nuances—things we assume go over their head. They may not know the significance of these signals they pick up, but I do believe they react to them. An introverted child, however, will usually keep most of their feelings bottled up inside. Because these anxieties aren't released through normal channels, they may manifest through changes in behavior, such as acting out or becoming unusually withdrawn...or even becoming subjected to nightmares."

"But we divorced a year and a half ago," Lawrence argued. "These nightmares have just started."

"There's no time frame," LaFreniere remarked. "Besides, we don't know the divorce is at the root of the problem. Perhaps it is, perhaps not. There may be several contributing factors and the dissolution of your marriage is just one."

Maureen finally decided to broach the subject she had been avoiding. She spoke almost reluctantly. "Doctor, what about the attack two years ago?"

LaFreniere's expression became grim. "Yes, of course I've considered that."

"And?" Maureen wanted to know.

"It cannot be discounted," LaFreniere said bluntly.

Lawrence responded like a man offended. "Whoa, wait a minute. She's forgotten all about that. Remember, Doc? Hell, you checked her and said so yourself. Don't tell me you've forgotten how surprised you were when within not even a week Krissie couldn't remember a thing about what happened. You yourself said it was like nothing ever occurred." He pointed a stiff finger at the doctor. "And what about the counselor you suggested who said the same thing?"

"Yes," LaFreniere said, "she did forget—outwardly. But the memory is still there, Mr. Carver, only locked away deep in her subconscious. You see, it's my belief that all our thoughts, even those random ones that seem completely insignificant, are kept stored in the brain. I'm sure this extends even to those primitive thoughts the child has while still in the womb—which may explain why there are people who claim to remember the moment of their birth. The writer Ray Bradbury is one."

Maureen nodded in interest. Lawrence's cigarette craving was growing.

"You could almost compare the brain to a storage closet," the doctor continued. "Although this metaphor is simplicity itself, I think it'll serve as an effective illustration. Let's say the closet is empty. Then one day you throw your baseball glove in there. As the weeks pass you continue to add things—clothes, toys, books—until soon that glove is completely hidden. Forgotten. But the fact remains it's still there, only buried under mounds of other items. Well, the same with our thoughts, only more so. Don't forget the brain is always working. New thoughts and ideas are constantly being introduced."

"That makes sense," Maureen said, nodding and casting at glance over to Lawrence.

LaFreniere continued. "And why is it that some days the most minute, insignificant things happen to us, things we forget about as soon as they occur…yet that same night we might dream about them?"

Maureen spoke slowly, careful to find the proper words. "So what you're saying is that even though Krissie can't consciously remember what happened to her, she still holds onto the memory?"

"And it's possible that the subconscious memory is being released through her dreams," LaFreniere finished. "Dreams can be like a release valve for suppressed memories."

"But why the weird lands and hideous monsters?" Maureen asked.

La Freniere lifted a shoulder. "Interpretation perhaps. The monsters could be how her mind envisions the attacker. The strange foggy lands perhaps where—"

Lawrence cut him off. "Listen," he said, annoyed, "all I want to know is what we can do to stop her from having these nightmares." He wanted to add: *So I won't have to take anymore three a.m. phone calls.*

"Mr. Carver," LaFreiniere replied, "I think it best if I refer your daughter. There's a specialist in the city who would be better equipped to deal with what your daughter has been experiencing."

Lawrence cocked an eye. "Specialist?"

LaFreniere nodded. "Yes."

"I assume you mean—psychiatrist?" Lawrence said.

"Dr. Warren Kinbrace, a man highly regarded in his field," LaFreniere said. "I think he would be of tremendous help."

Lawrence looked doubtful. "Well, isn't there something you could do? I mean, is a psychiatrist really the answer?"

"A psychiatrist is trained to handle problems like Krissie's," LaFreniere responded. "As a general practitioner I'm rather limited in what I can do. The root of this problem with Krissie requires a deeper examination by a qualified professional."

"But isn't there a pill or something you could give her?"

Maureen's expression reflected her impatience with the stubborn arguments of her ex-husband.

LaFreniere offered an indulgent smile. "I could give her something that would help her sleep, but it's doubtful that would prevent the nightmares. Besides I prefer not to prescribe drugs to children your daughter's age." Almost as an afterthought he added: "Unless it's absolutely necessary."

Lawrence refused to give up in his search for alternatives. "Well, as a doctor what would you advise? I mean, uh, what could Maureen and I do to maybe help her along?"

Maureen regarded Lawrence with quiet surprise. LaFreniere's eyes shifted from Lawrence to Maureen, then from Maureen back to Lawrence. He could detect the tension that still existed between them as soon as they walked through the door to his office. It didn't require a medical degree to determine their ongoing resentment toward each other was not helping the situation.

LaFreniere said, "As best you can try to reinforce a positive environment for Krissie. Show her that it's still possible for you to enjoy a pleasant time together even though you no longer live together as a family. But most important, and I know it might sound like a cliché, show her a lot of love and understanding."

Lawrence squirmed slightly in his chair. As had happened on previous visits, it sounded as if LaFreniere's advice was directed specifically at him.

Maureen turned to Lawrence; then she looked back at the doctor. "She knows we love her," she said softly.

"Yes, I'm sure," LaFreniere agreed. "But remember her 'radar.' Children, especially children like Krissie, are not so easily fooled." He smiled and said lightly: "They haven't yet learned how to become cynical."

Jesus, Lawrence thought.

Dr. LaFreniere told Lawrence and Maureen to give serious consideration to his recommendation and if they were agreeable to contact his office so that an appointment could be made with the psychiatrist. Even though Lawrence told him they'd give it some thought, he had every intention of swaying his ex-wife to his way of thinking. The idea of taking his daughter to a shrink did not sit well with him. Perhaps it was because of the way he felt; his failure not so much as a husband, but as a father. Guilt that he couldn't acknowledge and that he struggled to keep buried deep inside. If Krissie were to start these sessions Lawrence knew he'd also be urged to open up his thoughts. Of course Maureen had discovered the truth, but Lawrence suspected that despite all her open-mouthed surprise, she'd always had that spark of suspicion. But for him to admit this failing to a stranger? Even to help his daughter, Lawrence knew he couldn't bring himself to do it.

* * *

That night Lawrence took Maureen and Krissie out to McDonald's. Like any average kid, Krissie put away a cheeseburger, fries, Coke, and cookies. Maureen noticed her daughter laughing a lot that evening, something she hadn't seen her do much lately.

After dinner, Lawrence suggested a drive out to the park. The orange sun was just setting, casting its final fading light across marmalade skies and through the thinning branches of the trees. The early evening breeze was cool and comforting. They strolled to the little playground near the picnic area, and Krissie trotted off to play on the swings.

"Don't get yourself too active," Maureen cautioned her. "You just put away a big meal."

When she was out of earshot, Maureen turned to her ex and said, "Lawrence, I've been thinking. Maybe we should take Krissie to see that psychiatrist Dr. LaFreniere suggested."

Lawrence pulled out a blade of grass from the lawn and slid it between his lips. He sucked on it thoughtfully.

"What do you think?" Maureen asked him.

"No," he said firmly.

"But there are so many questions a man like Dr. Kinbrace might be able to answer for us. Lawrence, I think if he's as good as LaFreniere says—"

Again: "No."

Count to ten, Maureen told herself.

"Okay, then what do you suggest I do the next time Krissie wakes up in the middle of the night screaming?"

Lawrence turned to her. He spoke with confidence. "Y'know, I don't think there'll be a next time. I've got a feeling she's through with her nightmares."

"Forgive me if I don't exactly share your optimism," Maureen said sourly.

"Then shove it."

"Damn it, Lawrence! You did the same thing two years ago. After that terrible thing happened to Krissie and Dr. LaFreniere suggested we have her looked at professionally."

"I agreed to the counselor," Lawrence reminded her.

"But that's not the same," Maureen argued. "And Krissie wasn't having these awful nightmares at the time."

Lawrence didn't say anything.

Maureen drew a breath. "LaFreniere said it, you heard him—that there's a good chance her dreams are being caused by a subconscious memory of what happened."

Lawrence spit out a stream of green saliva. "LaFreniere's a quack."

"I don't think so." Exasperation came through in Maureen's voice. "Lawrence, I'm trying. Why won't you help me?"

"No, Maureen," Lawrence said stubbornly. "I think the headshrinker is out."

Maureen had avoided pulling out the heavy artillery but Lawrence's inflexible attitude left her no choice.

"Fine," she said. "You go ahead and think what you want. Just don't forget who has guardianship over Krissie."

* * *

That night Krissie slept peacefully. After another night with no interruptions, Maureen decided not to arrange for an appointment with the psychiatrist.

Lawrence swung it so that he could take a few days off work. He spent much of that time with his ex-wife and daughter, going on seemingly endless outings. The visit to the zoo was especially memorable, for Krissie. Thursday they drove out to the beach for a picnic. Conversation between Lawrence and Maureen was kept to a minimum, but what few words they did exchange were pleasant.

Maureen was both surprised and pleased to discover that Lawrence had turned out to be correct. For three nights in a row Krissie had comfortable, undisturbed sleep. A healthy color had returned to her face; the circles under her eyes vanished. Once again she was cheery and playful.

And she was no longer afraid to go to bed at night.

Dr. LaFreniere was right, Maureen thought, barely unable to contain her joy. The love and feeling of togetherness really did work wonders.

The Friday before the new school year started Maureen took Krissie downtown on a shopping excursion. They had a wonderful time. Maureen watched with loving maternal interest as Krissie tried on one school outfit after another. They spent the entire day together, browsing in the stores along the main avenue. When they finally got home that night—weary and footsore, Maureen with a wild headache—Krissie just had to call Daddy and tell him all about her exciting day. She told him about their delicious restaurant lunch and her special strawberry shortcake dessert. She giggled as she attempted to describe some of the crazily-dressed people she saw downtown (Mommy called them *Harry Kirshner*, or something like that). But she was particularly excited about her new blouse and jumper. She made her daddy promise to come over and see her new outfit before school started on Tuesday.

When Krissie finally crawled into bed, exhausted, she wrapped her arms around her mommy and gave her the biggest hug and kiss she could. She couldn't stop thanking her for their wonderful day and hoped they could do it again real soon. Maureen found herself fighting back the tears. She promised they would.

As she walked out of her daughter's room, Maureen let a few of her tears fall freely. She paused outside the open door and smiled heavenward. She was so thankful things were working out.

At 2:45 a.m. Krissie woke up screaming…

5 Introduction To Dr. Kinbrace

IF THE DECOR of a person's home or office reflected one's personality, then Lawrence immediately envisioned Warren Kinbrace as a young, hip, "with-it" type. His waiting room was furnished with a couch, two acrylic contour chairs, and acrylic-surface center table, all of ultra-modern design. Two gooseneck floor lamps were positioned at opposite corners of the room. And, to complete the flavor, two large works of abstract art (all meaningless swirls and globules in Lawrence's view) were mounted on the main wall.

Lawrence walked over to one of the uncomfortable-looking chairs and plopped down, not surprised to discover that its feel matched its appearance. He picked up a well-worn copy of *Reader's Digest* from the table and flipped noisily through the pages. Finding a "Drama in Real Life" article, he began reading... or at least he pretended to read.

Maureen and Krissie were seated on the couch. The little girl, looking drawn and tired, scared, rested her head near her mother's breast. Maureen gently stroked the soft, white hair and periodically whispered comforting words. Glimpsed over his

50

magazine, Lawrence's expression was dour. All he wanted to know was what the hell happened? Just a week ago Krissie was doing fine. What in God's name made these night terrors start up again?

A side door quietly opened and a thin, weathered, elderly woman gradually came into view. Lawrence could tell just by looking at her that she belonged in a head doctor's office. Maureen in fifteen years, he thought with a slight, wry smile.

"Next Thursday and I'll reschedule your appointment for eleven," a husky male voice said.

Lawrence glanced up over his magazine and saw—*the shrink?*

He wasn't all that taken aback by Kinbrace's appearance: his brown, gray-specked hair done up in a modish afro, heavy Libra medallion hanging loose around his neck. He wore a loud silk shirt, unbuttoned enough to expose a healthy baked-in tan and a chest full of curly black hair, and navy blue trousers that were just a touch too tight around the waist. He looked more like a rock singer than a professional man of medicine.

What did surprise Lawrence, however, was that this Dr. Kinbrace had to be around the same age as himself—late thirties. And next to this guy Lawrence couldn't help feeling stuffily conservative.

But I'm an executive, he reasoned silently. I'm supposed to look like I just stepped out of a boardroom.

Dr. Kinbrace waited until his former patient scurried out of the office. He then turned to Maureen and Krissie and brought his hands together in a soft clap.

"Mrs. Carver." He smiled at the child. "And this has to be Krissie."

Maureen stood up and extended her hand. It was dwarfed in the handshake. "Yes, Dr. Kinbrace." She gestured over to

Lawrence, who took his time in rising. "And this is my hus— uh, Mr. Carver."

Kinbrace spun around on his heels like disco king and clasped Lawrence's hand. Strange man, Lawrence thought. But at least he had a good firm handshake going for him. Lawrence placed value on a handshake. Eyes may shift; a smile can crack. But a person's grip never lies.

"It's a great pleasure to meet you both," Kinbrace said cheerily, in an obvious attempt to relax any fears or doubts they may have had about being in a psychiatrist's office.

Maureen returned, "It's our pleasure to meet you, Dr. Kinbrace."

Lawrence grunted out something.

Kinbrace moved across to Krissie and crouched down until he was at her eye level. "And I have a feeling that we are going to be terrific friends," he said.

Krissie managed a shy, seven-year-old smile.

"Tell you what," Kinbrace said to her. "Why don't you wait out here for a few minutes and read a comic book? I want to talk to your mommy and daddy inside my office." From an untidy pile he extracted a dog-eared magazine. "Of course you like Donald Duck," he said with a wink.

Krissie's smile broadened and she accepted the comic book.

"See you in a little while," the doctor said, giving the girl another wink. He then motioned for Lawrence and Maureen to follow him into his office. Closing the door, he settled behind his paper-laden desk.

"As you can see, I'm in desperate need of some organization," he joked. "Please, take a seat, both of you."

Lawrence did so, noticing that the office chairs were of a more comfortable design than those in the waiting room. Spotting an ashtray, Lawrence yanked out his cigarettes. "You don't mind," he said, after flipping one into his mouth.

Kinbrace cleared some space on his desk and smiled. "Feel free."

Maureen, too, lighted a cigarette.

Lawrence had to admit that he found the shrink a likeable sort. But there was no denying that he still felt ill at ease being here. These brain probers were too damn subtle. Just by asking a few seemingly harmless questions they could expose personality quirks that even you didn't know existed. He intended to remain on guard.

"Dr. LaFreniere explained to me that your daughter is troubled by a recurring nightmare," Kinbrace began, taking out his pen and a pad of blue-lined paper.

Maureen pulled a puff on her cigarette. "Yes, Doctor, the same horrible dream every night. She literally jumps up in bed, terrified."

"Also when we spoke, Mrs. Carver, you said that last week there was a brief period when Krissie didn't experience this nightmare."

Maureen nodded. "Yes, for a few nights. We followed the advice of Dr. LaFreniere, who suggested that Lawrence, Krissie, and I start doing things together—like a regular family. Lawrence took some time off work and the three of us went on outings to the park and to the beach." Her voice started to tremble and she spit out in frustration: "Damn, and it seemed to be helping."

Kinbrace paused a moment to allow Maureen to recover.

He said gently, "You two are no longer together, I understand."

Maureen frowned. "Lawrence and I are divorced."

Lawrence butted his cigarette, even though it was barely smoked, and struck up another.

"A year and a half ago," Maureen added.

Kinbrace resumed his writing. "How did Krissie react to this, your divorce?"

Maureen looked down to the floor, her expression pained. "We've already discussed this with Dr. LaFreniere," she said. "She was quite upset, of course, to learn her mommy and daddy weren't going to be living together anymore." She hesitated; then added: "But I think more confused."

Kinbrace nodded sympathetically. "Were there any noticeable changes in her behavior at that time, such as unusual aggression? Perhaps withdrawal?"

Maureen shook her head and sighed. "Krissie's always been quiet. No, I can't say she behaved any differently."

Kinbrace passed a quick glance over to Lawrence. He wrote something on the pad; then looked back to Maureen.

"Prior to the divorce, what was the situation like at home?"

Maureen stiffened, almost imperceptibly, yet a gesture noticed by Kinbrace.

"Between Lawrence and me?" she said.

"Yes."

Maureen coughed. "Well, uh, is a question like this really necessary?"

"Mrs. Carver," Kinbrace said calmly, "before I can help Krissie overcome her nightmares I have to first find out what's causing them. By asking you these questions I get probable bases on which to build. Now I understand that some of these questions may be difficult for you to answer, but just keep in mind that they'll help me in treating your daughter."

"Well, I can't deny there were some difficult times before the break," Maureen said softly. "Many difficult times, I suppose. But Lawrence and I both did our best to shelter Krissie from these." Smiling faintly, she turned to Lawrence. "I like to think that we did a pretty good job."

Lawrence looked back at her, his features set and impassive.

"So, then it's safe to say Krissie never saw or heard many of your, uh, disagreements?" Kinbrace presumed.

"No," Maureen replied, a tad too quickly.

Kinbrace flipped over to another piece of paper. "How does Krissie do in school, academically?"

A flash of pride crossed Maureen's face. "She's an exceptional student, Dr. Kinbrace," she answered without hesitation. "Her teacher last year, Mrs. Crampton, couldn't say enough about Krissie; about how bright and imaginative she was. Top grades in all her subjects."

"Does she have any problems relating to the other children?"

Maureen's expression grew golemn. "There was some difficulty last year. You see, Doctor, Krissie was somewhat above the Grade Two level, and I don't just mean with her schoolwork. She couldn't seem to get along with most of her classmates."

Kinbrace asked, "Is she ever teased or bullied by the other children?"

Maureen smiled an unfunny kind of smile. "Well, you know younger children; they can be extremely cruel at times. There was one boy in particular last year, Peter Grubbish. I think he got his kicks out of giving Krissie a bad time; you know, constantly pushing her around in front of his friends, calling her names."

"And what was Krissie's reaction to this bullying?"

"It's funny," Maureen said thoughtfully. "She never once mentioned it to me. I finally heard about it from her teacher. Krissie's really never been one to complain."

Kinbrace stopped writing. He lightly tapped the end of his pen on the desk. "So, Krissie doesn't usually talk to you about things that are troubling her?"

Maureen looked at Lawrence. "No, not really," she answered slowly. "Not as I think about it. She seems to keep a lot bottled up inside."

The doctor turned to Lawrence. "How about with you, Mr. Carver?"

"Huh?"

"When you're with your daughter, does she ever open up to you about problems she might be having?"

Lawrence responded with a shake of his head.

Maureen slid forward in her chair. "Dr. Kinbrace," she said uneasily. "There is something we should tell you—that might help you with Krissie."

"Yes?"

"It happened two years ago. On her way home from kindergarten… Krissie was… she had an 'incident.'"

"Yes. Dr. LaFreniere informed me."

We never knew all the details," Mo said, a pained look reflected in her eyes. "We never found out who was responsible."

Kinbrace maintained his professional demeanor, though his left eyebrow did arch slightly.

"She wasn't assaulted in *that* way," Mo added. "She was professionally examined and there was never any indication that… you know…"

"And this was two years ago?"

Maureen nodded.

"But Doctor," she said, "thank God, she seems to have no memory at all about it ever happening."

Kinbrace nodded. "So Dr. LaFreniere told me."

Maureen thought for a moment, then asked: "Tell me, do you find that—unusual?"

"No, not at all," Kinbrace replied, putting his pen aside and leaning back in his chair. "It's an amnesia. Sort of a mental defense. When an incident that traumatic happens to someone—and especially to someone as young as your daughter was at the time—it, plus the expected confusion, can prove too difficult for the mind to handle. Sometimes it becomes so hard to comprehend that it is pushed right out of the consciousness."

Maureen furrowed her brow and said, "But Dr. LaFreniere believes the memory of the attack is still buried somewhere in Krissie's brain."

"Yes."

"And that it's being released through her nightmares?"

"Very possible, Mrs. Carver. Dreams can bring back to consciousness deeply repressed memories which we would never otherwise permit to resurface. In handling cases like this—and I can assure you that recurring nightmares are not that uncommon—it generally is best to reintroduce to the conscious mind these locked-away memories."

"And that's what you're saying you'll have to do with Krissie? Make her remember the attack?"

"If I feel that it's somehow related to her nightmares, yes, I may make that suggestion."

Maureen shuddered. "I don't know which is worse… God, she's only seven years old!"

Kinbrace spoke reassuringly. "You forget, Mrs. Carver, I'm an experienced psychiatrist. I've been in practice for many years. If I felt that some part of my therapy might have negative effects, you can be certain I'd use discretion."

It was apparent from her expression that Maureen still wasn't totally convinced.

For the next several moments there was quiet. Lawrence, assuming, hopefully, that this preliminary questioning was over, started to rise from his chair. Maureen waited for a moment; then she also stood up. Kinbrace briefly glanced over his notes. He then pulled open the top side drawer of his desk and brought out a small cassette tape recorder.

"There won't be any objections if I tape my session with your daughter?"

Maureen looked at Lawrence, who responded with a shrug, and shook her head.

"Before I speak with Krissie do either of you have any questions you'd like to ask?"

Lawrence had one. He wanted to know just how long this therapy crapola was going to take. He was going to ask, but in the next instant decided against it. He'd purposely kept his mouth shut the whole time of Kinbrace's questioning, why say anything now?

"No," Maureen said, "I think that's all."

"Fine," Kinbrace smiled, lifting himself from his chair. "Would you send in your daughter, please?"

As soon as Lawrence and Maureen stepped out of the office, Kinbrace rushed over to the window and opened it; he didn't want the little girl to choke on the cigarette smoke that lingered in the room. He then emptied out the ashtray, and after pulling one of the chairs closer to his desk, returned to his own chair and set up the tape recorder. Once Krissie was seated across from him, Kinbrace switched on the recorder. They chatted informally for a few minutes before Kinbrace started with his questions.

"Krissie, what can you tell me about these bad dreams you've been having?"

Krissie: Well, I always remember them. When I go to bed at night I know I'm going to have one, and I know what's gonna happen in it. But when I'm dreaming them I forget everything and it's like it's all new.

Kinbrace: New? What happens in these dreams?

Krissie: I sorta feel like I'm in an elevator. I keep going higher and it feels like I'm never gonna stop. Sometimes, but not always, I get dizzy and feel like I wanna throw up. But then there's like a drumming noise and I get a cozy warm feeling. I see all these pretty lights and I get closer to them. Then I'm not scared anymore… well, not really… until *they* come.

Kinbrace: They?

Krissie: Uh huh. I'm in this scary place… there's all this cloudy stuff, but there are these bright, bright colors, too. Then I start to walk around— No, it's kinda like I'm floating. I never know where I'm going… until I get to more of this big bunch of cloudy stuff. But it's not white, like real clouds are. It's pink, and it kinda looks like the cotton candy you get at the circus. Uh, once I go through it, that's where I always see them. They come out of the fog, and there's a whole lot of them… and they just stand there and wait for me.

Kinbrace: What happens then?

Krissie: I go to them. I always go to them.

Kinbrace: Do you want to go to them?

Krissie: No. Something makes me.

Kinbrace: What do they do?

Krissie: Well, they wait until I'm real close to them. Then they try to grab me. Then I see their faces: they're scary, ugly monsters…a whole lot worse than the ones on TV or in picture books. I start to run away, but my feet aren't on the ground so I'm not really running but I move fast, and they chase me. It always feels like they're just about to catch me, then I start falling.

Kinbrace: And your nightmare is over?

Krissie: Yes.

* * *

Kinbrace: Krissie, how did you feel when you found out your mommy and daddy weren't going to be living together anymore?

Krissie: You mean when they got a divorce? Well, it's funny. I remember feeling really sad…but also kinda happy because I knew there wouldn't be any more fighting and yelling in the house.

Kinbrace: Did you hear a lot of their fighting?

Krissie: Mommy and Daddy don't think I did, but sometimes I couldn't help hearing them when it got real loud.

* * *

Kinbrace: Your mommy tells me that you do very well in school.

Krissie: Oh, I like school a whole lot. Last year all my subjects were so easy, 'specially arithmetic. But I think it's gonna be harder this year. I just started Grade Three.

Kinbrace: Do you have many friends in school?

Krissie: Not too many.

Kinbrace: Why do you think this is?

Krissie: Oh, probably because I do better than a lot of them and they just get jealous.

Kinbrace: When they get jealous do they sometimes pick on you?

Krissie: Some of them do.

Kinbrace: And does this bother you?

Krissie: Huh uh… Well, there is this one boy who gets me mad. His name is Peter Grubbish and we were in the same room last year. He sat in the desk right behind me. Sometimes he can get real mean. He calls me "weirdo Krissie" and all sorts of other names. But I guess he's the only one who really makes me mad.

Kinbrace: Do you ever wish you could do something to make him stop?

Krissie: That's funny because I used to have this storybook at home that was all about this ugly old troll that lived under a bridge, and if people didn't pay him to cross the bridge he'd eat them. I remember when Peter would pick on me lots I'd wish that that troll would come to life and eat him up. But I know that's not very nice of me.

Kinbrace: Well, not counting Peter how do you feel about the other boys?

Krissie: There are some boys in my school that I kinda like.

Kinbrace: Would you say that any of these boys are your friends?

Krissie: Oh, I don't know. Sometimes I'd like to talk to some of them, but I can't.

Kinbrace: Why is that, Krissie? Are you shy of boys?

Krissie: No, I don't think I am. I think it's probably because they like to play rough games. I like these boys, but they always want to play these games where you can get hurt.

Kinbrace: Yes, but don't some girls like to play rough, too?

Krissie: I know some who do, but that's different.

Kinbrace: How is it different?

Krissie: It's just—different.

Kinbrace: Have you ever played a game with boys where you've gotten hurt?

Krissie: I don't like getting hurt.

Kinbrace: And that's why you're afraid?

Krissie: I don't wanna talk anymore. Can we stop now? My head is starting to hurt...

Kinbrace: Of course, Krissie.

Krissie

"I LOVE YOU, MOMMY."

Maureen was in the kitchen putting away the leftovers from dinner: pot roast, mashed potatoes, peas and carrots. When she heard the soft, gentle voice of her daughter behind her, she turned around.

Dwarfed in the doorway, Krissie made a sad figure—clad in her nightwear, her little hands folded in front of her, as if she'd just been disciplined for doing something naughty. She was standing very rigid, and very still, her expression indicating that tears were not all that far away.

Maureen dropped what she was doing and went over to her daughter, scooping her up in her arms.

"I love you, sweetheart."

Krissie hugged her mother tightly, burying her face in her shoulder. Maureen lightly stroked her snow-white hair and carried her into the living room.

"Does your head still hurt, honey?" Maureen asked as she lowered them both onto the chesterfield.

Krissie looked up at her. Her left eye glistened as a tear formed but stubbornly refused to fall. "No, my head's fine now," she said quietly. "But Mommy, I'm so tired."

"I know you are, honey," Maureen said with a nod. "And that's why you have to get some sleep."

Maureen felt Krissie's fingers dig deep into her arms.

"No, Mommy," she said adamantly. "No. 'Cause if I do I'll have another bad dream. I don't want to dream again."

"I know, but soon you're not going to have to worry about that anymore," Maureen said with as much conviction as she could muster. "Dr. Kinbrace is going to help you."

"Is he?" Krissie asked weakly.

"Of course," Maureen answered. "And you do like Dr. Kinbrace, don't you?"

Krissie nodded. Her eyes suddenly brightened. "Mommy, do you think maybe he's helped me already?"

Maureen swallowed. Such desperation coming from a child whose only worry should be remembering how many letters there are in the alphabet. Grasping out, like Maureen herself had done so often, and yet the lies—telling them what they *wanted* to hear—were really so unfair.

"Honey," Maureen said with hesitation, "I really don't think you should expect too much from Dr. Kinbrace—*yet.*"

"But you said that Dr. Kinbrace is going to help me."

"He is, but it's just going to take a little bit of time." Deciding to offer Krissie something that might comfort her, Maureen pulled at the truth. "You know, Dr. Kinbrace told me that he thought you were a brave little girl."

Krissie looked down and mumbled, "I'm not very brave."

"Well, Dr. Kinbrace seems to think you are," Maureen said,

trying her best to sound convincing and encouraging, "and he's a very smart man."

Krissie yawned.

"Honey," Maureen said with concern, "you have to sleep, otherwise you'll get sick."

"I don't wanna, Mommy."

Maureen could feel emotion welling up inside her, and even though she felt sure her voice would falter, she knew she had to stay strong for Krissie. "How about if you just go to sleep in my arms? You know you'll be safe right here with me."

The strain of trying to fight sleep was becoming evident on Krissie's face. "Are you sure I'll be safe, Mommy?"

Maureen hugged her, and Krissie snuggled in closer.

"Close your eyes, sweetheart," Maureen said soothingly, beginning to rock gently and rhythmically on the chesterfield. "And don't you worry about anything."

Though Krissie felt herself rapidly surrendering to sleep, there still was a part of her that actively tried to struggle against it. But along with her worried thoughts, her resistance was weakening… weakening…

7 Tormented

"STOP TORTURING ME! Oh Jesus, please!"

Ernest flung himself onto the bed and rolled frantically about on the soiled sheets. Pulsing fingers grasping the sides of his head, the undressed Ernest continued to shout as the barrage of explosions went off inside his skull.

"Please… Stop! I—I can't take it anymore! I give up!"

At these words, almost miraculously, the pain began to subside.

But relief came slowly. Very slowly.

Ernest remained sprawled on the bed, his body half wrapped in a cocoon of sweaty blankets. Recovering from the agony he had just endured, he gently massaged around his head with the palms of his hands.

He was sobbing.

"Why? Why d'ya always do this to me?" Although he knew it would reignite his pain, he screamed: "Haven't ya done enough? What the fuck kind of game are yuh playing with me?"

As if in a mocking answer, the faint white ray of sunlight that was streaming through the window faded, and harsh gray shadows descended on the walls.

After about five minutes had passed and Ernest was once again free from his suffering, he pushed out of bed and headed for the cupboard at the opposite end of his room. He walked slowly and with careful steps, his head held upright, stiffly, ever on guard for the slightest indication of the pain returning. Once at the chipped, dusty wall fixture, Ernest reached inside and pulled out its solitary occupant: his bottle of rye whiskey. There was enough left in the bottle for two gentlemanly shots or one to-hell-with-everything drink. Without deliberating, Ernest unscrewed the cap and quickly gulped down its contents, greedily keeping the bottle tilted until the last drop had trickled down his gullet. He then muttered a disappointed expletive before dumping the bottle into the stinking, leaking garbage bag beside the sink. Within minutes he was pacing the floor.

"Damn, that ain't nowhere good enough," he mumbled through thick saliva, trying desperately to think of where he could lay his hands on a few dollars. Payment for his rat's nest of a room was six days past due, but so what? That wasn't important. Ernest wanted— needed!—bucks for another bottle... for just one more lousy drink!

His sanity restorer.

There was gentle rapping at the door. Ernest whirled around and impulsively brought his clenched fists up into an aggressive position.

He stood motionlessly.

"Hey in there?" a feeble voice called out.

Ernest recognized the voice and his tenseness eased.

"Yeah," he answered back.

"It's Danny. From down the hall." A prolonged wracking cough. "I heard some shoutin'. You okay?"

"Yeah, I'm—all right," Ernest replied. "I, uh, was just lyin' down for a nap an' I guess I musta had a bad dream or somethin'. Startled m'self. But I'm okay now."

"You sure 'bout that?"

"Yeh, I'm sure. Thanks."

"Okay then."

Ernest walked over and put his ear against the door. He could hear Danny's slippered feet shuffling back down the hallway.

That was when the idea suddenly dawned on him.

He quickly slipped into his tee shirt and trousers and rushed out into the drab, musty-smelling corridor. He called to Danny, who was just about to re-enter his room. Danny turned slowly around and started back toward him. Ernest invited him inside.

Danny O'Ryan was an old man, somewhere in his eighties, and claimed to be a veteran of the First World War. Through his occasional contacts with the man, Ernest learned that nothing gave old Danny more pleasure than having a glass of good whiskey while recounting his never-ending war exploits, all at great length—and all, Ernest was sure, greatly exaggerated. Today Ernest decided to give him an audience. Only there was one problem: he didn't have any refreshments to offer. Would Danny, if he had it, possibly consider supplying a bottle of something? The octogenarian agreed immediately, appearing overjoyed at having another opportunity to relive his past. He handed Ernest the key to his room and told him to bring back a bottle of whatever he could find.

…Seven o'clock ticked away into eight o'clock… eight o'clock into nine… and so on…

Ten-fifteen.

The bottle was empty and Ernest was just hanging on by a belch. He was slouched in his chair, feebly trying to focus his double vision.

But old Danny, surprisingly enough, was still animated; talking and talking, occasionally stopping to gag or snort. Although by this time the mush that Ernest called a brain was little more than an alcohol-drenched fantasyland of meaningless sights and sounds, he was still aware of Danny's presence.

Painfully aware.

Danny shakily lighted an unfiltered cigarette and his ancient road map eyes followed the trail of smoke that spiraled up to the ceiling, adding to the hazy cloud that enveloped the small room.

"Mike Reilly never did stop thankin' me for saving his life," he said. "Not 'til the day he died, which was in '64—the summer of." He paused to cough up some phlegm, which was promptly spit into his well-used handkerchief—and to take a long, reflective puff from his cigarette. "A lot of good boys, I tell ya. Damn good boys. Y'know, we shared everything together. Hell, it weren't even that uncommon for us to be sharin' our underwear if need be. Hey, speakin' of that, did I tell ya about Bobby Rhodes? Heh, heh, now there was a guy to write home about…"

Ernest knew he couldn't take much more of the old man's incessant ramblings. It was going on past the stage of human endurance. The booze was gone; Ernest was gone, and he no longer had any interest in the nostalgic reminiscences of an old geezer.

"Danny, stop it," he quickly muttered, brushing back his thinning hair with a flurry of quick, nervous strokes.

But old Danny just went right on with his gabbing, laughing aloud as he recounted how he lost his innocence—to a fifteen-year-old French hooker. About the fifth time he told the story that day, and each one a little different. The old bullshitter.

Ernest fidgeted in his chair, finally pulling himself to his feet, swaying uncertainly. When he regained sufficient balance he began pacing the floor. Danny didn't seem to notice.

"...and by God I'll never forget how pissin' drunk I got that night. Me and a few of the boys went to this little pub in the village...No, I remember it was 'bout three miles outta the village..."

"Danny, ya gotta go."

"...Hell, I bet I still hold that pub's beer-guzzling record. Kept it goin' all night and straight 'til the morning sun come up."

Ernest's body suddenly stiffened. His eyes widened to almost twice their normal size. It was there: a slight but steady tremor at the left side of his head, just above the eyebrow. A trembling that he recognized immediately: a forewarning of what was to come.

"... but when Frankie Lynn—we called him *the tenor*, but that's a story in itself—when he came back with this little mademoiselle and saw that I'd puked all over his bed sheets..."

Ernest clasped his hands against his head and slowly hunched over. The trembling was rapidly building in intensity. The tears were beginning to form in his eyes.

His sweat glands were starting to overproduce...his heart and lungs were pumping faster than normal...

Impulsively, Ernest swung his arm out and it connected with a vase on the shelf by the window, sending the flower-designed pottery crashing to the floor.

Danny shut up and very slowly turned his head in Ernest's direction.

"What's wrong with you, m'boy?" he asked in a voice that could best be described as mildly concerned.

Ernest swung around and faced him. A wild look of terror blazed in his eyes. "G-get out," he stammered. His voice grew stronger and he shouted: "Get out—NOW!"

Danny edged forward in his chair. "But you look sick," he said, casually rolling a fresh cigarette between his fingers. "Maybe I should get you help."

"Dammit!" Ernest shouted. "The only way you can help me... an' yerself old man, is by gettin' yer mummified carcass outta here."

Danny shook his head, strangely unaffected by his companion's outburst or urgency. "I could leave, but no—best if I stay with you 'til it passes."

"Till it passes..."

—the voice commanded—

Ernest was no longer in control of himself. He rushed forward, dug his fingers into the loose flesh of the old man's neck, and began applying pressure.

A look of panic now appeared on Danny's face.

Still, his voice had a strange calm. The words he spoke were even stranger.

"You can fight it," he said.

"No," Ernest snarled, his eyes wide and wild. "An' if you ain't gonna leave one way..."

Danny choked out his words. "But you don't..."

"Ya hear me! You—"

Ernest suddenly realized what he was doing and struggled to regain control over his action.

"God, you—you just don't understand... But I'll be alright... I just gotta be left alone."

He continued to hold the old man by the throat for several seconds longer. Then, gradually, he weakened his grip, finally releasing him. Danny's head dropped forward as he attempted to catch his breath.

"If it's what yuh want, I'll go," he sputtered.

Ernest turned away and staggered to the window. His own breathing was heavy and ragged as he looked out down onto the street.

Danny pulled himself up, quickly brushed off, and carefully inched over to the door. He stepped out of the room and quietly closed the door behind him. He remained stone-still for a moment, the trace of a curious smile beginning to stretch across his lips.

Ernest turned from the window and went to lie down on his bed. The pain had passed but he was overcome by distress, realizing how close he had come to killing Danny. He was reminded yet again of how he had no control over this sinister impulse—and how it possessed the influence to cause him to do whatever might be its bidding. He had no resistance against it. His willpower had been compromised and his strength defeated. He understood that he wasn't meant to kill Danny; it was merely a reminder and reinforcement of the power "it" held over him.

But Ernest also realized with a mounting dread that soon… soon it would compel him to commit murder.

* * *

Two men stood on the street in front of the run-down hotel. Both were tall, slim, conservatively dressed in black business suits. They had pale complexions and a narrow face… and each wore dark, oversized sunglasses.

They were staring up at a fourth-story window.

8 Meeting With Adamm

KRISSIE MOVED SWIFTLY, gliding frantically over the mist blanketing the landscape.

Once again the inhabitants of her nightmare world were chasing her. But for the moment they were unseen, their grotesque, subhuman forms concealed by the swirling veil of mist. Yet their marrow-freezing howls—persistent, growing ever more close—were frightening reminders to Krissie that she mustn't relax her guard… that they remained in determined pursuit.

Tendrils of mist slithered up around her, lazily drifting together and forming the heavy cloud that Krissie entered blindly into—lost, desperate.

She had to stop… to decide which way to go.

Only she found it impossible to think. She was exhausted, confused; her mind swirling like the mist that engulfed this strange and terrifying environment.

Scabrous, malformed hands reached through the milky clouds, and Krissie, to her horror, discovered that she was surrounded. She started to tremble as the threatening shadows moved in closer… closer…

Krissie swallowed her breath and once more glided through and above the mist. She was able to slip through the hulking forms and keep free of the slimy, pulsing fingers. But even as she deftly maneuvered, becoming ever more desperate in her attempt to escape, she knew she had a long way to go.

Then, off into the distance:

A clearing suddenly appeared where there was no mist.

Where she was sure she could define clear, cloudless skies and beautiful leafy trees. A place that she could recognize!

Krissie glided ever faster. She was determined to see whether this *paradise* truly existed—or if it was just a product of her desperate mind.

The ghastly creatures were rapidly getting nearer. At times Krissie was sure she could feel hot, fetid breath on the nape of her neck.

But she wouldn't look back. She had to keep going.

The welcoming land before her—

(*Please be real!*)

—was growing nearer.

Yet the grasping hands were also getting closer to her.

The mist slowly parted.

And Krissie glided through.

The creatures slowed their pursuit before stopping completely. They continued to howl, but they would not follow after her. Krissie halted and leaned breathlessly against a large, leafy tree—that really was there!—and watched as the creatures clawed away at their misty prison. They would not enter... but neither would they turn away.

After many long minutes had passed and Krissie felt quite certain that the creatures wouldn't follow, she moved ahead tentatively and began her exploration of this wonderful and welcoming oasis.

She was no longer gliding; her feet were now on firm ground, traveling along a narrow winding path. The air was pure and she breathed in its clean, fresh fragrance. Overhead towered countless majestic trees, dense and green, their lush foliage providing a cooling shade. Krissie moved slowly beneath the high branches, her mouth open wide and her eyes near-bulging as she scanned the landscape. It was all so impressive, like something out of a storybook. Peace and pristine beauty apparently reigned supreme here, but Krissie, in her childish, inquisitive way, wondered why this should be. It just didn't seem real.

She walked along until the path came to an abrupt end at a high barrier, a wall built of colorful stones. Krissie suddenly felt herself being lifted above this wall and taken to the opposite side where there was a lake. The widest, most beautiful lake she had ever seen!

She moved toward the shoreline to dip her feet into the clear, placid water.

The water was cool and Krissie gently knelt down and brought a cupped handful up to her lips. She smiled. The water tasted good—even a touch sweet. She slowly scooped up another handful to enjoy…

"Hello," a mellow voice said from behind.

Startled, Krissie's head jerked up and she whirled around.

Standing atop the wall of colored rocks was the silhouette of what appeared to be a small boy, dressed oddly in a flowing robe which danced around his form, even though the air was still and there was no breeze.

The figure then seemed to float down from the rocky perch. He started toward the girl.

Krissie carefully pulled herself to her full height and stood motionlessly in the water. She brushed her damp hair aside and squinted to see him more clearly.

It *was* a small boy. Yet he seemed to define no specific age. A strange-looking child, he appeared to Krissie almost like a ghost: his pale complexion and long cascading hair, whiter than the freshest snow. His skin was smooth and shiny, like porcelain, free of even the slightest trace of lines or blemishes. But perhaps the most striking feature of the boy were his eyes. There were no irises, no pupils—just two large, crystal blue orbs, possessed of a deep, hypnotic beauty.

Krissie was unable to look away from those eyes. Almost immediately she felt herself somehow being drawn into the very depths of them.

The boy stopped just a few short feet of her and extended his arm. His fingers were very long and lithe.

He spoke softly, in a smooth, clear voice that sent pleasant shivers through the girl.

"Welcome, Krissie."

Krissie snapped back to herself and pulled her gaze away from the magnetism of his eyes. A perplexed expression crossed her face.

"How do you know my name?" she asked cautiously.

The boy stepped closer, gently placing his hand upon her shoulder. "Indeed, I know much about you," he replied. He smiled warmly. "But you have no reason to fear me."

Krissie gulped back a quick breath. "Who are you?" she asked. She could feel herself being drawn into those eyes again.

"My name… is Adamm," the boy said. He looked out at the waters and then his gaze returned to Krissie. "And I suppose you could call this my home… rather, my reluctant home."

Krissie was puzzled. "Your *what* home?"

"Where I wish not to be," Adamm replied with a hint of sadness.

"But—where are we?" Krissie questioned.

"Of course it would be wrong to expect you to understand all at once," Adamm said. "But you might say we are a part of—*eternity*."

Krissie's features scrunched up into a look of utter bewilderment.

"Huh?"

Adamm merely smiled. "All the answers will come… in time."

"What about those—*monsters*?" Krissie asked, glancing back nervously over her shoulder as if expecting them to suddenly appear. She was surprised to see that the stone wall had vanished and the beautiful lush forest had become visible.

"Now that you have succeeded in breaking through, you will never again be bothered by the *guardians*. From now on you will come directly to me. You will have nothing to fear. They will be forgotten."

"Guardians?" Krissie said, flustered. "Oh, I don't understand any of this."

"As I said, the answers will come," Adamm offered. "What is important is that you have a new friend, and it will be my responsibility to teach and guide you."

"Teach me?"

"Indeed, there is much for you to learn—including how to appreciate a very special 'gift' you have been given. But for now, child, you shall play."

Krissie still couldn't understand any of what was happening: Why she was here, who this strange boy was and what he was telling her. But at least she wasn't afraid. She felt protected by him, even though he, too, was just a child. She looked at Adamm, whose serene smile radiated a warmth so comforting that it almost seemed to consume her—and decided she liked him.

And so Krissie played.

Adamm stood close by and watched approvingly as the girl splashed about in the waters of the lake; as she raced gleefully through the dense gathering of trees, stopping occasionally to climb one, never getting too far. Time, like a magical friend, seemed to stand still for Krissie as she completed her exploration of this wonderful place.

Finally Adamm gestured to her.

Breathlessly, Krissie scampered over to her new friend.

"You possess admirable energy," Adamm smiled.

"I've—never had so much fun," Krissie sputtered back.

"That is good," Adamm said. He then spoke with a slight regret in his tone. "However, the time has come for you to leave."

"No... I don't want to," Krissie protested, tears beginning to glisten in her eyes. "I—I wanna stay here, Adamm... with you."

Adamm placed both hands on Krissie's shoulders and lightly squeezed. "There is no need for you to be upset," he said comfortingly. "You will return to me."

"When?" Krissie asked eagerly.

"Tonight. And every night after. Already have you forgotten what I told you: That there is much for me to teach you?"

"But—how do I know for sure?"

"You *will* be back," Adamm said, rubbing his long fingers smoothly along Krissie's shoulders and up her neck. "Now you will close your eyes and relax."

"Do I really have to?"

"Relax," Adam whispered.

Krissie obeyed, reluctantly. She screwed shut her eyes and within minutes felt herself grow drowsy. Soon she was entering into a comfortable void…

Then she was spinning, descending deeper into the maelstrom. Then—blackness.

* * *

7:30 a.m.

Maureen was in the kitchen preparing Krissie's toast and juice and customary bowl of Cheerios, singing aloud with the vintage Beatles hit currently playing on the radio. She had slept well—never once waking to the now familiar, but no less upsetting sound of her daughter's screams—and was in a particularly bouncy mood this morning. Pouring herself a cup of perked coffee and setting Krissie's breakfast at her usual place on the oval dining table, Maureen didn't even attempt to question the grin that was steadily working its way across her face.

Damn, she just felt good.

"G'morning, Mommy!"

Maureen spun around and saw an equally cheery Krissie rush at her. Her grin broadening, Maureen lifted her daughter in her arms and hugged her tight.

"Mornin', angel. And how are you this fine day?"

Krissie planted a big, affectionate kiss on her mother's lips and giggled. "I'm real good."

"Real good, huh?" Maureen said in a lighthearted voice. "Well, does my *real good* daughter feel like some really good breakfast?"

Krissie nodded enthusiastically. "You bet. I'm starvin."

"Okay," Maureen said, easing Krissie down and patting her lovingly on her blue jeaned bottom, "then go sit yourself down at the table and dig in."

"French toast and bacon?" Krissie asked hopefully.

Maureen shrugged. "Cheerios and toast."

"Oh well," Krissie sighed, taking her place at the table, "I guess that's okay."

Maureen shook one of her bony fingers and pretended to mildly scold her. "Well, young lady, that just better be okay 'cause that's all you're gonna get. Until maybe Sunday."

"*Yipppeee!*"

Krissie giggled nasally and took a bite of toast, following with several quick sips of orange juice. Maureen brought her coffee over to the table and sat down across from her daughter. Sliding a cigarette between her lips and lighting it, she spent the next few minutes puffing leisurely and quietly studying Krissie, who was obviously enjoying a hearty appetite, and that was a good sign. What's more, no mention was made of any nightmare. Could it be?

Krissie gulped down the last of her orange juice, accidentally dribbling some onto her sweater. She looked furtively at her mother, who had both eyes focused on Krissie, but whose attention seemed elsewhere and her thoughtful expression didn't crack.

Krissie took her napkin and carefully, unobtrusively, blotted up the beads of juice. She then coughed and asked for another glass.

"Huh?" Maureen was slipping away from her thoughts. "Did you say something, sweetheart?"

"Could I please have another glass of orange juice?" Krissie repeated quietly.

"Oh, I don't know if that's such a good idea, honey. You don't want to be running to the bathroom all morning."

Krissie faked a disappointed frown and directed her attention to her bowl of Cheerios. She began shoveling the cereal into her mouth, barely stopping to breathe. Normally Maureen would have been quick to point out her lack of dining table etiquette, but just seeing her daughter with an appetite made her feel too good to complain.

Finally she had to ask.

"Honey, how did you sleep last night?"

Krissie's response was immediate, emphatically positive. "Oh, I had a real good sleep!"

Maureen sipped on her coffee. "You didn't have a bad dream?" she asked cautiously.

Krissie finished munching another mouthful of Cheerios; then she rested her spoon against the side of the bowl and gave her head a nod. At the same time her lips curved upward in a smile that, to say the least, puzzled her mother.

"You had another dream?"

"Yes. But I wasn't scared, Mommy."

"No?"

"Huh uh." Krissie looked briefly thoughtful. "Weeellll," she drew out, "I guess I was a little scared at first."

"Was it that same bad dream?" Maureen asked.

Krissie scrunched her brow. "It started off the same as always; you know, with those monsters chasing me. But then—my dream went kinda funny."

"How do you mean 'funny'?"

"Well, y'know how I tell you it's so scary—the place where I am?"

"Uh huh."

"Well, last night I was running away from the monsters and I came to this really pretty place. I remember there was this lake, and there were all these big trees... and Mommy, there was this little boy."

"Little boy?"

Krissie scratched her forehead. "Well, he didn't talk like a little boy, that's for sure. He'd use all these big words. But he looked like he was probably about seven... or maybe a little bit older."

Maureen regarded the long, curving ash on her cigarette and tapped it into the ashtray positioned in front of her.

"Did this boy talk to you?"

"Oh, he talked about a whole lot of things," Krissie replied, smiling broadly. "But a lot of the things he said didn't make any sense. But I remember him saying that I wouldn't have to be afraid of the monsters anymore. He didn't call them monsters, though. I think he called them... oh, I can't remember."

"Can you remember anything else he said?"

Krissie slowly shook her head and reached for her cereal spoon. "Not really." She took a spoonful of Cheerios, munched thoughtfully. She then said: "Oh yeah, I do remember something else. But I don't really know what he meant. He said he was going to teach me things."

"Teach you things?"

"Uh-huh."

"What sort of things, did he say?"

"All I really remember is that he said I was going to learn how to use some—special… I think he called it a…" Finally, becoming frustrated, Krissie grumbled, "Oh, I don't know, Mommy. I'm not really sure anymore."

Maureen butted her cigarette and glanced over at the pear-shaped wall clock. It was 7:50.

"Well, little darlin'," she said, "methinks you'd better wash up and start on your way to school."

Krissie nodded in half-hearted agreement. She took one last spoonful of her cereal, then stepped from the table and headed for the stairs.

Maureen smiled and said, "Love ya."

Krissie stopped. She turned around and, grinning playfully, ran into her mother's waiting arms for a hug.

A Day At School

JANET ROSSEN HAD TURNED twenty-six the past summer, but it still was not unusual for her to produce proof of age when going into a bar. She was a tiny creature, just making it to 5'1", with a non-maturing figure and delicate schoolgirl face.

She was to be Krissie's teacher for the new school year.

On this morning Mrs. Rossen stood at the blackboard and printed in large block letters a list of Grade Three level words. Her twenty-eight pupils, all present, were seated at their desks with their scribblers open, quietly copying down these written words.

After three neat columns of six words each were up on the board, Mrs. Rossen turned and faced the class.

"All right," she said, twirling the chalk stick smoothly between her fingers, "after you've finished copying all the words off the board I want you to make six different sentences using six of these words." She half-turned back to the board and pointed the chalk at VACATION. "For example, if one of the words you should choose is 'vacation' you could create a sentence like: *I spent part of my summer vacation at the beach.* Now do you all understand the assignment?"

The class responded with a collective: "Yes, Mrs. Rossen."

The electric clock over the side blackboard buzzed the lunch dismissal.

"Lunch already?" Mrs. Rossen muttered aloud, wondering what had happened to the morning. She checked her wristwatch against the clock; then smiled at the class.

"Okay gang, you're all dismissed. You'll work on your assignments first thing this afternoon."

Desk legs scraped noisily against the floor as twenty-eight eager children pulled free of their seats. There followed the hurried shuffle of sneaker-clad feet; the loud, spontaneous chattering.

"Quiet 'til you get outside," the teacher instructed them.

Grinning with the satisfaction of someone who truly enjoyed her job, Mrs. Rossen then sat down at her desk and shuffled through a stack of papers.

Krissie was one of the last pupils to leave. Before passing through the door, the little girl with the white hair and hauntingly pretty face turned to Mrs. Rossen and gave her a shy smile. The teacher returned it, along with a little wave.

She stopped what she was doing.

There was something about the Carver girl that suddenly set her to thinking. She seemed so unlike the other children in the class. Not a misfit really, but also not one for silliness, or even the typical schoolyard games, like hopscotch or jump rope. She was a quiet, maybe even an introspective child. Quite the opposite of tomboy Janet Palaniuk when she was the same age, for whom trouble could have been her middle name.

Mrs. Rossen had heard some circulating rumor about a medical problem, but she had never been fully informed. She wished she did know more; she found herself growing quite fond of the girl.

But Mrs. Rossen's thoughts concerning Krissie vanished once she remembered the lunch date she had—and that she was going to be late for! Glancing at her watch again, she picked up her purse and sweater and hurried out of the room, forgetting to shut the door behind her.

* * *

"Hiya Carver, I been looking all over for ya!"

Krissie's eyes rolled back in their sockets; she recognized that obnoxious cracking voice immediately. She told herself to ignore it.

"Aw, what's the matter, Carver?" the voice again called out. "Ya bein' stuck up or somethin'?"

Krissie wrapped the woolen sweater her mother had knit for her tightly around her shoulders and sped up her pace.

Peter Grubbish and a small gathering of his runny-nosed friends came charging up behind her.

"See, what'd I tell ya?" Peter said to his snickering buddies. "She's still the weirdest girl in school. She never talks to no one." He gave Krissie a sharp elbow nudge in the back. "Ain't that so, Carver? Ya never talk to no one?"

Krissie turned quickly out of the schoolyard. The boys, like a persistent pack of picking vultures, remained close behind, shouting insults—some surprisingly vulgar—and making all sorts of semi-human noises.

"Come on, Krissie!" Peter hooted, pulling hard on the back of her sweater. "I wanna be friends... just like last year."

Then began a high-pitched chorus of "Weird Krissie... Weird Krissie..."

The sharp honk of a car finally brought a halt to the cruel chanting and the jeers. Krissie meekly turned around and, spotting the familiar patchwork Chevy inching alongside on the road, breathed a heavy sigh of relief. Mrs. Rossen leaned out the open car window, a no-nonsense expression etched into her normally passive features. In her best disciplinarian voice she issued a stern warning to Peter and his friends: If they didn't leave Krissie alone immediately they'd all be staying after school for a week, cleaning chalk brushes! The boys took the message in the manner in which it was intended and sheepishly backed away. All except the orange-haired ringleader, who remained where he was for a moment, giving Krissie a threatening "I'll see you later" look.

Once the gang had dispersed, Mrs. Rossen tossed a reassuring wink to Krissie, and drove on to her appointment.

Krissie walked the rest of the way home with a toothy smile stretched across her face. With Mrs. Rossen as her teacher, she felt quite certain she was going to like Grade Three.

* * *

Janet Rossen took a tray and the necessary silverware and squinted into the shadowy darkness of the cafeteria. Unable to spot her lunch date, she started down the slowly moving line, waiting behind a couple who, if they had their way, would be sampling every item on display. Passing the tempting dessert window with some difficulty, Janet selected the spaghetti special and picked up a roll and butter farther along. It took a few seconds of debate, but she chose tea over coffee. She moved down to the aged, tired-looking cashier and paid her check.

Off in the far corner a lone figure waved to her. It was Michael. Janet waved back with a wide smile, then, taking her tray in both hands, carefully snaked her way through the maze of tables.

The well-dressed bearded young man stood up and pulled out her chair. "I was starting to think you weren't going to show," he said.

"Sorry," Janet apologized, "but I got caught up in some business at school."

"Oh? Anything important?"

"No, uh, just some paperwork I wanted to clear up before the weekend."

"You get it done?" Michael asked idly.

"No," Janet said, unloading her tray, "but I can work on it after class today; it shouldn't take me too long." She glanced about the restaurant. "Busy."

"Lunchtime," Michael replied. He pointed to her meal. "How much?"

"Three-eight-five," Janet replied. She hastily added, "But that's not including my very generous gratuity."

Michael's eyes squinted. "You left a tip?"

Janet smirked. "No-o-o-o."

Michael pulled out his wallet and removed four one-dollar bills. He had no change. "Keep it for the gas you used," he said with a slanted smile.

Janet grabbed the money and stuffed it into her purse. "You better believe I will," she said playfully.

Janet took her roll and carefully broke it in two, offering the larger half to Michael, who declined with a quick wave of his hand. Janet then noticed that he had only a cup of coffee and an untouched piece of banana cream pie sitting in front of him.

"Aren't you hungry?" she asked. "Michael, now I'm gonna feel not just guilty but gluttonous eating this."

"No, don't be silly, Jan. You go ahead, enjoy. I really don't feel like eating."

Janet eyed him with concern. "Is something wrong?" She probed a little deeper. "You seem to be preoccupied."

Michael brushed off her worry. "Naw, I just have sort of a queasy stomach."

"You're sure you're all right?"

Michael finished his coffee and pushed his cup to the far edge of the table. "I think I'll live."

Janet nodded faintly and buttered both halves of her roll. She then took her fork and began twirling the long strands of spaghetti around the prongs.

She noticed that Michael seemed a little uptight; fidgety, not as talkative as usual. Something definitely *was* troubling him.

"What's on your mind, Michael?" she asked quietly.

"Huh?" Michael cleared his throat. "Oh, I—I told you, Jan. It's just that my stomach is unsettled."

Janet slowly shook her head. "I'm not trying to put you on the defensive but…"

Michael sat motionless for a moment. He puffed out a breath.

"Okay," he then blurted. "Okay, you wanna know what it is? I'll tell you. I'm not sure about this weekend."

Janet creased her brow. "Not sure?"

"Jan, it's just that I've never… Well, Jan, you know."

"No, I don't know, Michael," Janet said straightly.

Michael shuffled in his chair. "Damn it, you're gonna make me say it, aren't you?"

Janet shook her head. "No. But I thought everything was decided. Chuck's going up north—"

Michael interrupted. "Just try to understand how it is for me."

"Oh, I think I'm beginning to understand," Janet said impatiently. "You've lost interest."

"That's not fair," Michael replied hastily. "How many times have I told you what I think of Chuck? The guy's an asshole. Living proof that Darwin was right. Hell, buggering off on you every other weekend on drinking excursions and then spending the rest of the time pub-hopping all across the city with his equally jerky friends, leaving you to take care of all responsibilities. Yeah, that's a sure sign of maturity all right. I mean, the guy's just never bothered to grow up."

"Don't you think I know that?" Janet grumbled, eyeing Michael harshly. "I've lived with it for six years. Six *long* years. But that's not what we're talking about."

"Yes it is." Michael lowered his eyes to the table. "It is because if I were Chuck I'd never think of treating you like that. You deserve more, Jan, a helluva lot more. So don't go saying I've lost interest in you."

Janet's features softened. Her lips pulled back into a smile and she blushed.

She spoke quietly. "I should have known what I'd be getting myself into. I still really don't know why I did it."

Michael reached across the table and tenderly closed a hand over Janet's.

"Well… maybe at that time you did love him," he said.

Janet shrugged. "Maybe." Then, after pondering for a moment, she shook her head. "No. No," she sighed, "I can't honestly say I ever did. I may have felt something, but it was never love. Never real love. I don't know, here I was: nineteen years old, going to university, planning to get my degree and become a teacher. Some of my friends from high school were already married; most were at least involved with somebody. But I was too heavy into my studies to develop any real relationship. Then one day I meet

Chuck—a guy who's always there to give me the encouragement I need. I guess deep down I was naive… or selfish. I wanted both my career, always number one, and a husband—but I guess mostly so I could feel I fit in with friends who I felt were starting to drift away because I was still single. Weird, huh?"

Michael replied with a mild shake of his head. "No."

"Of course Chuck happened along at the perfect time. He fit right in with my ambitions." She took a slow sip of her tea. "Then, not long after, I find out the only reason he was supportive was so I could someday carry the load. I got my degree, landed a teaching job and not a month later he either quit or got himself fired from his construction job. Never did know for sure what exactly happened."

Janet glanced down at her plate of spaghetti. It had gone cold. She pushed it aside, hesitated; then looked into Michael's eyes. They, in contrast, were warm.

"Tough break," he said.

Janet gave an empty nod.

Michael hesitated before he drew a breath. "About this weekend…"

Janet nodded hopefully, desperately.

"Yeah," he said, though he was unable to erase that reluctant edge from his voice. "But I'd be lying if I told you I feel all that comfortable about it."

"Michael," Janet said reassuringly, "there's nothing to worry about. Chuck won't be back 'til Sunday evening—late Sunday evening, guaranteed. It's going to be beautiful, you'll see."

Michael forced a thin smile.

"Yeah," he said.

* * *

Mrs. Rossen was going over the class assignment, calling on various pupils to stand up and read a few of their sentences. Dougie Purcell— by no means the brightest kid in the class, but a tryer— was struggling through the sentence using the word *prairie*. Mrs. Rossen couldn't be sure whether his difficulty stemmed from his inability to read his own writing or his inability to read, period.

"Dougie, would you please bring your scribbler up to my desk?"

Dougie's Adam's apple bobbed noticeably. He slowly shuffled up to the front of the room and handed the teacher his work. She examined it, shook her head.

"Dougie, I had *prairie* written up on the board this morning— in large, clear letters. How come you have it spelled P-R-E-I-R-Y?"

A few of the children snickered. Mrs. Rossen quickly quieted them with a firm, practiced look.

"But that's the way it looked to me, Mrs. Rossen," Dougie replied, his face flushed.

"Hmm, you've misspelled quite a few other words, too. Tell you what, Dougie. First thing Monday morning I want you to go to see the school nurse and have your eyes checked. Okay?"

Dougie nodded and returned to his desk. Mrs. Rossen scanned her class and finally called on Krissie to read next. The little girl timidly rose from her seat.

She spoke barely above a whisper. "One of the words I picked was *theater*. 'This summer my mother took me to the movie theater to see *Cinderella*.'"

"Very good, Krissie," Mrs. Rossen complimented. "But could you speak a little louder?"

Krissie nodded and cleared her throat. "Another word I have is *dream*. The sentence I made is: 'Now that I have a new friend I won't have bad dreams anymore.'"

Mrs. Rossen reacted with a quizzical look. What an odd sentence for a seven-year-old girl to write. For the moment, the teacher forgot about the assignment.

"A new friend, Krissie?"

Krissie nodded.

"And who might that be?" Mrs. Rossen inquired gently.

"His name is Adamm," Krissie replied with a beaming smile. "Adamm is my new friend."

* * *

For the children of Reuben Willis Elementary, the weekends officially started with the Friday three-thirty dismissal buzzer. At this time, four hundred-plus youngsters began the frantic race out of the school grounds.

Today, Ernest was standing on the other side of the wire mesh fence—his tense, sweaty fingers curled through the links. A cigarette butt dangling from the corner of his mouth, he watched the sudden avalanche of children pour out of the school.

He watched, and again he remembered.

Ernest didn't know what it was that brought him to the school grounds today. This time it wasn't the voice—*that damned voice!* It wasn't any conscious desire either. He figured it had to be some separate influence locked away deep inside, that somehow compelled him to return here… right back to the same wire mesh fence where it all began.

Two long, tortured years. But he still recognized the girl. She'd grown some, but that sweet trusting face had hardly changed at all.

She walked like all proper little schoolgirls: straight-backed, with her books held up close to her chest. She walked slowly, thoughtfully, with short steps.

Ernest heard a rasping whoop and he turned his attention toward the school. Three boys—one a rough-looking sort with a crop of tousled orange hair—came charging down the steps. They ran erratically across the hardtop, viciously shoving aside any children who happened to be in their way. Tearing onto the sidewalk, the three bullies headed straight for the little girl. The orange-haired one yelled some idiotic mock war cry. Then, jutting out his elbow and still going at full speed, he rammed his elbow into the girl's delicate back. Books and papers went flying into space as she shrieked and fell forward onto her hands and knees, ripping her palms on the rough pavement. The boys ran off laughing, but not before finishing the job of kicking her books onto the road.

A crowd of children and a few passersby gathered around to help the weeping child, and soon Ernest's view of her was blocked. He was about to take a few steps in that direction, but paused, thought about it, and, lighting a fresh smoke, turned the other way.

A sleek, jet-black Lincoln Continental sat parked across the street. The two male occupants—both of whom wore oversized sunglasses—weren't watching the crowd. Their attention was focused on Ernest.

* * *

Janet Rossen pulled her Chevy into the driveway and coasted to a stop. Shifting into neutral, she allowed the engine to idle for a few minutes while she prepared to face her husband. She was worried about that today. He'd know the minute he set eyes (probably heavy-lidded and bloodshot) on her that something wasn't quite right. Janet was afraid that she wouldn't be able to fake it. How could she? Her other feelings toward the man she really did care for were too strong. How could she be convincing?

Not that Janet had ever felt any great affection for Chuck, but when the honeymoon (a drunken weekend at a rundown lakeside cottage) had ended so had Chuck's romantic considerations for her. For six years she had lived with a beer-guzzling, foul-mouthed slob, whom she'd find either slouched in front of the TV set or passed out, often stark naked, snoring loud enough to bring down the walls of Jericho. Or else he'd be off drinking with his buddies. Sometimes he'd be gone for days on end and Janet wouldn't have any idea where he was (not that she was ever all that concerned, but it did get annoying fielding all of his telephone calls from his fun-loving friends). Then he'd come home, always without an apology or explanation, and get liquored up all over again. On very rare occasions he'd take a menial job for maybe a week to earn drinking money; most often she would be handing over cash from her paycheck to keep him satisfied. So what if they fell behind in their bill payments…

Fortunately, Janet's schooling, and now her career, had always been of primary importance. Because of it, she managed to tolerate the lifestyle she had so unwisely stepped into. But now that there was Michael she found it nearly impossible even to look at Chuck; to fake a smile required a huge effort.

Janet gazed at her reflection in the rear view mirror and sighed. Well, she thought, you made your bed. You damn well can't blame anyone else.

One comforting thought, however, was that if things worked out with Michael, she wouldn't hesitate to ask Chuck for that divorce she had so long considered. She truly believed Chuck would not miss her as much as the money that funneled through her.

Janet switched off the ignition and got out of the car. She slowly crossed the lawn, which was badly in need of a trim, to the front steps of her orange bungalow. Hesitantly, drawing a breath, she inserted the house key into the lock and turned it till she heard a 'click'. She pushed open the door and stepped inside.

The house was still.

Janet removed her shoes, placed them neatly on the plastic mat, and padded into the living room.

No one was there… though it was apparent something had gone on earlier. Overfilled ashtrays and empty bottles of beer littered the coffee table; the couch pillows were scattered across the floor; there was a big black stain of something on the carpet— and it had just been shampooed the week before!

Janet bit down on the inside of her mouth and then called for Chuck. She waited, but there was no reply. She called again, moved into the bedroom. Called yet again, went down into the basement. Finally Janet returned to the living room, figuring that Chuck and his cronies must have already gone off on their weekend drinking party.

Janet's ire gradually eased. She went over to the telephone and dialed a number.

After a few moments she spoke into the receiver:

"Michael? Come on over."

10 The First Lesson

TOGETHER THEY SAT by the still waters of the lake surrounded by a surreal and multicolored twilight: the boy, cross-legged, in a stiff meditative pose; the girl, cross-legged as well, but more loose and relaxed.

The boy, Adamm, was speaking.

"...and I was exiled by the evil society that once existed upon your planet. The society consisted of ambitious, corrupt individuals, and I attempted to halt their advances. Unfortunately, what chance had I—one—against the forces of so many?"

Krissie's eyes grew large. "But you're just a little boy!"

"Yes Krissie, I suppose you could say I am. And I was but a boy then, during that great struggle for dominance—so very many years ago."

Krissie's features expressed her bewilderment over what the boy was saying.

Adamm explained. "Do you recall when you asked me where we were—what place this was—and my answer to you was that we are a part of eternity?"

Krissie nodded, uncertain.

"It may prove difficult for you to understand, Krissie, but eternity is such that physical age is non-existent. As you can see, bodily I have not aged. Of course mentally and emotionally I have grown. I have advanced rapidly. Indeed, I have acquired much knowledge through all the years I have been part—" He opened his arms to their widest separation to indicate their surroundings. "—of this."

"You are very smart," Krissie said.

"Yes. Much time was spent learning… and observing." He added: "And planning."

Krissie squeezed her eyes. "Planning?"

"Yes Krissie, planning my return to the world I was made to leave. Your world. And this is why you were brought to me."

Krissie shrugged her shoulders. "But I'm only a little girl. You're the one who's smart."

"Yes, I possess the intelligence to know that I cannot free myself on my own."

"But what could I do?" Krissie asked.

"Again, do you recall when I told you that you were in possession of a very special gift?"

"Yes."

Adamm smiled; his strange eyes seemed to glow.

"Krissie, your 'gift', if used properly, could help me… so that I might come with you to your world, where I could continue to teach you and be your friend—always."

Krissie asked, "What kind of a gift is it?"

"Child," Adamm replied, "Simply your gift is this: *If you will it, so shall it be.*"

"Adamm, you're not making any sense again," Krissie said, flustered.

Adamm rose, taking Krissie's hand and gently pulling her up with him. In silence, they walked to the edge of the lake. There, Adamm stretched wide his arms and said: "Krissie, if I told you that you could make this entire lake vanish merely by wishing it, but wishing it hard, would you believe me?"

Krissie took a moment before answering. Then: "I don't know if I'd want to do that, Adamm. It's my favorite lake in the whole world."

"Indeed. But what if I told you that it was possible, that simply by wishing it you could transform all this before you into a barren desert?"

"I don't know," Krissie said, shrugging.

"Krissie, you possess the *ability*."

"Huh? The ability? What's that, Adamm?"

"Your gift, child. A most rare and enviable talent. It is the power to effect any change simply by willing it."

Krissie thought for a moment; a gleam came into her eyes.

"Do you mean I could really make this whole lake disappear... just by—thinking about it?"

"Indeed."

"Okay, I'll try."

Krissie closed her eyes tightly and thought about the lake drying up. In her mind she pictured the water evaporated, replaced with miles of beach sand, exactly like the photographs she'd seen. When she again opened her eyes, after several seconds of not very strained concentration, she saw that the calm blue waters were still before her. Her face dropped.

"Adamm, I thought you said—"

"Young Krissie. You possess the *ability*, but you must learn how to channel it. Your mastery over your power must be gradual."

"Can you teach me how to—channel it?"

"Yes, I can and I *will*."

Krissie was starting to grow excited. "When can we start?"

"It is apparent one of the first things I must teach you is patience. To use your gift effectively requires concentration. To concentrate effectively, you must first master patience."

Krissie's eyes drifted down toward the waters. "Sorry," she muttered.

Adamm took her by the hand and together they walked along the beach. It was cooler now and the yellows, reds, and lime greens of the surrounding skies were losing their hue and a curtain of more subdued blue began to paint the horizon.

"Sorry?" Adamm echoed. "Child, you will learn that with the *ability* you needn't ever be sorry. Indeed, when you have mastered your power and to call upon it becomes as simple as humming a tune, it shall be others who apologize to you."

Krissie's face scrunched up and her lips tightened. "I know one boy I sure wish I could make sorry. He's always picking on me and today after school he pushed me on the cement and hurt me real bad. Mommy had to put medicine on my hands because they were bleeding and that really stung."

"And you would like to punish this boy for hurting you?

"I sure would," Krissie said with emphasis.

Adamm said, "Very well. Perhaps that shall be our first test—when the time is right."

"Huh? What do you mean, Adamm?"

Adamm turned to Krissie and slowly closed his long fingers over her shoulders. "This boy," he said. "You shall use your gift to ensure that he never troubles you again."

Krissie's eyes got wide. "You mean I could really do that? Make sure that Peter Grubbish never picks on me anymore?"

Adamm merely smiled.

An eager look blossomed on Krissie's face. She still couldn't understand all that Adamm was saying, regarding this strange power of hers. What he called her... *ability*. But she did know that she must be pretty special if she could just think about punishing the boy who tormented her and it would happen. And Peter Grubbish deserved it!

Krissie's joy suddenly merged with a new confusion and she cocked her head and looked at Adamm.

"Adamm," she said thoughtfully, "I don't understand something. How is this *ability* going to help you come with me?"

Adamm said: "We shall not worry about that yet, child, for not until you have completely mastered the *ability* will it be of use to me. All I will say is this: When that time comes, when you have complete and absolute control over your gift, then it will require every ounce of the power. That is why it is necessary for us to begin with small exercises—to build up to that glorious point where you will be able to help me."

Krissie asked, "How long will that take?"

"Be patient," Adamm replied quietly. "The time is not very far off."

11 Saturday Barbecue

LAWRENCE CARVER CAME RIGHT out and angrily asked himself, "What the hell am I doing?"

He had accepted—much too hastily—his ex-wife's invitation to come to a backyard barbecue, and was now questioning his decision. What good could possibly come out of his going there? He and Maureen would just argue, as usual, and compete to see who could rack up the most points in the put-down department. Lawrence grumbled out an expletive, shook his head, and brought a fist down hard on the table beside him. Not only did he have difficulty understanding the actions of certain people around him (namely an ex-wife who extended barbecue invitations), lately he was having a hell of a time understanding the actions of *Lawrence Carver*!

It was a sunny and very dry Saturday afternoon. The curtains in Lawrence's apartment were drawn and the air conditioner was going full power. The scenic design clock over the television read 2:30, exactly. Nothing on the tube held his interest. Using his remote control, Lawrence absently switched through all the channels, twice, then finally clicked off the set. He remained seated in his chair for a moment, then forced himself up and went into the kitchen to fix that drink he'd been convincing himself he needed. He mixed a tall rum and Coke, swirled the drink around in the glass and returned to his chair. He lit a cigarette and leaned back.

But any relaxation he was hoping to capture was dashed as his brain was suddenly besieged by thoughts: some pleasant, others less so. But no matter what form they took, they all grouped around the same nucleus:

His daughter Krissie.

The pleasant thoughts were like brief, random excerpts from long ago memories. Quick flashes of events that, for the most part, seemed only to exist in a parallel world. The almost forgotten happy times spent before it all came tumbling down.

There were the Christmases, made extra special by the baby's presence... and Lawrence was remembering how he used to rush home from work, every day, just so he could hold that cuddly little bundle in his arms. He was remembering the day Maureen dressed up the three-year-old Krissie (she was such a curly top) in her best little outfit, a yellow frilled concoction, for that family portrait. And of course he was remembering the first day his little girl went off to kindergarten, so happy and excited because she felt so grown up...

Maybe he was feeling the effects of the alcohol, but what Lawrence found himself reflecting on were those times when he was sure no father loved a daughter more.

But Lawrence's lips drew tight and his eyes creased as those thoughts were overtaken by the deluge of unpleasant memories; painfully, they were all too vivid.

The assault on his daughter. And the mixture of responses that followed: the grief, confusion, concern. The consuming hate and guilt. The frustration at being so helpless.

But most prominent and lasting—the sickness that, like a cancer, spread rapidly through his system and chose to remain. Plaguing him endlessly as he became overwhelmed by a sense of self-loathing, brought on by feelings of revulsion.

Revulsion... toward his own flesh and blood.

Lawrence's thoughts traveled back even further; it was as if he were regressing through a series of doors, each one swinging open to reveal a dark and disturbing memory...

He was a little boy. It was a specific day in the spring of his eleventh year.

The day his sister came home.

Jeannie had just turned fourteen, but in many ways she looked more like a woman than her own mother. And she was a beauty. Slim, flaxen-haired, with soft blue eyes and features that could only be described as pure and angelic.

But despite the innocence of her looks, she had a rebellious side and chose to associate with a less than desirable crowd. Although she had been raised in a strict Protestant household, Jeannie began to exhibit undisciplined behavior once she reached her early teen years.

She knew that her parents would certainly have disowned her had they found out she was running with a wild bunch, so she was careful never to cause them suspicion. At this time she discovered another facet of her personality—the ability to lie convincingly.

But after about three months had passed, Jayne and Douglas Carver began picking out strange irregularities in their daughter's behavior; slight things, like the use of words and phrases they'd never heard her utter before. Never anything particularly offensive, just so unlike the child they had raised. However, being stubborn and old-fashioned (and strong in their conviction that their children could do no wrong), they directly attributed this to her school environment.

Lawrence remembered it as a Saturday. He had just come back from seeing a matinee featuring a science fiction picture about an invasion of giant mutant insects and was excitedly revealing the plot to his patient but less-than-interested mother, whom he remembered vividly as engrossed in the baking of a mammoth chocolate cake for a church luncheon. Lawrence remembered building dramatically to the climax of the movie when the back screen door slammed shut and Jeannie stumbled inside the house, sobbing hysterically. Her skirt and blouse were soiled and, revealingly, torn, and Lawrence recalled seeing something thick and red trickle down her legs (raspberry jelly, he kept thinking and not knowing why). His father came charging into the kitchen, his omnipresent pipe spewing cheap tobacco fumes, with a look in his eyes that gave Lawrence the impression he was ready for the kill. The moment he set eyes on his daughter, he ordered young Lawrence out of the room. The boy protested, out of brotherly concern for his sister, and his care was promptly rewarded with a sharp backhand swat (later the old man would make a half-assed attempt at an apology, but Lawrence could never really forgive him).

Lawrence ran sobbing to his room, but through the paper-thin walls he heard his sister's story.

Jeannie, out of fear and anger, didn't hold anything back. She admitted that she had been fooling around with a rough crowd, smoking and drinking and hanging out at disreputable night spots. Then she tearfully told her parents how two of the boys had lured her into the back of a clubhouse and spent the better part of the afternoon violating her. She went into graphic detail, and Lawrence could only imagine the look on his parents' faces as they listened to her story. Jeannie had hoped for understanding—for sympathy—but neither Mother nor Father was prepared to offer their daughter any comfort. Instead, shocked out of their comfort zone, they attacked her, calling her a "whore" and "a disgrace to the good name of Carver." Her mother spat on her and her father replaced compassion with two good slaps to the face. Lawrence remembered cringing as he heard his sister plead for forgiveness, only to fall under the barrage of accusation.

There was never any question about Jeannie keeping the baby. Nor was adoption a consideration. Despite his parents' strong religious convictions, arrangements were made immediately to terminate the unwanted pregnancy. A child conceived under such brutal circumstances was an abomination, an insult to God.

After the abortion things were never the same—not between Jeannie and her parents, nor between Jeannie and Lawrence. They had always enjoyed a special bond, but his parents had drilled it into him that his sister was no better than a street tramp. In the two years that followed, the girl underwent a drastic personality change. Once so fresh and lively, she became unnaturally withdrawn, almost catatonic. "I don't live in this house, I only exist here" was the one phrase she would periodically repeat to her brother.

But Lawrence likewise offered her no sympathy. Due to his parents' influence he no longer regarded Jeannie as his sister. She had selfishly brought shame to the family. While Jeannie was allowed to stay in the house, she was rarely acknowledged. Both Mother and Father explained in their unyielding way that any girl violated in such a manner was now unclean. The gray, solemn words of his old man still echoed in Lawrence's mind, like the fading but never totally dissipating knell of a distant bell: "I don't care how old she is, or what color she is, or even what religion she is. When a thing like that happens to a girl, she's been touched by the hand of the devil. Son, you never have anything to do with her after that."

And harsh as they were, Lawrence grew up remembering those words. He could never feel the same about Jeannie.

Less than four years later, early on a November morning, Jeannie, aged eighteen, was killed in a two-vehicle accident on a lonely stretch of road leading into the city following a weekend party. Jeannie had moved out with some friends by then. She just never cared anymore and gave vent to her rebellion. Her companion and driver of the car, Charlie Hendricks, had obviously enjoyed himself too much because, according to the one witness to the accident, he was "weaving and doing a lightning bolt across the road." Until his vehicle hit a patch of ice. His T-Bird swerved over the center line and collided with an oncoming semi. The driver of the semi survived. Charlie and Jeannie were killed instantly.

Jeannie's funeral was a closed casket affair; Lawrence heard the rumor that his sister's body had arrived at the mortuary in bags…

While his parents were devout churchgoers, they decided against the service being held at their regular parish; instead, the funeral was held at the mortuary itself, where Lawrence remembered his mother and father sitting in rigid impassivity, politely if coolly accepting the condolences of those mourners in attendance…

As these disturbing memories faded, Lawrence discovered that he was standing in the kitchen, preparing another drink.

He shook his head rapidly, as if trying to physically shake away those tragic images. But what he could never erase from his mind was the crystal clear image of his sister, stamped indelibly on his brain… and how much his daughter Krissie resembled her when Jeannie was young.

When his head was clear, Lawrence turned and contemplated his empty glass. Passing up the Coke, he knocked back two ounces of straight rum. Another straight shot before the empty bottle went into the trash can.

* * *

It was after three. Maureen told Lawrence to be at the house no later than three-thirty. However, he decided not to go straight there. Instead, Lawrence stopped off at his favorite watering hole and slammed back a couple doubles.

By the time he arrived at the duplex it was 4:15, and he was hardly sober. Maureen knew instantly by the heavy smell of alcohol that wafted from his breath that he had made a detour. While upset, she decided not to say anything because earlier she, too, had indulged in a few afternoon libations in preparation of his visit.

She did, however, ask him if he wanted some mouthwash; Krissie was sure to notice the odor of booze.

Lawrence responded in predictable fashion.

"Maureen," he slurred, "why don't you just get the fuck off my back."

Maureen tensed. "If you're planning on using your PR language around here, you might as well leave now," she said, standing her ground.

Lawrence hesitated, caught unprepared by the sternness of her attitude, and for just a moment Maureen thought he was going to turn back to the car. But he looked at her, nodded slowly, and started into the house. Maureen stood aside and held the door open for him. She didn't want him to leave, but she wasn't pleased at having their daughter see him in this condition either.

One thing Maureen did know for certain—and it made her resentful. This was not going to be the pleasant visit she had been planning for.

Damn it, Lawrence, I'm doing my part.

"Barbecue's out back," she said coldly, stepping in after Lawrence. "Cheeseburgers and hot dogs."

"Sounds quaint," Lawrence said.

Maureen held up her hands and worked them against each other. "How about a cup of coffee?"

Lawrence came back quickly with, "How 'bout a brewskie?"

Maureen pushed out a breath. Against her better judgment, but attempting to forestall the inevitable argument, she crossed over to the bar. She opened the fridge and peered inside.

"Any preference?" she asked, biting her bottom lip.

"You mean I've got a choice?"

Maureen sighed. "Not really."

"As long as it's cold," Lawrence replied.

Maureen popped the cap off a bottle of domestic ale and asked, "Glass?"

"Yeah, sure," Lawrence nodded. "It's not so—" he deliberately brought up a belch "—gassy that way."

Maureen grimaced. She poured the beer into a mug and handed it to Lawrence who raised it in a mock toast.

He sipped off the foamy top. "Hits the spot."

"Yeah, I'll bet," Maureen muttered under her breath. She lighted a cigarette and went over to the chesterfield.

Lawrence spun around on his stool. "Where's the kid?"

The kid? That struck Maureen as being somewhere between uncaring and cold-blooded.

"Your daughter," she replied deliberately, "is out back watching the barbecue."

"Is that such a good idea?" Lawrence asked absently, patting his pockets for his smokes.

"She's not exactly a baby, Lawrence. Besides, she's just looking at the coals."

"Well, I guess you'd know," Lawrence mumbled miserably.

Maureen pretended not to hear. She was not going to acknowledge an invitation to an argument.

"So I was going to ask," Lawrence next said as he twisted the mug of beer between the palms of both hands. "This Kinbrace character. Do you feel that he's doing anything for Krissie?"

"It's only been one visit," Maureen replied with knowing suspicion.

"Yeah, I know. But d'ya think anything is gonna come out of it?"

"It's not costing you anything," Maureen retorted.

"I'm not talking about that," Lawrence said with emphasis.

Maureen softened. "Lawrence, I don't know. But Krissie seems to be comfortable with him."

"That doesn't answer my question."

"Lawrence, if anybody can help, I think Dr. Kinbrace is the one," Maureen said with a sigh.

Lawrence sipped on his beer. Stubbing out her cigarette, Maureen headed for the kitchen. She began placing the hamburger patties on a tray.

"I'm going to start barbecuing the burgers," she said, adding: "If you're ready to eat."

"Shit," Lawrence grumbled. "I can't remember what I did with my friggin' smokes."

Maureen rolled her eyes. "Oh, take one of mine," she said. "And when you come outside do you wanna bring the wieners and buns with you? They're on the counter."

Maureen hadn't told Krissie that her daddy was coming to the barbecue; she wanted it to be a surprise. But when Lawrence appeared in the backyard and said "Hi" to his daughter, Krissie's reaction was not quite what Maureen had been expecting. She seemed strangely distant. Not at all excited to see him.

It was an awkward dinner. They ate quickly, and in relative silence. Lawrence's attempts at conversation with his daughter went nowhere. She either ignored him or answered him shortly. He'd noticed that the palms of her hands were badly scraped and asked what had happened. She wouldn't tell him; Maureen had to explain the incident with Peter Grubbish. She noticed the color in his face start to darken and worked to calm his temper, which could turn unpredictable with all he'd had to drink.

"If I ever see that little punk," Lawrence said through gritted teeth…

* * *

At 6:30 the skies turned gray and there was a sudden cloudburst, so the rest of the dinner moved indoors. Immediately after finishing her meal, Krissie asked to be excused. Maureen said no, that her father had come over especially to see her. But Lawrence managed an indulgent smile and told Maureen to let her go play, there'd be plenty of time to see her later. Maureen could see that Krissie's behavior had made it uncomfortable for Lawrence and so she reluctantly gave her daughter permission to go to her room. Krissie then kissed her mother on the cheek, thanked her for dinner, and went skipping off to her room.

Maureen was about to call after her to say goodnight to her father, but Lawrence halted her, taking his ex by the arm and giving his head a shake.

"Let her go," he said.

Lawrence and Maureen both found that they had lost their appetites.

It was hard to tell who was the more embarrassed, but Maureen decided to replace her usual after-dinner coffee with something a little stronger. Of course Lawrence didn't have to be coaxed into joining her.

There was a long strained silence between them. Finally Maureen felt that something had to be said, but a weak "I'm sorry" was all she could manage.

"Is this the work of that psychiatrist?" Lawrence asked abruptly.

"You can't blame Dr. Kinbrace," Maureen returned.

"No? Well, she wasn't acting this way before she started seeing him."

For a brief moment Maureen considered that Lawrence had a valid point. But in the next instant she refused to accept it.

"He wouldn't turn Krissie against you."

Lawrence wore a slanted smile. "Maybe not deliberately, but who knows what Krissie has been telling him."

Maureen said, "Maybe... it's because of the way you were today." She offered a meek smile. "You weren't at your best."

Lawrence refused to acknowledge that possibility.

"Krissie loves you," Maureen assured him.

Lawrence finished his drink, hotly. "Yeah. She sure showed it tonight."

* * *

At 9:30, long after Lawrence had left, Maureen tiptoed into Krissie's still-lighted bedroom, expecting to find her fast asleep. But the little girl was lying atop her Cinderella comforter, reading aloud from a picture book. Maureen sat down beside her and began stroking her hair.

"Whatcha reading?" she asked, picking up Mr. BoBo Jones, Krissie's ragged teddy with her free hand.

"Oh," Krissie replied softly, "just an old storybook I found in my closet." She held up the worn cover and Maureen saw that it was *Pinocchio*.

Maureen said, "You know, when I was a little girl that was my favorite story."

Krissie rolled over onto her side. "Really!"

"Sure," Maureen laughed. "Let's see if I can still remember: Jiminy Cricket, Papa Gepetto, oh, and that whale—"

"Monstro!"

"Yeah," Maureen said, waving her index finger. "Boy, he used to give me a scare."

"He doesn't scare me," Krissie said proudly.

"No?"

"Huh-uh, not anymore," Krissie said with a determined shake of her little head. "No monsters scare me anymore."

"Really?"

"Nope. Not since I met Adamm."

Maureen frowned. "Adam?"

"My new best friend."

"Oh…?"

"He protects me from those awful monsters that used to chase me and he tells me he always will."

Maureen didn't quite know what to make of what Krissie was telling her, and it was too late to start asking questions. She was tired, a little drunk and she had something a little more important to say to her daughter.

"Honey, I think you hurt your daddy's feelings tonight."

Immediately, Krissie's cheery disposition vanished and she turned back to concentrate on her book. With a light finger she began tracing the comical figures on the cover.

"Do you wanna talk about it?" Maureen asked her.

Krissie shook her head.

"Is it maybe because of the way Daddy was when he came over tonight?"

Maureen heard a few faint sobs cough out of the little body beside her. She turned her daughter toward her and held her tightly in her arms. Krissie cried freely.

"Don't be mad at your daddy," Maureen said, herself starting to weep. "He loves you very much."

Krissie rubbed her eyes with tight little turns. She looked up at her mother. "I know he does," she stammered.

Maureen patiently waited for Krissie to get it all out of her system. She then asked her to tell her what happened.

"I don't know, Mommy," Krissie said with a sad sigh. "But when I saw Daddy in the backyard tonight I felt—so funny. I really didn't want to see him."

"But darling, there has to be a reason," Maureen said. "Has Daddy done or said anything to upset you lately?"

"Huh uh." A sob was creeping back into Krissie's voice. "Mommy, I don't know what it is. Honest. But you know how sometimes you know you're doing something wrong and you don't really wanna do it, but you can't help yourself? That's how I felt."

Maureen nodded. She decided not to pursue this any further; Krissie was clearly bothered by these unpleasant yet strange emotions she was dealing with. Instead, Maureen tucked her daughter snugly under the covers and told her not to worry. She explained to her that she was just growing up and experiencing new and confusing feelings. Maureen didn't know if that truly was the case, but it sounded like a good explanation for now. Krissie seemed to accept what her mother was telling her and cheered up a bit. In a steadier voice, she told her mommy that she was sorry and that she would call Daddy tomorrow and also tell him that she was sorry for being bad.

Maureen kissed her tenderly on the forehead and urged her to go to sleep. "Things will be better in the morning."

She was hoping they would be.

12 Janet and Michael

THE BEDROOM WAS VEILED in velvety black, a faint aroma of honeysuckle lingering pleasantly in the air. The clock radio on the bedside table was turned on and the relaxing strains of an instrumental rendition of *Scarborough Fair* came drifting through the speaker, only occasionally mixing with the irritating crackle of static.

Michael Daley was lying on his side, his right arm positioned between his head and the pillow. He squinted his eyes (he was nearsighted, a contact lens wearer) to make out the time indicated on the luminous face of the clock. It was now Sunday morning: 12:04 a.m. Michael sighed quietly and rolled over onto his opposite side, so that he was now facing Janet. He'd hardly slept five minutes, but here she was—dead to the world. And, judging by the puckered smile on her lips, obviously *satisfied*.

Satisfied? Michael thought. Hah! That was a laugh and a half. How did it go: *Slam, bam, thank you, ma'am…* Those old words of "bedroom business" summed up exactly what Michael thought of his performance (and it was a performance!) earlier. In-out-cigarette…

116

(*But you're in another man's bed*)

Michael rolled over again, more forcefully.

(*With another man's wife!*)

Michael sat up quickly and exhaled long and hard, as if he had just wakened from some terrible dream. Well, it was terrible all right. But it was no dream.

He looked over at the still, peaceful form lying next to him and muttered a throaty "I'm sorry." Janet seemed to respond to his words. Her left eye pried open, closed; then both eyelids fluttered open.

She stretched and smiled up at Michael. "Mmmm, hi."

Michael didn't return the smile. Had Janet been able to focus through the hazy darkness, she would have noticed that all his features were working together to form the frown now highlighting his expression. His arms were folded around his raised knees and he was gently rocking back and forth. Janet pulled herself up and hooked an arm around his neck.

"What's wrong, honey?"

"Do you really have to ask?" Michael replied miserably.

"No," Janet said with a sigh, slowly pulling her arm away. "No, I guess I don't."

"I—tried," Michael whispered, the frustration seeping through with his words. "Jan, I really tried."

"I know you did."

"It's just not going to work." Michael stepped out of bed and crossed the old linoleum floor to the light switch. He flicked it on and it took a minute for him to adjust to the sudden flood of illumination.

"I can drive you," Janet offered half-heartedly, hoping that he would change his mind and just crawl back into bed beside her.

"No, I'll call a taxi," Michael said, reaching for his shirt and jeans; hesitating. "Damn, I wish to hell I knew what to do." He whirled around to Janet. "I want nothing more than to stay here with you. But—well, look what happened. Last night I couldn't even get it up and tonight I performed worse than some faggot monk."

"It wasn't that bad, Michael," Janet reassured him, though it was obvious she was merely trying to appease his manhood.

"Yeah, well of course you'd say that," Michael said with an unfunny smile.

"I'm serious."

Michael turned back around and slipped into his jeans.

"You don't have to leave because of… *that*," Janet argued. "Michael, for now it's not important."

Michael stared down at the floor and shook his head. He had known since the beginning that this moment was inevitable, and he had carefully prepared what he was going to say.

"But don't you see, Jan? The reason it didn't work is because I shouldn't be here—not tonight, not ever. I guess there's no way I can say this without coming across as a triple square, but over the past few weeks I've discovered I have these—I dunno, principles I guess you could call 'em. What's more, they keep gnawing away at me. Look, you're a married woman. Yeah, Chuck's a horse's you-know-what and I'd trade places with him in a heartbeat, as far as you're concerned. But dammit, it's just not in me to mess around with another man's wife." He paused; then spoke less intensely. "If you were to leave Chuck for good—well… Jan, I love you. You mean more to me than anyone. But I can't, not under this arrangement."

Janet murmured, "You're making it sound—so final."

Michael eyed her sternly. "That's gotta be up to you."

13 Incident at Reuben Willis Elementary

MONDAY MORNING WAS GLOOMY.

There was a heavy overcast that shadowed most of the city in a cold, depressing gray. A September wind gusted strongly from the east, scattering dead leaves and loose garbage along the streets and sidewalks.

The schoolyard of Reuben Willis Elementary was especially dark, as if the blackest clouds chose precisely that location over which to hover, like a portent. In fact, if one were superstitious, it would be hard not to think back to a day very similar to this, almost four years before. The day of the only fatality ever associated with Reuben Willis. Ten-year-old David Reardon was just leaving the school grounds with a group of his friends when a sudden gust of wind grabbed hold of his handful of papers and sent them scattering. Immediately, without thinking, David rushed after some onto the road and was struck dead by a van.

Principal Wiley and his staff were hit hard by this tragedy, but rumor had it they were affected more by the black mark against their school's safety record than by the loss of a student.

* * *

Principal Harriman Julius Wiley was, in appearance, the epitome of conservatism. He was a tall, broad man in his late forties, with neatly-combed hair graying in just the proper pattern to make him distinguished. He dressed soberly; always in dark, three-piece suits with plain white shirts and simple neckties. Principal Wiley was also a man highly educated, with almost as many letters behind his name as there are in the alphabet. Of course he was a strong proponent of the values of education and, where appropriate, the strict discipline of children.

The wind was howling, banging against the office window that overlooked the playing field. It was a continuous and unsettling sound.

Seated behind his desk, Mr. Wiley was giving his early morning face the once-over with his cordless Remington. He clicked off the razor and ran a hand along his cheeks and neck. Nodding slightly to himself, he returned the razor to its case which he then carefully placed into the side drawer of his desk.

He now felt ready to face the challenges of the day.

There was a light tapping at the door before Mrs. Grywinski, his hatchet-faced secretary, stepped into the office.

"The boys you wanted to see are waiting in the outer office," she announced.

"Thank you, Mrs. Grywinski," Mr. Wiley smiled. He took a sip of his coffee. "You can send them in."

The old secretary left the office, leaving the door slightly ajar, and almost immediately Peter Grubbish and his two pals from the previous Friday's incident filed in. Mr. Wiley set aside his coffee cup, then leaned back in his chair and eyed each of the boys sternly. There was the customary moment of silence that had become a familiar prelude to all of the principal's disciplinary meetings.

The boys were standing side by side in a straight line, like soldiers awaiting inspection. Despite the probable severity of what was to come, not one of the boys appeared to be overly nervous.

The principal said, "Well Mr. Grubbish, I see we're starting this year off on the wrong foot."

"Yessir, Mr. Wiley," Peter said, his play at politeness not fooling the principal.

"Mmmhmm."

Mr. Wiley glanced down at a yellow sheet of paper on his desk, looked across to the other two boys.

"Tom Dwyer and Greg Crowley," he said, nodding in recognition. "I don't suppose I have to tell you boys either that I'm not too surprised to find you here."

The boys shook their heads.

"I couldn't hear that," Mr. Wiley snapped.

"No sir," Tom and Greg mumbled in unison.

Mr. Wiley rose from his chair and started toward the coat rack at the opposite end of his office. His expression was unflinching.

He said, "I don't know if you boys realize the seriousness—not to mention the stupidity—of your actions on Friday. What if one of the children you pushed had fallen and been seriously injured? As it is, I understand that one little girl got her hands cut quite badly. Do you have anything to say for yourselves?"

The boys remained quiet, and stood motionless, though the faint trace of a smile was beginning to appear on the corners of Peter Grubbish's mouth. Mr. Wiley caught that smirk and managed to wipe it off with a hard-eyed glare.

He then said, "I hope you boys realize that you're going to have to be disciplined for this. I feel that a week-long detention should also be in order." He then reached for his strap hanging from its place on the coat rack. "And a more immediate punishment is also in order."

* * *

Janet Rossen wasn't quite herself that morning. She taught her class as usual, but was merely going through the motions, like a well-oiled piece of pre-programmed machinery.

She was preoccupied with a troubling personal matter. So it had finally come to her making the choice. Of course she had been expecting it—but now it seemed too sudden even for her. The problem was that Michael had issued the ultimatum without his offering any real commitment. Oh, perhaps there was some suggestion of a future together, but Janet had to be honest. She had always hoped to make her decision to leave her husband with Michael waiting with the promise of marriage.

…the *promise*…

Johnny Lancaster finished answering the last arithmetic problem on the board and was repeatedly clearing his throat to get his teacher's attention. Mrs. Rossen snapped back to herself and blushed in subdued embarrassment. She warned Robert Schroeder about whispering in class—unnecessary, since he wasn't, but she wanted to show her pupils that she *was* paying attention. She got up from the desk and examined Johnny's chalked-in answers…

But it was difficult for her to stay focused…

On the other hand, perhaps she had never been all that optimistic about her future with Michael. Now that it had come down to her making the choice, she was afraid, more than a little hesitant.

But the question she kept asking herself was *why?*

After all, she was in love with Michael, of that she was sure, and she never had any doubt the feeling was reciprocated… and she certainly placed no importance on her marriage.

Was it fear of how Chuck might react?

Yes! Yes, that was her worry—and she knew it all along. Chuck didn't know how to treat a wife, how to be gentle. And if Janet were to disappear for a few days chances were he wouldn't even notice, provided he had access to some cash for his own amusements. But how would he respond if she were to tell him she was leaving him for good? She understood it wouldn't be her he'd miss so much, but her bank account. Chuck had a temper, one that he never took great pains to control. She remembered the night he was out drinking with his cronies and a waiter accidentally overturned a filled ashtray onto his table. Janet wasn't there, but she heard the story from the two police officers who escorted Chuck home that night. The way she understood it, it was a miracle he didn't hospitalize the poor man.

Janet shuddered just recalling this and other incidents that occurred whenever his temper would ignite.

Her concern shifted to Michael. If she told Chuck she was leaving him for someone else and he were to find out whom, what might Chuck do to Michael?

The 10:15 buzzer sounded. Recess.

Once again Janet was snatched from her thoughts; this time mercifully. She was surprised to find herself trembling, feeling emotionally drained. She glanced at her watch, worked on a smile for her class.

"Okay, we'll do the rest of these problems right after recess."

* * *

Peter Grubbish was leaning against the outside wall of the school, on the side that faced the gravel parking lot and the playing field. His two buddies, Tom and Greg, were standing on either side of him. All three had their hands buried deep in their pockets, each still aching from Principal Wiley's punishment.

"It's all that Krissie Carver's fault," Peter snarled. "She probably finked to Wiley."

Greg shrugged his shoulders and said, "So whatcha gonna do 'bout it?"

Peter spit out a missile-like stream of saliva and popped a wad of gum into his mouth. "Aw, I dunno," he said, putting an exaggerated effort into his chewing. "But I sure know I gotta do somethin'." He chewed more vigorously on his gum; then said miserably, "Now a week's detention. My old man's gonna kill me."

"You aren't the only one," Greg said.

Tom started walking away, toward the hardtop. Peter called after him.

"He's chicken," Greg sniggered, bending his arms at the elbow and flapping them against his sides, mimicking the bird. "He told me he don't want no part of anymore of your ideas."

Peter stared after Tom, popped a large pink bubble.

"Aww, let him go," he said. "As long as he don't start finkin' on us."

A large group of boys from Grades Four to Six came storming onto the field with their baseball equipment. They momentarily congregated at the backstop to choose up teams and distribute the gloves. Peter, who boasted of failing two years consecutively and should now have been in Grade Five, watched as half of the boys scattered onto the field and their assigned positions. The other group, with the exception of

Raymond Gautron, who was first at bat, stepped behind the backstop, awaiting their turns.

The wind was still gusting. Peter and Greg doubled over in laughter as they watched class klutz Todd Adotta chase after his bouncing and rolling baseball cap that a sudden harsh sweep of wind had caught and blown off his head.

"Wanna go watch 'em?" Greg asked.

"Yeah, I guess so," Peter shrugged. "Nothin' else goin' on."

The two youths scurried across the field, kicking up light showers of gravel as they ran. Peter happened to glance back at the school and saw Mr. Wiley peering out his office window, looking as austere as ever. Peter had the urge to pull down his pants and wave his dick at the principal, but didn't want to press his luck.

When they got to the backstop, there were a few low rustles of "Hi Pete" and "Hi Greg," but most of the players chose to ignore the two boys. They were wise enough to know that Peter Grubbish and anyone who bothered to associate with him were bad news.

Raymond Gautron already had two strikes against him. Pat Corbett was pitching and all the boys were betting that he'd strike him out. Peter started snickering and making cracks about Raymond's holding the bat like a fairy. The other Team I players tried to shut him up, but it was no use. Once Peter Grubbish got on a roll nothing could turn him off.

It took a long time for the final pitch. Unbearably long for Raymond, who was steady in his pose, trying to shut out Peter's comments, and failing. Pat Corbett could see that Raymond was stressed and nervous and, in all fairness, gave a few seconds before delivering the pitch.

—"Throw the ball, Corbett!"—

—"Yeah, c'mon and strike him out so's we can get on with the game!"—

Pat couldn't wait any longer. He wound up, and pitched the ball. To Raymond, the ensuing split second slid into slow motion action: a 78 r.p.m. record revolving down to 33 1/3. He could see the ball coming at him. It was a perfect pitch. Smooth. He knew he could hit it. *He could*! His arms swung out powerfully with the bat… and then the record switched back to its normal speed and Raymond heard a *whoosh* and a soft thud as the ball hit dead on—right in the back catcher's mitt.

"Yer out, Raymond!" someone with an irritatingly scratchy voice yelled; probably Reg Underwood because his voice had started to undergo a premature metamorphosis the past summer.

Peter slapped Greg on the back and laughed so hard that he practically fell to the ground.

"Didn't no one ever tell ya, Goat?" he hooted. "Fairies don't play baseball—they dance ballet!"

No one else on the playing field was laughing, not even his buddy Greg.

Raymond Gautron swung around and glared at Peter. He was turning quite purple and the veins in his forehead were beginning to swell.

His teammates were prepared to draw blood, but instead of ganging up on Peter and beating the crap out of him, they just angrily shouted for him to get lost. Peter, doubled over in laughter, pointing his finger mockingly at Raymond, pulled himself upright and stumbled away from the backstop. As he moved onto the gravel parking lot, he happened to glance up.

Standing on the very edge of the hardtop was the little white-haired girl: looking very rigid, glaring under hooded eyelids at Peter, with an expression so unnerving that the boy felt an unexpected chill creep through his body.

And suddenly he wasn't laughing.

He tried to project his cockiness, stare back at the girl, but found that his eyes kept veering away from her.

A weird sort of feeling was starting to overtake him. A feeling so strange and unnatural that it was impossible for Peter to comprehend.

Peter swallowed a heavy breath and turned to Greg—but his friend wasn't there. His eyes darted about the field and he finally saw him—still at the backstop, apparently ignoring him. Peter was feeling really uneasy. Almost against his will he found his eyes sliding back over to the hardtop.

The girl still was glaring at him, her expression growing ever more intense.

His focus remained so steady on Krissie Carver that Peter didn't acknowledge the shouts that suddenly erupted from the boys in the field... as Raymond Gautron slowly crept up behind him, brandishing the baseball bat like a club.

* * *

Usually Mrs. Rossen, when she wasn't on recess duty, spent break periods in the staffroom, chatting with the other teachers. Today, however, because of the mood she found herself in, she decided to spend this recess alone in the quiet of her classroom.

She was munching on a coconut granola bar, not really tasting it, still trying to sort out her conflicting thoughts. The problem she was now dealing with was entirely of her own making: constant dwelling on her situation; blowing her concerns so completely out of proportion that she couldn't conceive of any satisfactory solution. She knew that she had to empty her head of this clutter of worries; give herself a break before she drove herself right up the wall—sideways!

Not surprisingly she could feel a headache coming on; minor now, but she recognized this kind of pain and knew that by noon she could be in the throes of a major migraine.

A two-month vacation would be good right about now, she thought with a sigh.

A series of screams coming from outside pierced the silence.

Mrs. Rossen had just tossed away her snack wrapper when she heard it. Before she knew how to respond, there was more screaming—continuous—all merging together into a single shrieking cry of distress.

Mrs. Rossen shot up from her desk. She darted for the door.

A few teachers were already in the hallway, moving around in a lost, confused sort of way.

—"What the hell is that?"—

—"Who's doing all that screaming?"—

—"My God, one of the children must be hurt!"—

Mr. Wiley came charging out of his office. His usual calm demeanor had vanished and he rushed frantically out of the building.

Mrs. Rossen and other teachers followed close behind.

The activity was at the far corner of the parking lot, by the field. There was an ever-growing circle of children: some were hysterical, a few throwing up; others were merely wandering around in a wide-eyed daze. Mr. Wiley grabbed one of the kids randomly: twelve-year-old Phillip Mann. The principal asked him what happened; no answer; shook him; no response. The boy was clearly traumatized by whatever he had seen.

Mrs. Rossen had kept on going forward. The circle of children was so thick that it was impossible for her to see what was going on. She started pushing her way in, using more muscle than was needed. Young bodies were shoved aside as the teacher waded in deeper. At once, this all dissolved into a nightmarish kaleidoscope… of frightened young faces…

Mrs. Rossen could feel her heart beating more rapidly with each step she took. Whatever had happened, she was expecting the worst.

It was the worst that she got.

Some intuition told her that it was the Grubbish boy, but she never would have known by the body that lay sprawled on the ground—

Because there was no face, just an opaque veil of crimson.

There was not much left of the head at all. It had obviously been crushed, likely repeatedly, by some heavy instrument…

…and Raymond Gautron was standing not three feet away, his face devoid of any expression, holding a baseball bat that was dripping gore all over his running shoes. Mrs. Rossen could only mouth:

"Raymond…"

14 Changes

KRISSIE CALLED: "Adamm, where are you?"

There was the sound of her own echo, far off and fading into the distance, but no reply.

For the first time since she had met the strange little boy with the soul-consuming eyes he was not present to greet her. Krissie was growing concerned. Scared. She went over to the lake and stood with her feet just dipping into the water, surprised to find the comfortable currents unusually cold.

She glanced about in every direction. But all was still. The little boy named Adamm was not to be found.

The chill from the water was beginning to creep up her spine, so Krissie stepped back onto the sand—so warm beneath her feet. She turned and looked into the forest of trees. She could not spot the boy but of a sudden the trees appeared different to her. They seemed somewhat darker, the branches not as sturdy and proud; the color of the foliage not as vibrant.

"Adamm?" She was now merely whispering the name.

"Hello Krissie."

The familiar voice came from behind, drifting up from the waters.

The little girl quickly spun around, but the eager smile she was wearing abruptly vanished.

Adamm was standing waist-high in the lake. He was naked, and one of the first things that Krissie noticed was that there were no markings on his torso; he possessed no nipples—or navel. But what was particularly puzzling to her young eyes was that he was now completely bald, devoid of the flowing white locks.

Krissie queried, a little unnerved, "Adamm—what—what happened to your hair?"

Adamm was wading toward her, his arms raised high over his head, as if he were preparing to dip in an exaggerated bow.

He was smiling at her in a peculiar sort of way.

As he came nearer the shore, exposing more of his physique, it was revealed that he possessed no genitals!

Adamm walked up to the girl. He cupped his hand around hers; Krissie experienced a cold shiver at his touch and abruptly, instinctively, drew back. Adamm's unsettling smile widened.

He said: "What one sees is not always what is. Or what one chooses to show another."

Krissie didn't understand what he meant by that. All she knew was that her friend Adamm seemed different to her on this meeting—and it went beyond the obvious physical change. He exuded a darkly mysterious presence; there was something frightening about him. Even his eyes failed to radiate the warmth that Krissie had found so comforting—they had taken on a harsher, colder hue.

Adamm said: "The *ability* has worked for you." There was a slight harshness to his tone.

"Peter Grubbish is dead," Krissie said quietly, haltingly.

"And was it your wish that he die?"

"No!" Krissie shook her head emphatically. She turned away from Adamm so that he wouldn't see her eyes begin to grow moist.

"Tell me why you turn away?"

Krissie's voice was wavering. "I—I only wished for him to stop picking on me. But... when I saw him in the field... I—I couldn't stop myself from wanting him to be hurt."

Adamm's hands closed over Krissie's shoulders. He gently turned her back to face him.

"The *ability* has worked for you and yet you are sad."

"Adamm, I don't want this *ability* anymore! Ever since you told me about it things have been going all wrong. First I get mad at my daddy and I don't know why. Then—then I make a wish for Peter to never pick on me again —and I wished for it just like you taught me, Adamm—and something awful happened to him today at recess... and now even you seem different to me."

Adamm brought a finger up to Krissie's face and tenderly wiped away her tears.

"You only feel this because the *ability* is still so new to you. Listen, child. As you learn to control your gift you will find that many of your present feelings will change. Many situations that you are familiar with will change. But you will also discover that with mastery comes acceptance. Again, you must be patient."

"But I didn't know the *ability* would be like this," Krissie argued. "I never made a wish for Raymond Gautron to kill Peter, honest I didn't!"

"Let me try to explain to you, Krissie. You willed a change. You were not specific in your thoughts, and since your control is limited at this point, your change did indeed occur... only in the most extreme manner."

"Then I just won't use it anymore," Krissie said definitely. "I don't wanna hurt anyone else ever again."

Adamm said: "My promise to you is that you won't. And you will indeed employ the *ability* again, but not until I feel you have gained a sufficient command over it. Child, you must never ignore your gift—it is much too valuable." He paused before adding: "Besides, you *do* wish to help me?"

"Yes," Krissie whispered. "But when? And how can I... control it?"

"You *will* control it by applying concentration. By focusing firmly on that which you desire. At that moment that one thought must take precedence over all else. Do you understand what I am saying?"

Krissie nodded faintly. "I think so."

Adamm continued. "You must never allow one unfortunate experience to deter you. Indeed, when I was involved in the great power struggle, combating the aggressors, there were many times when I felt ready to surrender; when I found myself questioning the wisdom of my actions. But I did continue to fight... until, by force, I was taken captive and exiled—" He made a wide, sweeping gesture with his hands. "—to this. Krissie, if you were to deny your wonderful gift I would have to remain here—a prisoner of eternity... and all of my fighting will have been in vain."

Krissie spoke with hesitation. "Would... you die here?"

"Perhaps... eventually. But to live on eternally, alone, as a prisoner of this world would be a much worse fate."

Krissie lowered herself onto the sand, sitting cross-legged. She scooped up a handful of sand and watched as the golden granules slipped smoothly between her open fingers. She looked up at Adamm and her eyes were sorrowful. At the same time, deeper, they seemed to project a new understanding.

She broke into a smile.

"I want you to come with me," she said.

13 The Voice

THURSDAY, 2:00 P.M.

Krissie Carver's second session with Dr. Kinbrace.

Krissie was telling the psychiatrist about the tragedy that occurred at her school the previous Monday. Kinbrace had his tape recorder going and was periodically checking to see how much time he had left on his 60-minute cassette. He figured there to be about five minutes.

Krissie concluded her account of the incident. "...so they had to send us right home after it happened and some of the teachers had to drive some of the kids... those who were really sick. Greta Illson had to go to the nurse's office because I think she fainted. She hasn't been back to school yet."

Kinbrace nodded slowly; he'd read about the murderer, eleven-year-old Raymond Gauntron. According to the shaken youth, he had absolutely no recollection of the killing. He was presently undergoing a psychiatric evaluation.

"How do you feel about what happened to Peter?" Kinbrace asked Krissie, remembering what she'd told him about how the boy teased and taunted her.

Krissie shrugged tightly. "I'm not really sure. After it happened I know I felt 'specially bad; pretty scared, too. But that night I talked to Adamm about it and he explained things, so it really doesn't bother me now."

"Adam? The friend in your dreams?"

"Yeah," Krissie said with a wide smile. "Only he's more real to me than that, though."

"Oh? Let's talk a bit about Adam," Kinbrace suggested. "For instance, how would you describe him? What does he look like?"

Krissie managed to stifle the giggle that was pinching her throat.

"Well," she began, tightening her features in thought, "he used to have this long white hair—almost like mine, but even whiter—but he doesn't have any hair at all now. I remember when I first saw him like that it really scared me. But now I think it's pretty funny. Uh, I think I told you that he's just a little boy, probably just a bit older than me. But you know, when he talks and explains things to me he sometimes uses these big words that I've never heard before. What's kinda neat, though, is that I still think I know what he means—well, most of the time."

Krissie paused, scratched her head, trying to remember where she left off in her description. "Oh yeah," she grinned, "I almost forgot these—" She pointed to her eyes. "He's got these really weird eyes. They're not like ours—they're just a straight blue color, and sometimes it's almost like they glow... Oh, and they're really round!" She frowned. "But they looked kinda different last night."

"Different? How?"

"Well... they didn't really look so nice like they usually do."

"Did that frighten you?"

"Maybe a little—at first. But I guess I sorta got used to them. Even when he sorta scares me he always makes me feel better before I have to leave."

"Hmmm, that sounds like quite an interesting little boy." Kinbrace glanced down at his recorder again. "Krissie, do you ever see Adam when you're awake?"

"Huh uh," Krissie was shaking her head. "Nope, I only go to him when I'm sleeping."

"You said before that he sometimes uses big words. Can you remember any of these words?"

Krissie thought for a moment. She slowly shook her head.

"Huh uh," she said, "I can't think of any right now."

"Well, what does Adam talk to you about?"

Krissie suddenly seemed unwilling to respond. She dropped her gaze to the little hands folded in her lap.

Kinbrace spoke quietly. "If you'd rather not say just yet…"

"I-just-don't-know-if-I-should," Krissie said, her words halting, brow furrowed and legs starting to swing.

"Why is that?"

"Well… because," Krissie muttered, her eyes lifting back up to the doctor—slowly. "I don't think Adamm wants me to."

Kinbrace offered an understanding smile.

Krissie grimaced, and began rubbing her hands against her temples.

"Can we stop talking? My head hurts."

Kinbrace nodded. "Okay Krissie, we'll leave it at that for now."

He clicked off the tape recorder.

* * *

Maureen was answering the question that Kinbrace had put to her.

"...I think in the past week she's mentioned this Adam to me—oh, maybe a half dozen times. I have to admit, though, that I really haven't been paying that much attention to it. I guess that's because I'm just so glad she isn't having those awful nightmares."

"I can understand that," Kinbrace said with a smile. He then asked, "What about this incident at her school?"

"Peter's murder?" Maureen lowered and shook her head disbelievingly. "Oh God, yes. That was horrible. When Krissie came home early on Monday and told me what had happened—well, I assumed that she was telling some cruel made-up story to get back at Peter because of the way he treated her. But... she isn't like that. And then when the news started spreading—and isn't it amazing how fast news like that travels? I remember one of my first thoughts was that Krissie's nightmares were going to start up all over again. A seven-year-old girl witnessing such a thing! She was right there and saw it all."

"Yes, so she told me," Kinbrace said, nodding. "Mrs. Carver, Krissie also told me that she's no longer troubled by what happened."

"I know," Maureen said with a push of breath. "And don't think I don't find that—unusual, though I have to admit I'm also glad for it. You see, Dr. Kinbrace, Krissie is such a sensitive girl basically. I suppose I could say hypersensitive without too much exaggeration. Why, I can remember just last year when she found a dead kitten on the front street... it took her almost two weeks to get over it. But with Peter's killing, and so horribly... Doctor, it's just so unlike her."

"The way Krissie explains it, she had this talk with Adam and—"

Maureen slid forward in her seat. "But who, or what, is Adam?" she asked with concerned impatience. "I mean, how would you explain what he or *it* is?"

"Adam?" Kinbrace leaned back in his high-backed chair and made a tent with his fingers. "In simplest terms, Adam is Krissie's imaginary friend."

"That's pretty well what I figured," Maureen said, nodding. "But doesn't it strike you as odd, an imaginary playmate that she only communicates with when she's dreaming?"

"It's not so strange, Mrs. Carver. In the first place, I don't think that Adam is Krissie's quote, playmate, unquote. I believe he serves another, more important purpose."

"I don't understand."

"Just a week ago Krissie was terrified of going to bed and having one of her nightmares. Then Adam appears and suddenly Krissie's bad dreams come to an apparent end. My feeling is that Adam was created by Krissie's subconscious to combat her nightmares. He's become a most welcome reassurance to her that her fears can be overcome."

"Well, if that's the case it certainly seems to be working," Maureen said, sounding relieved.

"And of course he has become very real to Krissie. Her description of Adam is quite vivid, and imaginative. Although she was reluctant to talk about it, I feel that Adam has since helped Krissie with a few other problems. I'm basing that on the way she's changed in the course of just one week."

"You've noticed a change?" Maureen said hopefully.

Kinbrace nodded. "A subtle one, but a positive change nonetheless. Overall, she seemed calmer and happier than when we last spoke."

Maureen blew out her breath. "You don't know what a relief it is for me to hear you say that, Dr. Kinbrace." She frowned. "But I still don't know if I'm entirely happy with her having an imaginary friend. Even one that she meets only in her dreams. Couldn't that lead to something like autism?"

Kinbrace smiled and replied, "I wouldn't worry about it. Because I feel that as soon as your daughter finds she can handle different problems and situations on her own, Adam will have served his purpose and simply fade away."

"How long should that take?" Maureen asked eagerly.

Kinbrace spoke in a formal tone. "Mrs. Carver, my advice would be not to try to rush it with Krissie. Allow the changes to occur naturally, and they will. I know of similar situations where the parents had become scared and anxious, and in their rush to obtain quick results—even though their intentions were well-meaning—they caused more harm than good. The human brain is a complex and delicate piece of machinery. If it weren't, why, then there wouldn't be a need for us shrinks," he added with a good-natured smile.

Maureen returned the smile—but shallowly.

"However," the doctor continued, "I would like for Krissie to continue sessions. Her creation of Adam is helping her to overcome some basic fears, but I feel there's still work to be done. I would like to try to get her to open up more."

Maureen lifted her purse to her lap. "Certainly, Dr. Kinbrace. Whatever you think is best."

Kinbrace rose from his chair and walked Maureen to the door. After he said goodbye, he returned to behind his desk and sat quietly, in contemplation. While he tried his professional best to ease Maureen Carver's concerns, there were details that he found curious and that he would have to examine further.

* * *

He stayed late that night, reviewing the tapes of the day's sessions. It was past ten and the large window overlooking the west side of the city revealed that the skies were an inky black, pinpricked by scattered lights emanating from other occupied city buildings. His office, too, would have been shrouded in darkness but for the eerie light provided by the fluorescent desk lamp.

Kinbrace pressed down on the button marked *fast forward* and there was a steady muted whir as the mechanism wound the tape quickly to its end. A short way before the tape ran out he clicked the *stop* button, then pressed *play*. He pushed back from his desk and stiffly crossed his legs. He indulged himself to a smoke, withdrawing a thin cigar from the pack inside his top drawer and lighting it.

Krissie Carver was speaking.

"...I can't think of any right now."

Kinbrace: "Well, what does Adam talk to you about?"

There followed the pause that the doctor remembered: Krissie's reluctance to answer his question. Only there wasn't the total silence that he recalled. Kinbrace was sure he heard—

A voice.

A whispered, somewhat shadowy-sounding voice.

Krissie began talking. But the voice spoke again, overlapping her words, repeating the same phrase as before:

You will not speak to him

Kinbrace frowned in bewilderment and rewound the tape a bit. Clicking it back to *play*, he moved closer to the recorder and listened intently.

...not speak to him

There could be no mistaking it—an additional voice *was* coming through on the tape. A voice that he clearly determined spoke with a dark edge.

Kinbrace stiffened. He felt a chill shoot up his spine. He shut off the recorder—*click*—and collapsed back into his chair, letting out a long, heavy breath. For the next several minutes he remained motionless, the fingers of both hands pressed tightly into a steeple, positioned under his chin.

...A voice...

Belonging to whom...?

Or *what*?

16 Danny

DANNY O'RYAN WAS PUTTING all of his limited energy into beating his hands against the door. For the first few minutes he had used a closed fist—pounding, pounding. But the side of his arthritic hand soon began to hurt, so he now was hammering away with his palms; they, too, were beginning to throb.

"You must open up!" he demanded, his weak voice now forceful and urgent. "It's important that I talk with you—*now!*" He jerked into a violent coughing spasm, spitting up thick globs of brownish-yellow bile.

Ernest was inside his room, sitting on the very edge of his unmade bed, staring blankly out the window. The late night view was hardly spectacular. From his angle, all he could see were a few old buildings and a smattering of dark clouds, gliding across an even blacker sky. But Ernest wasn't paying any attention to what was outside.

He heard the old man slamming at his door but tried to ignore both it and the sound of the man's desperation.

"Please, m'boy," Danny pleaded. "Please open the door!" His voice seemed to falter slightly as he added, "Th-this'll be the last time I'll have—to talk to you."

Ernest's Adam's apple bobbed once, but other than that reflexive movement he appeared stiff and uncaring to Danny's demands.

(*No old man, I can't... leave me alone... Please, leave me alone*)

Suddenly the pounding ceased.

Danny turned from the door but stayed where he was. He understood that it was no use.

A single warm tear streaked a line down his tired and craggy face as he thought once more of what was to be. Of what *had* to be.

Perhaps he was being selfish. His thoughts concerning his own well-being were hardly worth considering. At the same time, Danny O'Ryan was only a man, a flesh and blood being, and, therefore, he felt entitled to have a moment of fear; a moment of regret. To reflect once more on the years left behind...

Where it all began: in a six-family tenement in East Brooklyn; his adventures in war-ravaged Europe; his girl, later to become his wife of forty-eight years, beautiful red-haired Patricia; his two boys, James and Matthew (tragically, he had outlived his sons; one was a casualty of World War II, the other died in a construction accident); his move to Canada at the start of the last decade to spend his remaining years with his sister; her death in the spring of '74; finally to now...

Danny's cloud of memories faded... faded...

They evaporated as completely as the smoke from his cigarette. A deep, personal ache as he knew he'd relived them for the last time. Rather too quickly, but the recollection of the triumphs and tragedies of those long-ago days hadn't dimmed.

He was satisfied—as satisfied as a man could be under these circumstances.

And then Danny's thoughts returned to the moment and the reason why tonight he'd made the decision he had, beginning with a horrendous revelation which had determined his seventeen-year mission.

He had come close, but he'd failed. He became almost angry at himself because it had taken so damned long. So needlessly long. He should have gone with his instincts when they first started pecking at him. But he'd made mistakes before. So he waited; waited for the signs that he himself had agonized through... the signs that would tell him for sure. And they had come. Only now it appeared too late.

Danny started down the narrow, dimly-lit hallway. He turned at the stairs, taking tight hold of the banister railing, and slowly clumped down the creaking steps. His breathing was labored and his heartbeat greatly accelerated, thudding heavily in his chest.

He was a man preparing to meet destiny.

* * *

Ernest finally maneuvered his gaunt frame off the bed; his muscles and joints were aching so that even that simple action required a straining effort. He was also feeling terribly chilled.

He finished smoking his cigarette—his last, right to the filter—and hobbled over to the rusty old radiator in the corner. Unmindful of his pains, he gave the pipes several furious kicks.

thump, thump, thummmmppp

A short hiss... then nothing.

"Bug me for the rent, will they," Ernest grumbled. Swearing ambitiously, he went across to the wooden coat rack and yanked off his ratty yellow sweater. He wrapped the clothing around himself, as he prepared to go out to buy another pack of smokes. He moved over to the cupboard, reaching into the top side shelf where he removed a little painted tea cup. Inside was a wad of cellophane. He took this out and brought it over to the kitchen table where he carefully peeled back the wrapping. He counted out forty-seven dollars and twelve cents—in bills and change.

"Yeah, thank Jesus for welfare," he mumbled.

Only rarely did Ernest suffer an attack of conscience and feel guilt at living off the generosity of the working taxpayer. To Ernest, convinced long ago that through no fault of his own he had become a physical and emotional wreck, these dollars meant continued survival (not that his needs were all that complicated: rent, occasional transportation, very little food, but as much liquor and cigarettes as possible. Putting aside a buck or two was never a consideration).

And yet the irony was that at any time he could have it all.

He had the power.

The power, Ernest thought bitterly. To him, it was better called *the curse.*

Even though he'd made a vow never to call upon his power, it still succeeded in bringing him an endless misery. His chronic drinking, his headaches; basically his whole deteriorating physical and mental condition he could attribute to his *gift.*

And he knew that possessing it had brought anguish to others. It began with a woman named Jolene.

God, he'd almost forgotten about her...

He remembered he'd met her during the closing days of 1975. Both were celebrating a lonely holiday season at the Tobian Hotel. She was far from the best-looking female in the world, what with her bloated belly, hardened features and cratered skin, and it was true that she was one of the few people—let alone women—who could match Ernest drink for drink. But she *was* a woman. And Ernest, at least at the time, was a man with basic urges, and he started seeing her. They were compatible enough when sober. But the tables turned when both were drinking… which was how they spent most of their time together.

The lonely strains of a forgotten Frank Sinatra Christmas song played on. They were chugging down glasses of beer and consuming straight shots of gin up in her room. Getting drunk. Talking loud. The talk turning into arguing…

…when Ernest's head began to hurt.

At first he thought nothing of it, having been used to almost daily hangovers.

But with each passing second the pain grew more intense, developing into something more than a mere headache.

Ernest didn't know what was happening to him. He started to panic. It felt like a six-inch steel spike was slowly being driven through the center of his skull. He feared he was dying.

He begged Jolene to stop her nagging. But for some reason his pleadings only made her angrier. Her voice grew louder.

Ernest didn't want to hurt her… he *didn't*! But the bitch just wouldn't shut up. Her persistent shrieking seemed to drive that spike in deeper.

And that was when:

—the voice commanded—

What followed Ernest remembered through a crimson haze, as if his vision was filtered through blood-stained gauze. He remembered leaping across to where she was sitting, grabbing the woman around the neck, and viciously thrusting her rag doll body to the hardwood floor. Her head hit with two reverberating thuds. Ernest could remember hearing her gag, as if her tongue had folded over into her throat. Then her eyes rolled up in their sockets until only the bloodshot whites were showing. And although he struggled to fight against this sinister impulse that was guiding him, he couldn't. The voice in his head wouldn't allow him to stop. He became like some destructive wind-up toy with a spring that had not yet wound down. He pounced on her, landing on her heaving, gas-bloated belly with almost his full weight. The entire room reeked from her escaping flatulence.

—the voice commanded—

Ernest was now totally out of control. Still on top of her, he grabbed a beer bottle from the table beside him and rammed the stem several quick times into her mouth, knocking out the few front teeth she had remaining. He then grabbed a thick handful of her hair and began beating her head rhythmically against the floor. He had no idea how long this went on, but when he was finished Jolene was bloody and quite unconscious.

It was only then that the pain faded and the voice disappeared...

Recovering from this terrible memory, Ernest felt physically sick. The image of Jolene's limp form lingered in his brain. He had never been a violent person and the voice or whatever that evil influence was that compelled him to behave so viciously terrified him. He could never explain it. He could never have known that it was only the start to an ongoing nightmare.

No! He had to stop thinking.

Back at the kitchen table, he checked his alarm clock. It was almost twelve, just a few minutes to the hour. Good, that still gave him plenty of time to get down to the Tobian Hotel and buy his cigarettes—plus maybe stop for some needed drinks before the 2 a.m. closing. He grabbed a five-dollar bill and five singles from the table and shoved them into his back pocket. The rest of the money he rewrapped in the cellophane which he returned to the shelf.

As Ernest stepped out of the hotel into the windy cold of the night, he noticed how the street seemed unusually quiet.

He walked two blocks to the Tobian when he saw the familiar figure up ahead, starting slowly across the road.

It was Danny.

Ernest didn't want to be recognized by the old man, so he quickly bowed his head and sped up his gait. He was just about to pass through the smoked glass doors of the hotel when he heard that ancient voice cry out:

"M'boy!"

"Damn," Ernest muttered through clenched teeth, and his hands tightened into fists as he paused briefly, trying to decide whether to ignore the old man or acknowledge him.

Before he could decide, Ernest heard the sudden shriek of tires burning rubber, the sound slicing through his head with the impact of a jet on takeoff. Ernest jerked, startled, then whirled around to the road.

His eyes bugged.

"Danny!" he shouted, taking a few awkward steps forward.

It seemed to Ernest that the old man wasn't even putting an effort into moving out of the path of the rapidly advancing—

Black Lincoln!

Danny stood on the road, motionless, almost in defiance to the car's approach, and it was only in the split second before the screeching black monster was upon him—in the blinding glare of its headlights—that his face registered panic.

Ernest heard the powerful bone-crushing thud and watched in numb shock as Danny's body was tossed up into the air, the arms and legs flailing wildly. He landed in a twisted heap about twenty feet from impact.

Ernest rushed over.

He was surprised to find that the old man was still alive, and conscious. He was coughing up throaty gurgles and struggling to move. When the exertion finally became too much, he dropped back limply to the concrete.

Ernest knelt next to Danny and gently took his hand, unable to resist giving it a squeeze. He stared helplessly at the broken body. Rivers of blood were pumping thickly out of an ugly wound in the old man's chest. Ernest knew he couldn't last much longer.

But the old man wasn't ready to give up the ghost. To Ernest's amazement, Danny's eyes suddenly took on an intense, almost transcendent glow and they fastened into Ernest's own eyes; within seconds Ernest felt as if his brain were on fire. Soon he was in excruciating pain, but whatever force had locked into him wouldn't release him. The pain quickly heightened and Ernest felt that at any moment he might pass out.

Then, as quickly as it came—the severity subsided.

Danny managed a vague smile.

It was then that Ernest heard the old man's voice, speaking to him not through speech, but reaching him as if through a long, deep echoing tunnel and entering directly into the brain.

(*Thank God you've come, m'boy*)

Ernest nodded. All at once he understood.

(*I'm dying, so please listen to what I must tell you*)

Ernest felt his body begin to tremble.

(*You've also heard the voice?*)

Ernest nodded.

(*And you listened?*)

"I had no choice."

(*The voice spoke to me, long ago. It tried to take control. But I didn't listen. No matter what it did to me, I didn't listen! I fought it... and I defeated it. I possess it, just as you do. The power*)

"I figger that now," Ernest said. "An' I guess that's why yuh had to talk to me tonight."

Danny's physical strength was rapidly ebbing. But his concentration held.

(*It took too long. First to find you, then to make certain you were the one*)

"How did ya know it was me?"

Danny smiled; his head began to quiver.

(*The headaches, m'boy... and when you tried to kill me. You listened... it has control of you*)

"Yes," Ernest said, bowing his head.

(*Reach into my shirt pocket*)

Ernest did and his hand withdrew a key.

"A key?" he said, bemused.

(*The key to my room. Inside, on the top shelf of my closet, you'll find a book. A very old and valuable book. Read it, m'boy. You must read it! It—it'll explain to you what I can't. You'll understand*)

A small crowd of people had begun to move in around the scene: the city's nightwalkers, the drunks, the derelicts with no place to go. Many were babbling incoherently, but Ernest was oblivious to their presence.

(*But you must take care. Now they'll do whatever they can to stop you*)

"Who? Who'll try to stop me?"

(*You've taken over, m'boy*)

"Who are *they?*" Ernest asked again, desperately.

(*But prepare for your soul to be eternally damned... as is mine. That... is the price we must...*)

Danny's body suddenly stiffened and his concentration broke. Ernest experienced a reversed head rush, as if some powerful suction was pulling the last thoughts of the old man out of his brain.

A look of terror, the wide-eyed expression that accompanies impending death and perhaps the fearful approach of an uncertain afterlife, etched itself into Danny's features.

And with this expression frozen upon his face, Danny exhaled his final breath.

Ernest felt his own body tighten, stiffen—then undergo a momentary paralysis. He stayed with the corpse until he heard the faraway wailing of sirens. With unsteady fingers he closed Danny's sightless eyes.

He then pulled to his feet and hurried away.

17 The House On Queenston

THE HOUSE WAS A RAMBLING old structure. It would have seemed overly spacious for a well-to-do family of six. As it was, the three-storied house was the residence of only one man. Yet because of who he was, the structure never took dominance. He not only controlled, but fit into every shadowed corner of his sprawling estate. He felt a communion with it. His only companions were a vast library of esoteric books dealing with mysticism, spiritualism, and the paranormal.

Privacy—of the utmost importance to its owner—was provided by the six-foot high wrought iron fence that encircled the property. An expected visitor would announce his arrival by way of an elaborate intercom system that would respond even if the owner was absent, precluding any attempt at a burglary.

Because this evening had been pre-arranged, Dr. Kinbrace knew that his long-time friend was at home. Lifting his coat collar against the slashing wind, he pushed the black intercom button a second time.

A crackle, then: "Yes?"

"Kinbrace."

A buzzer sounded and the gate opened.

Ten minutes later, Kinbrace found himself comfortably seated in the parlor, warmed by the heat generated by the crackling corner fireplace and the snifter of brandy offered by his host.

Dr. Walter Barton was in appearance the antithesis of Kinbrace—short, corpulent, bespectacled with bottle-bottom lenses that gave his eyes an almost deranged look. Yet he had gained respect as a dedicated academic who had left his work at the university to devote his time fully to the study of parapsychology, in which he had become a noted expert. For many years he was in demand throughout North America (and occasionally beyond) as both a speaker and an investigator, researching such strange phenomenon ranging from alleged hauntings to spirit possession to individuals supposedly endowed with psychic powers.

But what fascinated Dr. Barton most—and Kinbrace had been aware of this since their university days—was the disembodied "spirit" voice, just recently gaining recognition as EVP: Electronic voice phenomena. Barton had investigated only a few such incidents where recordings were presented, but he was never able to offer a logical explanation for these occurrences. Even his more mundane theories crossed the boundary into the preternatural.

...*You will not speak to him*

Kinbrace stopped the tape. Barton slowly sipped at his brandy.

"There were just the two of us in the office," Kinbrace said. "Besides—well, as you can tell, that is neither my voice nor that of a seven-year-old girl."

"No," Barton agreed, "it certainly isn't."

"Well, discounting ghosts, how would you explain it?"

Barton smiled indulgently and pressed some tobacco into the bowl of his pipe. He paused before lighting it. "Of course I can't discount ghosts, my friend. Or perhaps the presence of a disembodied spirit."

"There's a difference?" Kinbrace asked.

"Between a ghost and a spirit? Distinctly." Barton said.

Kinbrace looked dubious.

Barton noticed his friend's doubtful expression and continued. "The unexplained is my life and I've always found it best to keep open to all possibilities, whether in the earthly realm or beyond. But I have always understood your skepticism regarding the latter."

Kinbrace waved his hand in defense. "Our paths diverge only when it comes to the subject of these otherworldly manifestations, Walter. I've always agreed and even defended you when you began expounding on the unlimited powers of the mind."

"Which I've appreciated," Barton said. "Still, in listening to this tape I am reminded of the experiments of Jurgenson and Raudive."

Kinbrace shook his head. "I'm afraid I'm not familiar with the names."

Barton drew a puff from his pipe. "Friedrich Jurgenson and Dr. Konstantin Raudive—pioneers in the field of EVP. Both men claimed to have established electronic communication with the dead."

Kinbrace gave a noncommittal nod, saying only: "I recall how the subject became your fascination."

"Let's say a long-standing interest," Barton corrected with a subtle smile.

Kinbrace shifted in his seat. "I am curious, what type of equipment did they use?"

"You're willing to consider this as a possibility?" Barton questioned with a cock of his head.

Kinbrace merely answered with a vague smile.

Barton said, "Although Jurgenson's experiments predate Raudive's by nine years, both consisted of simply sitting by a tape recorder with a group of people carrying on an average conversation."

"And on replay these voices would appear?"

"Yes, but more than that, often they would receive a direct communication. These voices would answer specific questions asked during the recording."

"What about the clarity of these voices?"

"Again, these experiments certainly weren't carried out using the type of sophisticated recording devices we have today. Often the voices they recorded were merely whispers, sometimes difficult to decipher. But other times these voices were astonishingly clear. And it's difficult to discount those instances where answers to specific questions were provided, or when the names of people sitting in the room would be acknowledged."

Kinbrace sat with his features creased in contemplation.

Barton added, "Also worth noting is the fact that these voices often claimed outright to belong to the deceased."

"Walter," Kinbrace finally said, expelling a breath, "I still can't accept it's a spirit voice that I picked up on my tape. I'm sure it's something equally fantastic, just not as otherworldly."

"I don't know in which direction you want to go with this," Barton said with a neutral nod. "But since it appears you're insistent on leaning toward a less 'cosmic' explanation, just keep in mind that there were only the two of you in the office. The voice apparently was speaking directly to the girl, instructing *her* not to talk to you. You asked for my opinion and it stands that the voice on that tape belongs to a third party."

Part Two

One Month
Later...

18 The "Ability"

KRISSIE WALKED SLOWLY along the edge of the billowing mist, humming and mumbling the lyrics of some song that she remembered from kindergarten.

The hideous creatures on the other side of the "wall" were howling, and still attempting to claw through the curtain of mist that held them back.

Vast multitudes. All waiting. All eager.

Krissie stopped, inched back a short way, and stood wide-eyed, completely overwhelmed by their infinite number—a number that continued to grow!

Yet—it appeared to Krissie as if many of these creatures were attempting a kind of communication with her—with their awkward and exaggerated gesticulations, and desperate, almost beseeching expressions. Krissie was unable to understand what they might be trying to say to her, but in that instant, in her naïve innocence, Krissie had the feeling that they meant her no harm, and her fear became mixed with a strange pity.

And instinctively she ventured to take a step forward.

A powerful hand clamped down on her shoulder and held firm. Once the grip weakened Krissie whirled around.

"Adamm!" And she started to giggle, nervously.

"That was extremely foolish, Krissie," Adamm said in a stern voice.

Krissie was disturbed by the harsh tone, and the intense expression that shadowed his features frightened her.

Her voice trembled. "But they wouldn't hurt me, Adamm. I don't know why I'm so sure of that, but they *wouldn't*."

"They would destroy you without hesitation."

Without saying more, Adamm took Krissie by the hand and guided her away. They kept walking until the eerie, desperate wailing was left far behind—through the now-darkening forest and across a peacefully flowing stream… continuing on through what seemed like miles of vast grassland. Finally they came to a magnificent hill, an emerald green outcropping on an otherwise unblemished landscape.

When they reached its height, both settled into meditative poses on the cool carpet of grass. Adamm stared silently at Krissie for a long while.

Finally, in a gentle, comforting voice he said: "I do much of my thinking here."

"It's real pretty," Krissie said in wonderment, "just like the lake. But I haven't been here before, have I?"

"No Krissie, I've purposely kept this part of my world from you. You are here now only because it is apparent that you are gaining a mastery over your power. Happily, it has become possible to expedite your progress."

"Ex-pedite…?"

"Hurry, my child," Adamm clarified.

"Does that mean that soon I'll be able to bring you back with me?" Krissie asked. Her voice was tinged with growing excitement.

"Yes child, soon."

"Boy," Krissie sighed, "I thought it would take a whole lot longer."

"You have proven to be an exceptional student," Adamm said. "Without much practice you have acquired impressive control over the *ability*."

Krissie shrugged. "Well, I really haven't used it much, except for some of the stuff that you teach me, and when Peter Grubbish..." Her voice trailed off.

"Yes, but the control, as with the *ability* itself, is inherent. I have watched you. Indeed, I am aware of all your activities. The time is not too far off."

Krissie grinned. "I'm so glad."

Adamm said: "Can you not feel the power surging within you?"

"Yes," Krissie said with a slight lift of her shoulder. "I guess I have been feeling kinda different."

"Not merely different, child," Adamm said with enthusiasm. "You should be feeling charged with energy, for that is a sure sign of the strength you now possess."

Reacting to Adamm's fervor, Krissie practically shouted: "I can feel it, Adamm! I really can!"

Adamm's tone abruptly shifted. His voice became grave. "However, there is something that I must warn you of."

"What's that, Adamm?" Krissie asked.

"Krissie, there are people who will try to prevent my entry into your world... if they should be made aware of my existence."

"Who are they?"

"Most especially, the doctor you have been seeing."

"Dr. Kinbrace?" Krissie looked puzzled. "I know you don't like me to talk to him, but why would he—"

"Your Doctor—Kinbrace, and others like him, do not understand as you understand. Krissie, you look upon me as a friend, which is how it should be. Which is how it *is*. But there are many who would not regard me as such."

"But why, Adamm?" Krissie wanted to know.

"Indeed," Adamm whispered, smiling forlornly. "Why?"

Krissie lifted a shoulder. "Well, then I just won't go to see Dr. Kinbrace anymore. Anyway, every time I go there I come home with a really bad headache and have to go to bed."

"Soon that will no longer be a concern," Adamm assured her.

* * *

It was 7:40 a.m. and Krissie still hadn't come down to breakfast. And a hearty breakfast it was this morning, all her daughter's favorites: pancakes with maple syrup, bacon, toast and milk, with orange juice to start it all off. Maureen was sitting at the dining table, drinking her coffee and absently rubbing her cigarette stub around in the ashtray. She'd knocked on Krissie's door about twenty minutes ago and Krissie had told her that she'd be right down... so what was keeping her?

"Krissie," Maureen called out, "your breakfast is getting cold."

She didn't get a reply.

Maureen started to grow mildly concerned. And gradually she began to worry, her hand instinctively tightening its grip on the handle of the coffee cup.

Oh, settle down, she scolded herself. There's nothing wrong. She's probably just being tardy.

She finished the last drops of her coffee and pushed her chair away from the table. She started upstairs to the bedroom.

When Maureen finally reached the top of the stairs, she stood outside of Krissie's room, listening.

But the room was completely quiet.

Had Krissie maybe fallen back asleep?

Maureen gently knocked at the door.

tap, tap, tap

No answer. Maureen frowned as her worry set in deeper and her heart began to beat a little faster.

"Krissie, honey?"

Then: "Come in, Mother."

Mother?

Maureen shivered from the sudden blast of cold that seemed to penetrate through the door and tightened the tie around her housecoat. She turned the knob...

Krissie was sitting cross-legged in bed, still in her pajamas, staring directly ahead. As Maureen entered the room, she followed her daughter's concentrated gaze to the mirror perched on the dresser. For a split second, the briefest of moments, she thought she caught the reflection of—

A face... but a face not belonging to her daughter.

Maureen convinced herself she had just imagined this peculiar vision, though it still unsettled her.

"What do you want, Mother?" Krissie's head turned slowly toward Maureen. There was no expression on her face.

Maureen forced a smile.

Mother??

What do you want??

Maureen tried to speak calmly.

"Honey, your breakfast is getting cold. You'll have to come downstairs to eat. You'll be leaving for school soon."

"I'm not going to school," Krissie replied defiantly.

Maureen felt the muscles at the back of her neck tighten.

"What's the matter, honey?" she asked with concern. "Aren't you feeling well?" She stepped over to the side of the bed and placed the back of her hand against her daughter's forehead. Krissie shrieked—

"Mother!"

—and with a vicious swipe, pushed the hand away. Startled by the outburst, Maureen swayed, grabbing the back of a chair and holding tight. Eyes wide, she gasped:

"Krissie?"

Once again the little girl's face went blank. She turned her head the other way so that she was again facing the mirror, staring intently at her reflection.

Maureen waited a moment, standing back, vigorously rubbing her sweaty palms together.

She asked, "Baby, what's wrong?"

Krissie didn't answer. But even from behind Maureen could see the slight body tensing.

Again she waited. Then, finally managing to work up some semblance of courage, she demanded: "Young lady, I've had it with this foolishness. You get off the bed right this minute and get yourself ready for school."

Krissie didn't budge.

Maureen, her breathing heavy from frustration and uncertainty, said in an even stronger voice: "Did you hear what I said?"

No response.

"Damn it, Krissie!" And Maureen stomped over.

Krissie's upper body whirled around, and with burning eyes—contracted, wolf-like, filled with indescribable menace—she glared at her mother.

"Go away!" she howled.

Her eyes sparked into diamond-like brilliance.

And, incredibly, Maureen felt her feet lift high off the floor as some violent force sent her crashing to the far wall by the door. She fell to the floor in a crumpled heap.

She lay still.

"M-Mommy?" The voice was suddenly that of a scared little girl. "Mommy, get up... please get up!"

After several moments a stunned Maureen groaned and blearily opened her eyes. She slowly raised her head, and tried to focus on the bed. Her little girl was sitting with arms outstretched, her body trembling with sobs.

Using the wall for support, Maureen pulled herself up.

"Krissie, baby..."

"Mommy, I'm sorry... I don't know what happened. I really don't. Please don't be mad at me, Mommy. I love you."

Staggering slightly, Maureen moved back over to the bed. She threw her arms around Krissie, and her daughter hugged back, tightly, refusing to let go.

"Oh, I—I love you," Maureen cried as she smothered her baby with kisses. "You know Mommy loves you."

She could never stop.

19 Lunching With the Shrink

IT HAD BEEN THE KIND of morning that Lawrence Carver would spend a week trying to forget. One of those mornings when everything that could go wrong did. Appropriately enough, it began with the clock alarm going off an hour late. Next, he had to pass on his shower not just because of the time but there was no hot water in his apartment. He didn't even want to think about his drive to the office: construction, plus a minor collision farther down, had slowed traffic to a virtual standstill. It was at this point that the first symptoms of a tension headache (usually reserved for the hour before quitting time) presented themselves. Greeted by his wiseacre secretary ("Almost ninety minutes late, but who's counting, eh, Mr. Carver?"), he was immediately instructed that his boss, Mr. Sanborn, wanted to see him, where he was promptly reprimanded for his careless handling of the Jarvis account.

By the time twelve o'clock rolled around, Lawrence was anticipating a long liquid lunch.

He headed toward the newly-opened Picador Restaurant. The downtown lunch bunch were out in full force and Lawrence was hoping that he'd be able to find a solitary booth, preferably in some back corner where he could be alone with his misery.

Just the thought of a double scotch was doing wonders for his frazzled nerves.

"Mr. Carver!"

Lawrence half-recognized the voice, but he couldn't immediately place it. It was coming from somewhere in the table-waiting crowd ahead. Lawrence stopped just inside the front entrance to the restaurant and waited there, his eyes squinting into the crowd.

Then a muttered: "Oh hell."

Dr. Kinbrace emerged from the mass and stepped quickly to the double doors. He offered his hand.

Lawrence shook it, unaware that he was going against his long-standing rule by accepting Kinbrace's handshake with a weak grip.

Kinbrace asked, "Going for lunch?"

Lawrence nodded. Had he been able to think quicker, he would have told the shrink that he was expected at a business luncheon.

"Mind if I join you?" Kinbrace asked. "I'm in the mood for Mexican."

"Uh, well..."

"Good, my table should be ready soon." Kinbrace, his smile now proudly exposing his pearly whites, guided Lawrence to his spot in the line-up.

Lawrence's headache, which had been starting to ease, threatened to flare up again.

The interior of the restaurant was comfortable, but in no way elegant. Huge murals depicting hearty peasants in sombreros were intended to create an exotic Latin ambience, but to Lawrence these portraits just looked like cheap art.

He was also irked to discover that the only seating available was at one of the center tables—on display, in other words. So much for the out-of-the-way solitary lunch he was hoping to enjoy.

Kinbrace left his heavy olive green overcoat at the coat check. Lawrence couldn't be bothered and carried his into the dining area, slung over his arm; he figured it was faster and cheaper to simply drape it over the back of his chair. Besides, after lunch he wanted to make a quick getaway and not dawdle with Kinbrace at the coat check.

Kinbrace looked curiously different from the last time Lawrence had seen him and he quickly detected what that difference was. The psychiatrist was wearing a conservative three-piece suit—with a hanky neatly tucked into the breast pocket. Studying him as they were escorted to their table—obliquely yet thoroughly—Lawrence decided that he liked him better in his casual clothes. He felt they at least suited his personality.

They sat down and Lawrence immediately picked up the over-sized menu and buried his face behind it. He wasn't reading the items; he'd just decided that he was going to try and avoid conversation until he first had a good strong drink in front of him.

Kinbrace on the other hand studied his menu intently.

The waitress, a petite and pretty girl, came over to their table, order pad in hand.

"Would you gentleman care for something from the bar?" she asked.

"Yeah," Lawrence said, responding too quickly. "A double scotch." Why not? He'd already made up his mind to take the rest of the day off.

The waitress turned to Kinbrace.

"No thank you, water's fine," he smiled politely. "I'll have coffee later."

Kinbrace placed the menu back on the table, eased forward in his seat and folded his hands in front of him. Shortly after the waitress left, he said gravely, "I'm very glad I ran into you today, Mr. Carver."

"Yeah?" Lawrence mumbled, still appearing to be checking out the menu.

"I've come across some interesting developments in your daughter's sessions."

"Yeah?" Lawrence said again. He finally put the menu aside.

"Mr. Carver," Kinbrace said, "are you aware that your daughter's nightmares have apparently ended? That they've been replaced by dreams in which she encounters an imaginary figure she calls Adam?"

Lawrence cast his eyes about the restaurant, hoping to spot the waitress bringing over his drink. "Well, I suppose that's better than what she was having," he said with a casual shrug.

"I'm not totally convinced that it is."

"No?"

"In the beginning I thought so too," Kinbrace said, settling back into his chair. "I felt that these dreams were actually of benefit to her, at least the way I initially interpreted them. But I've since found there are a few details that I'm concerned about."

"Like what?"

"For one thing, Krissie has become strangely silent about Adam; I'd say almost protective of him. You see, at first she was willing to discuss him with me, almost excitedly, although she wasn't keen on telling me what they talked about."

Lawrence shrugged and said, "Maybe she just couldn't remember. Hell, who can remember dreams half the time anyway?"

"No," Kinbrace said in disagreement. "Her encounters with Adam are as vivid to her as her nightmares were." He watched as Lawrence pulled a cigarette from his pack. "Would you mind?" he then said, gesturing with a point of his finger.

"Huh?"

"Was wondering if I could trouble you for a cigarette?"

"You smoke?"

"Hardly ever," Kinbrace replied. "But on occasion."

Lawrence passed over the pack. Kinbrace withdrew a cigarette which Lawrence lighted for him.

Kinbrace took a drag and continued. "But as I was saying, about all I can get from Krissie is a 'yes' or 'no' if I question her about Adam."

"Yeah, well, I really can't say much about that," Lawrence said in a dismissive tone.

Kinbrace spoke pointedly. "You haven't talked to your daughter?"

Lawrence immediately prepared his defenses, anticipating a subtle probing from the psychiatrist.

Fortunately, the waitress came over with Lawrence's drink. She placed it in front of him on a red leatherette coaster with "Picador" emblazoned across it. She then took out her order pad. "Are you ready to order?"

Kinbrace looked at Lawrence, who invited the doctor to go first, and he placed an order for a steak sandwich, medium rare, with a side order of French fries and a ginger ale.

Lawrence frowned, remembering that Kinbrace said he was in the mood for a Mexican meal. He took a swallow of his double scotch and ordered another. For his own lunch he chose a cheeseburger and fries. He, too, decided against a Mexican lunch.

After the waitress had collected their menus and departed, Kinbrace took a final drag from his cigarette and butted it. He'd barely smoked half of it.

Once again Lawrence readied himself but he was relieved when Kinbrace didn't pursue the topic.

Instead: "As you know, I prefer to record my sessions on tape. It was my second session with Krissie—when she first told me about Adam. That night I was alone in my office playing back the tape, and I heard… I suppose you could call it a *phantom voice.* The voice was clearly not your daughter's."

Lawrence looked quizzically at the doctor.

"It spoke twice," Kinbrace said. "Both times it said the same thing, a command, I guess you'd say: 'You will not speak to him.'"

"How d'ya explain that?" Lawrence asked, suddenly realizing the absurdity in what Kinbrace was telling him.

"As of now I can't, not conclusively. Of course I do have some theories, the most probable of which is that it's Krissie—or to be more precise, the projection of Krissie's subconscious—coming through on the tape."

"What?" Lawrence got a little annoyed. "What kind of crap are you handing me? You just finished saying that it wasn't Krissie's voice you heard."

"No, it wasn't," Kinbrace said. "I'll go one step further: It was most likely Adam's voice that was recorded."

Lawrence downed the rest of his scotch and was impatient for his second round.

"Krissie's subconscious…projecting this, uh, other voice onto your tape…" Lawrence dismissed the whole idea with a cutting wave of his hand. "Shit, it all sounds like something out of the *Twilight Zone* to me."

"It's not as incredible as it might sound, Mr. Carver. Not if you consider psychokinesis."

"Psycho-*what?*"

"Psychokinesis, mind over matter. Krissie may have unwittingly used a form of PK to imprint the voice of Adam directly onto the recording tape."

Lawrence snorted. "Okay Kinbrace, I'll play along. Let's say this theory of yours is right. Why this Adam's voice?"

"Let me try to explain. To a child, an imaginary friend always takes on some—semblance of existence; that's to be expected. However, for the most part it's controlled, up to the point where many parents may not even be aware that this imaginary friend exists to their child. But with Krissie… well, you must remember that her subconscious created Adam at a time when she was very troubled and afraid—by her recurring nightmare. Because he helped her get over this frightening experience he has indeed become a very real friend to Krissie, one whom she doesn't want to lose. Perhaps because of my probing to find out more about Adam, Krissie saw me as a possible threat to his existence. Naturally that was unacceptable to her. So much so that she may have unconsciously allowed Adam to surface momentarily…to have it be *his* voice to instruct her not to talk to me. And, as I said, Krissie may have used her own psychic ability to impress his words, as well as the voice *she* hears, onto the tape."

"Sounds almost like you're saying my daughter is—schizo," Lawrence said miserably.

"Well, at this point that is an extreme. But as a projected prognosis, yes, I'd have to say that is a possibility," Kinbrace admitted. He edged forward in his chair. "Mr. Carver, can you ever remember your daughter complaining of sudden, intense headaches?"

"No, I don't think so."

"That's what I figured. Your ex-wife, of course, was more definite."

"Why are you asking?"

"In our sessions I've found that whenever I start probing a little too deeply Krissie complains of these spontaneous headaches. Psychosomatic, I'm sure. Physically your daughter was given a clean bill of health by Dr. LaFreniere."

Lawrence shook his head and gazed into his empty glass. His brow furrowed before he spoke hesitantly:

"I still can't buy this mind over matter stuff. But if what you're saying is true... Jesus, I didn't know Krissie was so screwed up."

Kinbrace spoke encouragingly. "I do feel that if she keeps up our sessions, and if I can get her to open up more, there's an excellent chance Krissie can return to being a normal, happy child who can deal with difficulties on her own, not reliant on this 'friend' her mind has created."

Lawrence suffered the sting of guilt when he heard the word "happy." Neither he nor Maureen had contributed much in that way.

Lawrence glanced up. "Tell me, does Maureen know anything about—any of this? What you say you found on the tape?"

Kinbrace hesitated in his reply. "No," he then said. "I haven't wanted to tell her much."

Lawrence nodded thoughtfully. Without Kinbrace having to explain his reasoning Lawrence understood. It was doubtful Maureen would be able to deal with what the psychiatrist had just told him.

"Maybe it would be better if you kept it from her for now," he said.

* * *

Kinbrace was back in his office by one-thirty. His next appointment wasn't until two—and, knowing the habits of his patient, understood that meant at least a quarter after—so he sat at his desk and sorted through the day's mail. While doing this, he switched on his telephone answering machine to play back his taped messages.

Following the beep, Mrs. Dixon's low, monotone voice came over the speaker droning that she had urgent family business to attend to and would have to cancel this week's session. Kinbrace smiled to himself. The call was completely unnecessary; she'd spent practically all of her last appointment telling him the same thing.

There was a second beep. Just the dial tone.

After a short silence that followed the third beep, a hushed female voice spoke. The caller failed to identify herself, but Kinbrace recognized the voice as belonging to Maureen Carver.

He laid the mail on his desk and listened to her message.

"Dr. Kinbrace, I'm frightened...I—I don't know what's happening. It's Krissie. Please Dr. Kinbrace, please call me as soon as you can..." Then she gave her number.

beep

Kinbrace snapped off the answering machine and dialed the number. Four rings before the phone was picked up.

"Hello?" There was a distinct caution in the voice.

"Hi, Mrs. Carver? Warren Kinbrace. I just got your mes—"

"Oh Doctor, you don't know how glad I am that it's you. I've been in a state of distress all morning."

"What seems to be the problem?"

"It's Krissie," Maureen said, speaking quickly, urgently. "Something happened this morning. Something that… Oh God, I still think I must be losing my mind." She started to sob.

"Take a moment, Mrs. Carver," Kinbrace said compassionately.

He could hear her breathing through the receiver; it was choppy, erratic.

Finally, in a more composed tone: "I'm sorry, Doctor. But I just had to talk to you. I don't know what else to do."

"I understand. Now what's this about Krissie?"

"You're not going to believe me." Maureen paused briefly and Kinbrace heard a match strike up on the other end. "This morning I went into Krissie's room to get her ready for school and… and she seemed so strange. Not at all like my little girl. And then she got mad and—she threw me against the wall! Somehow she just lifted me off the floor and threw me!"

"You mean to say she actually *physically* picked you up—"

"No, not like that!" Maureen interjected hastily. "She—she was sitting on her bed. But she did it! I don't know how exactly, but, Doctor, you should have seen her. She looked so—I can hardly say it, but *evil*. Not like Krissie at all. Oh, you must think I'm crazy."

Kinbrace disregarded her remark. Instead: "Is Krissie home now?"

"No. No, she's at school. You see, right after this happened she was herself again. She was crying and asking me to forgive her. Dr. Kinbrace, I don't understand any of what's going on."

"I'm booked for today, Mrs. Carver. Would it be possible for you to bring Krissie down to my office—" He flipped through his desk calendar. "—say tomorrow at three-thirty?"

"I don't know, Doctor. I don't think so. Krissie said that she doesn't want to go to any more sessions."

"Oh? Did she tell you why?"

"No… and—I didn't ask. I couldn't… not the way she's been acting. Her mood always seems to be changing… and… frankly, I'm scared of her."

"Well, would you prefer if I visited her at home?"

"Doctor, would you?" Maureen said hopefully.

"How does tomorrow afternoon sound, around five?"

"I appreciate it, Dr. Kinbrace. You don't know how unsettling all this is."

"On the contrary, Mrs. Carver," Kinbrace said in a low voice, "I think I do."

20 A Bad Day For Janet

BRADLEY COINER WENT AROUND to all the desks and passed out large 16" by 24" sheets of Manila paper. Mrs. Rossen had instructed her class to draw pictures that had something to do with their school. The five best drawings, selected by the class, would then be hung on the blackboard for Parent/Teacher night, coming up in just a few weeks. To the children this project was a welcome goof-off; usually at this time they were stuck with some boring Nature Studies assignment.

But then it seemed that Mrs. Rossen's classes had been getting easier—for about a month.

Very little *real* classwork; there were more art and creative composition assignments than anything else. And three days of substitute teachers in as many weeks!

Principal Wiley had become aware of Mrs. Rossen's neglect of her teaching duties after a few parents called the school complaining that their children were bringing home work sheets that were incorrectly graded. During a twenty minute chat in Mr. Wiley's office, Mrs. Rossen explained to the principal that she

179

had been having some personal issues but they now seemed to be working out.

She wasn't being entirely honest… but she also didn't care.

No, in actuality a month had passed and there was still no change in the life of Janet Rossen. Michael remained adamant; their future together depended on her making the move to leave her husband. And as if to convince Janet of his unyielding position, he'd been keeping his distance for the past couple of weeks.

God, she missed him! For the first time in a long, long while Janet became aware of a void in her life. This emptiness was like some terrible disease. Day by day it ate away a little more of her. She hadn't even had the consolation of knowing whether Michael was hurting just as much. The few times they did speak Janet detected a hint of indifference in his voice.

No, it wasn't fair! None of it! And she couldn't —she wouldn't—let it happen!

The thought of life without Michael… a lifetime with Chuck was too painful even to contemplate.

And it was at that moment that Janet became filled with a sudden rush of confidence… even if she could not totally free herself of apprehension.

But there was no other way. It had to be done. And it would all begin with a phone call.

"Class," she said, smiling, getting up from behind her desk, "I'm going to be leaving the room for a few minutes. Now I want you to work on your drawings, and absolutely no talking." She emphasized this last point by lifting a stiff finger.

She left the class and walked briskly to the staffroom. She was hoping that the phone was available because she didn't know how long her determination might hold.

But she hadn't hoped hard enough.

Old Mrs. Wishnowski, the school librarian, was engaging in one of her frequent conversations with her daughter who, rumor had it, had recently separated from either her second or third husband. From what Janet could pick up, this call had to do with something naughty Mrs. W's little granddaughter had done. Janet went inside anyway; maybe a little eavesdropping would prompt a quick end to the conversation.

The old librarian looked up, green eyes sparkling from behind her horn-rimmed glasses, and flashed a toothy smile. Janet smiled back politely, then went over to the percolator and poured herself a cup of coffee.

She sat down at the long lunch table and let her eyes wander aimlessly around the room.

Janet's presence obviously made no difference to Mrs. Wishnowski, who just went right on gabbing, once in a while glancing over and giving a smile. Soon five minutes had ticked by. The coffee was gone, though Janet could not remember drinking it. With growing impatience, she began to recognize one of those few instances when she wished that she smoked… she was starting to worry that her confidence might be fading.

She also was concerned that Mr. Wiley might walk in. After his earlier talk with her it wouldn't look good for him to find her sitting idly in the staffroom while her class went unattended.

And still Mrs. Wishnowski talked. *Another* five or so minutes, with no end in sight.

The minute hand on the dusty old wall clock continued to jerk forward. Janet felt her cheeks grow warm…

The door opened, and in an instant her worry materialized. Mr. Wiley stood in the doorway, rigid, his left hand thrust deep into his trousers pocket. Disapproval showed in his eyes. But he didn't utter a word; he simply gestured with a hand movement for the young teacher to follow him out into the hall.

As Janet rose from her chair she felt a rapid pulse at the side of her head. She released a forced breath as she started out of the staffroom to join the principal to likely receive another reprimand. Had she chosen to look back, she would have caught an oblivious, still chattering Mrs. Wishnowski giving her another smile.

Mr. Wiley stood outside, a few feet from the door. As he stared down at her, he seemed to grow several inches taller.

Then he said, in his usual officious manner: "I just had to give your class a warning about the disturbance they were making."

"I'm sorry," Mrs. Rossen mumbled, unable to meet the principal's critical stare. "But I had to make a very urgent telephone call."

"I see. And you thought you'd just wait around the staffroom until Mrs. Wishnowski was finished her call." His words came out in a more condescending manner than perhaps he had intended. He might as well have been talking to some troublesome pupil.

"Well yes, but—"

Mrs. Rossen cut herself off. She could sense that no matter what she told him it wouldn't excuse her. She suddenly felt herself deflating; she didn't have the energy to try and explain herself. And what good would it do? Mr. Wiley was a proud man, the type of person who was always right and would never permit himself to lose an argument.

She nodded weakly.

"I'll get back to my class."

"Yes, that would be a good idea, Mrs. Rossen." Mr. Wiley watched her turn away; then added: "I'm sure this won't happen again."

Mrs. Rossen half-turned toward him and mumbled something to the effect that it wouldn't, but she couldn't be sure if he heard.

When she returned to her classroom, it was obvious by her expression that she was not going to tolerate even a hint of misbehavior. She closed the door behind her with a slam that nearly rattled the glass. With the corners of her lips pulled down in a frown, she went to her desk. She looked out over her class and young, *innocent* faces stared back. Twenty-eight of them.

Finally, in a voice uncharacteristically harsh, she said, "Mr. Wiley just got through telling me that he had to come in here and give you all a warning." Her voice got louder and demanding. "*Now what is going on?*"

The silence she had requested earlier was more than evident now.

"Okay," she said, "as punishment you'll *all* be staying fifteen minutes after class today."

A heavy, disappointed group groan came from her pupils.

"You wanna try for a half hour?" she snapped.

The children became quiet, sitting in an almost stunned silence since they'd never seen their teacher in this kind of mood before. Gradually their heads bowed back to their art work.

Mrs. Rossen picked up a pencil and pressed it hard between her fingers. She was not given to outbursts of obscene language, but at this moment she struggled against opening her mouth and spewing out every expletive she'd ever heard Chuck use.

Closing her other hand around the pencil, she flexed her wrists and—*snap!* She scanned the class, almost hoping to find one set of little eyes focused on her. But no one was looking up. Mrs. Rossen redirected her attention to the top of her desk. She tried to find something to busy herself with… so that she could get her mind off—

A quick whisper passed between two children in the center of the room: Jeremy Westmacott and Krissie Carver.

"Jeremy, out in the hall!" Mrs. Rossen ordered, speaking so loud and suddenly that the other pupils sat bolt upright in their seats.

Jeremy whitened. "But I was just asking if I could borrow a crayon," he whined.

"Do I have to come over there?" Mrs. Rossen was stone serious.

Jeremy slowly rose from his desk and started down the aisle to the door, shuffling his feet. Most of the other children sat with their mouths hanging open. They were genuinely puzzled about what was going on with their teacher. They understood that she was upset about their behavior, but they'd been rowdy before and Mrs. Rossen had never reacted quite like this. Usually she would scold them mildly, always with a twinkle in her eye, never raising her voice. And never sending someone out into the hall just for asking to borrow a crayon! Mrs. Rossen's attitude was so unlike her that it scared them, as if a friendly pet had suddenly and inexplicably gone savage.

The teacher's eyes shifted from Jeremy, who had just stepped from the room, to Krissie Carver.

"I'm sorry, Krissie," her voice was softer but still firm, "but you were talking, too."

The little white-haired girl slowly raised her head from her work and looked at the teacher. Her mouth stretched into a smile.

"But I wasn't talking, Mrs. Rossen," she said sweetly.

"Yes, Krissie, I heard you."

"No, Mrs. Rossen, you couldn't have."

"Krissie—"

"No!" the little girl shouted.

Mrs. Rossen felt herself tensing. Her left hand involuntarily balled into a fist. "Don't get loud with me, young lady. Not in my classroom."

"But I wasn't—"

Before she could finish, the teacher's fist slammed down on the desk.

She heard a startled gasp from the children. All except Krissie, who merely continued to smile at her.

"You shouldn't lose your temper, Mrs. Rossen," she said.

Shouldn't lose... Why, of all the impertinence!

"Krissie Carver, not only will you stand out in the hall, you'll also remain *extra* late today."

A short pause, then:

"No I won't, Mrs. Rossen."

Mrs. Rossen could scarcely believe her ears. This couldn't be sweet, quiet Krissie Carver speaking.

All the same, she didn't have to put up with this kind of insolent behavior in her classroom. She didn't have to, and she certainly wasn't going to. She was the one in charge, not some little seven-year-old. The children sat with mouths agape as the young schoolteacher forcefully pushed away from her desk and walked with determined steps over to Krissie.

Although she put an effort into controlling her temper, she couldn't.

"Young lady," she barked, "I don't know what's gotten into you, but I won't stand for this—"

Krissie blinked. "If I were you, Mrs. Rossen," she said, speaking very slowly, "I wouldn't get mad at me."

Mrs. Rossen appeared incredulous.

"Don't you dare tell me how to behave," she sputtered.

Time froze for an instant. A disturbing silence descended over the classroom. The children sat numb and still, nervously waiting to see what was going to happen. They waited, but no one was particularly anxious.

Then Krissie started to laugh, the sound growing to an eerie, almost maniacal pitch. Not the laugh of a little girl.

Mrs. Rossen opened the palm of her hand—

"Krissie!"

—and before she could think, the teacher slapped Krissie hard across the face.

The class reacted with a collective gasp.

But the little girl didn't so much as wince. Still smiling, she just fastened her soft blue eyes into Mrs. Rossen's. Eyes that quickly changed to a harsher hue before becoming luminous.

The teacher's lips parted...

Suddenly, with a convulsive jerk, she drew back—but not voluntarily. It was as if invisible hands had suddenly grabbed hold and were urging her away from Krissie Carver's desk. She was stepping backward, rapidly moving to the front of the classroom.

And she couldn't stop herself!

She tried to protest, to cry for help, but found that she couldn't utter a sound. The words just wouldn't come.

A few of the children snickered. To them it appeared as if their teacher was doing some erratic, comical dance. They could not see or understand the confused terror that blazed in her eyes.

Krissie remained seated at her desk, now grinning broadly, with her glowing eyes still fixed firmly on the eyes of her teacher.

Mrs. Rossen was up against the blackboard…and still she was being pulled! She felt sure that at any moment the pressure might snap her spine.

Then, slowly, Krissie's grin vanished, and her eyes returned to normal and they once again drifted down to her drawing.

Mrs. Rossen's shoulders dropped and her body slid slightly forward. After steadying her footing, she stood quiescent. Beads of perspiration dotted her forehead. With her green eyes opened wide and her bottom jaw gone slack, she looked straight at her class. Most of the children who were snickering before now quickly changed their expressions. Mrs. Rossen eyed them collectively, hard. And then she focused on the Carver girl.

She was the only one of the class not looking back.

She was too engrossed in her coloring.

* * *

Somehow Janet Rossen made it through the rest of that afternoon. But promptly at 3:30 she left school, forgetting about the class detention. She dashed to her car, locked herself inside, and started to cry. Maybe she was feeling sorry for herself, but this had not been one of the worst days of her life… it was the worst! First: her run-in with Wiley… and that frightening incident in the classroom, which had left her bewildered and still shaken. Janet was by no means a religious person, but she couldn't help wondering whether her relationship with Michael had received the disapproval of some higher power. After all, didn't all those television evangelists preach that in the eyes of God infidelity was one of the cardinal sins?

She decided that a drink would go down good. Maybe she'd drive to some out-of-the-way cocktail lounge, call Michael, and ask him to join her. She felt she'd go mad unless she talked to him.

During the drive, Janet decided to tell him everything that had happened, and then she immediately changed her mind. He'd simply never believe what happened to her in the classroom. Janet herself was no longer sure that *she* could believe it.

Michael reluctantly agreed to meet Janet for a drink—but only because she sounded desperate and said that it was urgent they get together. He came straight from work and arrived at the bar a little after four-thirty. He found Janet sitting off at a booth in the corner, sipping what looked like a Tom Collins. As soon as he reached the table, Janet lifted her eyes and smiled. Michael didn't slide into the booth next to Janet; instead he pulled out a chair and sat across the table from her.

"You said it was important," he said curtly, in a tone that Janet didn't immediately recognize.

The temperature in the room dropped five degrees.

Michael signaled for the bartender to bring him the same drink as whatever Janet was having.

After a brief silence Michael pulled a cigarette from his gold case (a gift from Janet) and lighted it. He turned his head away from her as he blew out a stream of smoke; then looked straight at Janet. His eyes were strangely distant, but not empty. Janet could read a dozen thoughts in those reflectors of his soul. Only each seemed to suggest that something was troubling him.

"Well?" Michael asked, not hiding his impatience.

Janet spoke nervously. "I—I was going to call Chuck this afternoon… and tell him."

"Over the phone?" Michael had a critical note to his voice.

"I had no other choice, Michael. That's been the hard part: bringing myself to come out and tell him that it's over. I was all set to do it, but I couldn't just leave school." She paused for a moment. "Besides... I just didn't know how he'd react if I broke it to him in person. I was afraid."

Michael lifted his head and blew out another stream of smoke. "That's always been the problem, hasn't it?"

"And you can't understand that, knowing the way that Chuck can be?" Janet said.

Michael sighed. "We've already established that he's a Neanderthal. So, what happened?"

"I... couldn't make the call," Janet replied meekly, her eyelids lowered.

Michael sighed and gave his head a mild shake.

Janet then told him about Mrs. Wishnowski and her encounter with the principal.

Michael was unsympathetic. He waited for a moment before he said, "I guess I should tell you. I'm moving out at the end of the month, getting my own place."

Janet looked crestfallen. "So, I suppose that means..."

Michael said, "I've said it before. It has to be up to you."

Janet's expression grew taut. She then said in a firm voice, "I am going to do it. Michael, I will."

Michael responded with a look of doubt.

"No, Michael, I *will*," she said definitely. Her eyes glistened, reflecting a pathetic look of desperation. "But until then... Oh, Michael, you don't know what it's been like this past month."

With all her heart she was hoping he'd respond with an understanding: "Yes, I do."

Instead: "Things been tough with Chuck?"

Janet shook her head. "No, not really. That hasn't changed much. As long as I keep financing his drinking and stall with the bill payments, he's happy. It's just that… I've missed you so much."

Michael didn't have to be convinced of Janet's sincerity. But he remained set in what he wanted.

He had his reasons.

Nothing more was said until after the bartender brought Michael his drink. He sipped it, stubbed his cigarette, and blurted:

"Janet, I've been seeing someone else."

It came out perhaps too harshly, but Michael knew that he had to be honest with her. He couldn't keep it from her any longer.

"What?" Janet said uneasily, feeling an impact, but not certain she'd heard him correctly. "Michael, what are you talking about?"

"It's true," he breathed, suddenly experiencing a strange surge of relief. "For about three weeks."

He deliberately avoided the expression on Janet's face, which was probing, subtly accusatory.

"Her name is Maggie," he told her outright, feeling he at least owed her this, plus some kind of explanation. "I met her at a get-together one of the salesmen had. I don't know… something just happened between us. Besides," he added with self-righteous emphasis: "there was no commitment."

If not for the subdued lighting in the lounge, Michael would have noticed the color fade from Janet's face.

"Michael…"

Michael cleared his throat and reached inside his case for another cigarette, hastily lighting it.

"Well, dammit, what do you expect from me?" he said, jumping to the defensive. "Hell, I can't sit this out forever. Think of me, will you."

"I'm always thinking of you," Janet murmured.

Michael waved his hand sharply. "Oh no, don't try to lay a guilt trip on me."

Janet stiffened as her attitude shifted. "Why shouldn't I?" she said indignantly. "All the lines you handed me, about my meaning so much to you."

"I never lied to you," Michael said gently. "But even if things hadn't happened as they did this is something we would have had to face eventually. Really, I'm doing us both a favor. You could never bring yourself to tell Chuck, be honest."

"Oh sure," Janet said, grinning hotly, rubbing her hands together. "Sure, that makes it easy for you. I mean, convince yourself of that and then you can go merrily on your way with your... what's her name: Maggie?"

Michael shuffled in his chair. "Look, I don't need this."

Janet grabbed her purse and started to rise. "You know something? Neither do I."

Janet was too overwhelmed to notice how successfully she was concealing her emotions: a loss so great she could cry for days; an anger so intense she was tempted to throw the contents of her glass right into Michael's face.

Michael reached over and took her arm. "Listen, Jan, I know there's no great consolation in this, and I wouldn't expect you to find any, but it was the hardest decision I ever had to make. I mean that."

Janet gave him a narrow stare. She wanted to say something—*anything*—that would let Michael know what she felt. But pulling her arm free, she instead walked silently to the door.

She didn't look back.

* * *

Janet was nearing her house when the first signs of a thunderstorm appeared. A striking blue flash of lightning lit up the eastern skies, lashing out like the forked tongue of a serpent while the gray clouds moved steadily westward. There was a distant, muted rumbling of thunder. Then, as Janet turned her Chevy off onto the road heading for the twin bridges, the storm really broke. The rain hit suddenly with blinding intensity. How appropriate, Janet thought with bitter irony: A perfect reflection of my day.

Peering through the relentless sheets of rain, Janet was receptive to the drumming on the roof, of the rapid, rhythmic swishing of the windshield wipers, of the smooth whirring of the recently tuned-up engine—

Chuck!

Oh God, she thought with a sudden dread. What if Chuck should suspect?

Janet eased up on the accelerator pedal and swallowed back a lump in her throat.

swish ... swash ... swish ...

A honking car startled her back to the moment, and Janet saw that she was crossing the center line. She responded fast, spinning the wheel to the right, tires squealing. Sweating slightly, she let out a slow breath and tightened her grip on the wheel.

When Janet reached her neighborhood, the rain was still pouring heavily. It was only five-thirty, but already lights winked from inside most of the houses on her block. Janet's bungalow was an exception. She could see that even before she pulled into the driveway, and she dearly hoped that meant she wouldn't find Chuck home.

She popped off the headlights; switched off the ignition. Before she got out of the car to make her dash for the house, a different image of Michael and their relationship gradually seeped into her thoughts.

She considered the age difference: he was only twenty-one, a full five years younger than her. And if she really were to be truthful, it didn't say much for his maturity that he still lived at home with his parents…

But she knew she was kidding herself, just trying to come up with reasons to comfort the hurt she was feeling. His age made no difference. How could it? Boy or not, Michael had twice the maturity and sensitivity of her so-called husband. And as for his living at home, in a month that would have been taken care of.

Janet drew in a shaky breath, a possible prelude to a release of tears.

All right now, she scolded herself, stop thinking about it. You're home now and you know that Chuck must never find out about Michael.

As for her situation with Chuck, eventually she'd work out some plan to make her break, but for now she had no choice but to make the best of it.

Janet fished in her purse for her house key.

A clap of thunder jolted her.

"Steady, girl, steady," she uttered.

Then, like a shot, she was out of the car. She had her sweater pulled up over the back of her head as she bolted across the lawn. The grass was wet, and twice she nearly slipped and fell. Scrambling up the front steps, she pressed against the heavy inside door and thrust her key into the lock. Before she turned it, she tested the knob; the door was locked, which meant Chuck probably wasn't home and that prompted a sigh of relief. She unlocked and opened the door and stepped inside, securing the door behind her. She then slid out of her shoes and shook off a spray of water. Her clothes were drenched and the first thing she thought of was a bath. Yes, a relaxing bubble bath. Dinner could wait until she first soaked in that hot tub.

Janet dropped her sweater and purse on the hall chair; then she gazed into the plastic-bordered hallway mirror and fluffed her hair back into shape. Turning, she stepped into the darkened living room and—

There was a movement... in the corner, in the easy chair.

Janet squinted, trying to adjust her eyes to the dark. She made out a large shadowy form seated in the easy chair.

"Chuck?" she ventured.

She cocked her head and stepped inside a little farther.

"Chuck, is that you?"

A sharp flash of lightning momentarily illuminated the figure in the chair:

It was Chuck... holding a double-barrel shotgun!

"Hello, slut."

Janet didn't have time to make a sound or even allow the reality of the moment to register with her.

There were two powerful explosions—

A fitting end to her terrible day.

21

Kinbrace's Visit

THE SMELL OF PIZZA baking in the oven drifted out through the kitchen and into the living room, filling the house with a tempting aroma. From where Maureen was sitting she could watch the progress of her browning dinner through the oven window. A half-smoked cigarette in one hand and a double vodka with just a dash of ginger ale in the other, she was impatiently awaiting the arrival of Dr. Kinbrace.

Usually at this time she was engrossed in some late afternoon situation comedy or game show, but, as it had been all day, the television set was turned off.

And the house was completely silent.

There were no classes at Reuben Willis Elementary given the tragic news about one of the teachers, but Maureen had thought it best not to tell Krissie why she would be home for the day. Her behavior had been so unpredictable that Maureen was worried how this news might affect her. She knew how much her daughter liked Mrs. Rossen.

Krissie had been up in her room all day, completely quiet behind her closed door. Maureen was embarrassed to admit that after that last episode she was reluctant to check in on her.

Not until Dr. Kinbrace arrived.

Draining the last drops of her drink, Maureen felt that she could really use another. Initial numbing effects were evident, and just one more double—perhaps even a single—should help her reach that desired state of mental ease.

But with Dr. Kinbrace soon to arrive, she knew she had to be sensible.

Maureen leaned forward, placed her tumbler on the coffee table, and mashed out her cigarette. For about the fiftieth time that day she remained momentarily still, not twitching a muscle, and listened carefully for any noise coming from upstairs. There was the faintest ringing in her ears, probably resulting from the silence, but she heard nothing else. She pulled up the sleeve of her sweater and checked her wristwatch. Three minutes to five. God, she thought, that last half hour went by slowly. Maureen sat back on the chesterfield and patted away beads of nervous perspiration from her forehead. She couldn't deny her unease. Maybe just one more quick drink, she considered. After all, vodka's not so noticeable on the breath, she reasoned. Maureen almost had herself convinced and was beginning to lift from the chesterfield… No, she shouldn't. The doctor would be arriving at any minute.

And through the picture window Maureen saw a flashy green Grenada pull up to the curb. She recognized the afro immediately. Kinbrace stepped from the car and started up the walkway. He was dressed in a suede pigskin coat and was wearing a pair of mirror shades.

Maureen was at the door before he even started up the steps.

"Dr. Kinbrace," she greeted, holding the outer door open for him. "Please come in."

"Thank you." He stepped inside.

Maureen took his coat and hung it up carefully in the landing closet. She offered him a refreshment (halfway hoping he would ask for a highball, in which case she could join him) and he said maybe a cup of coffee, after he saw Krissie. Maureen led him into the living room and offered him a seat.

"Doctor," she said, reaching for a smoke, "I really can't thank you enough."

He smiled. "No thanks are necessary, Mrs. Carver. Is Krissie home?"

"Yes. There was no school today. Maybe you heard about what happened to one of the teachers yesterday."

"Yes, I did," Kinbrace said solemnly.

"Her name was Janet Rossen… she was Krissie's teacher."

Kinbrace blinked, then he gave a slow nod.

"Krissie was very fond of Mrs. Rossen," Maureen added. "I admit I'm quite concerned about how she'll deal with it."

"She doesn't know?" Kinbrace asked her.

Maureen gave her head a slow shake. "No. I didn't want to tell her. I thought it best if you see her first." She paused before she went on. "I haven't seen Krissie since I went up to her room this morning and told her that she could stay home today. She hasn't been out of her room all day—not for breakfast or lunch. It's been so quiet up there." She paused again. "I—haven't wanted to go up."

"Does she know that I was coming?" Kinbrace asked.

"No," Maureen said. "I'm sorry. Maybe I should have told her."

Kinbrace dismissed her apology with a smile.

Maureen spoke hesitantly. "Doctor, about what I told you over the phone yesterday—I don't know what you think… but it really *did* happen."

Kinbrace smiled again and said simply: "I think I should go see Krissie."

Maureen stood up with the doctor.

"Just tell me where her room is, Mrs. Carver. It might be best if I introduce myself alone."

Maureen sat back down and began to roughly scratch the back of her hand. "Up the stairs," she directed. "It's the first door to your left."

Kinbrace started up the stairs. Maureen watched, her gaze steady, until he disappeared from her view. She heard his muffled footsteps on the carpet as he moved toward the room. Then gentle knocking.

Kinbrace waited for a moment.

Then—

"You shouldn't be here, Dr. Kinbrace."

The doctor's hand had closed around the knob, and for another moment it remained there. He frowned, curiously. If her mother hadn't told Krissie about his visit, how did she know it was him?

The voice inside the room spoke again.

"Go away."

Kinbrace slowly turned the knob and stepped into the room. The curtains were drawn and gloomy shadows shifted and danced on the wallpaper. There was a palpable chill permeating the air inside the room.

Krissie had herself buried deep under the covers, a writhing and wiggling hump. Kinbrace gently closed the door and stepped over to the little desk set. He pulled out the small wooden chair, moved it to the side of the bed, and sat down.

The blanket-covered hump stopped twisting and squirming abruptly, and for several moments there was complete stillness and quiet in the room.

Then slowly: "Get out, Dr. Kinbrace."

"I don't understand, Krissie," Kinbrace said calmly. "Why do you want me to leave?"

"Because you shouldn't be here," came her muffled reply.

"Hmmm. Your mother seems to think I should be here."

"Yes, well, Mother's just scared because I got mad at her yesterday."

"I thought you and your mother always got along very well. Why did you get mad at her?"

The figure under the blankets began swimming out. Kinbrace watched as a sheaf of white hair came to the frilled surface. Krissie's hands popped out from under the covers and slowly pulled the blankets and her comforter down. When her little sweaty head was completely exposed, she turned to the doctor and said:

"Because she wouldn't leave me alone."

Downstairs, Maureen was in the kitchen checking on her pizza. She felt much better knowing that Dr. Kinbrace was with Krissie. Happily, her lost appetite had returned and she found herself really looking forward to biting into a big, cheesy piece of the pie. Just as she shut the oven door and rechecked the timer, the front door buzzer sounded. Maureen pulled off her thick oven mitts and went to see who was there.

"My father's come," Krissie said to Kinbrace.

"Lawrence," Maureen said with genuine surprise as she opened the door and saw her ex-husband standing on the porch.

"Hello, Maureen."

Lawrence's arrival was so unexpected (since when did he ever *voluntarily* drop over?) that Maureen neglected to invite him inside.

"Y'know, winter's on the way," Lawrence said with the trace of a smirk.

"Oh, I'm sorry. Come on in."

And to Maureen's relief he appeared to be sober. She made no attempt to hide her surprise at his visit. "What brings you here?"

Lawrence shrugged. "Just thought I'd drop by," he replied, in a tone that Maureen found refreshingly free of cynicism. "I—hell, do I need a reason?"

"Well, I am glad to see you," Maureen said. "Dr. Kinbrace is upstairs with Krissie."

"Kinbrace?" The skin around Lawrence's eyes creased. "Why is he here?"

"Maybe you'd better come inside," Maureen suggested. "Uh, do you want a drink?"

"Yeah, I guess I'll have a beer."

Maureen nodded and obliged. She went into the kitchen and brought him a bottle that she'd taken cold from the refrigerator. Lawrence took a seat on a barstool.

"Well, what's Kinbrace doing here?" he asked, and there was displeasure in his voice.

Maureen poured his beer into a glass and handed it to him.

"Lawrence," she began, "I have something to tell you about Krissie…"

* * *

"Everybody's always making me mad," Krissie was telling Kinbrace, "that's why *I* get mad. Nobody leaves me alone."

Kinbrace said, "I don't think people mean to get you upset, Krissie. I think it's just that they care about you."

"No," Krissie grumbled. "That's not true."

"Why do you say that?"

Krissie turned her head away from the doctor and paused. Then she slowly looked back at him and said, "Mrs. Rossen didn't care about me."

"Mrs. Rossen. Your teacher?"

Krissie shook her head. "Not anymore," she said softly.

"What do you mean by that?" Kinbrace asked.

"By what?"

"What you just said about Mrs. Rossen."

Krissie smiled. "Oh, it doesn't matter."

"Yes, it does."

"All right, then," Krissie huffed. "She's dead."

Kinbrace was startled by her words, but he maintained his professional approach.

"How did you find out about Mrs. Rossen?" he asked her carefully.

"Oh, I just know," Krissie said in a sing-song voice.

"Your mommy said that she didn't tell you."

"No. But she didn't have to."

"Well... can I ask you how you feel about what happened to your teacher?"

Krissie responded with an unsettling smile. "Oh, you can ask... but I don't have to tell you."

"No, I suppose you don't," Kinbrace said. "But sometimes it helps if you talk about how you really feel."

It was then that Kinbrace saw Krissie's little features take on a slight look of discomfort.

"Does your head hurt, Krissie?"

"Please, Dr. Kinbrace," she muttered. "Please go away."

"Would that make you feel better?"

"Please…" Krissie said as she laid her head back onto her pillow.

Kinbrace rose to his feet and for a moment just stared down at the little girl in the bed. She was lying very still, almost too still. Her eyes were shut tight and there was a slight frown on her face. The doctor returned the chair to the desk and quietly stepped out of the room. He closed the door.

* * *

"Hypnosis?" Lawrence was echoing the doctor's suggestion, and not reacting positively. "You want to put her into some kind of trance?"

As Kinbrace had told Lawrence the day before at the restaurant, he had not wanted his wife to know immediately about his concern with Krissie. However, becoming increasingly involved in what was happening to the girl, he now felt it would be best if he were upfront with the two of them—or at least as much as he could be at this point.

The atmosphere in the living room was tense. Maureen sat on a kitchen chair, staring numbly at the blank television screen. Lawrence was at the bar, working on his second beer. Kinbrace sat on the chesterfield, stirring his coffee… and observing the couple.

"I'm going to be honest with you both," the doctor said. "This is a unique case. I've never before come across a situation quite like Krissie's."

Maureen, still gazing emptily ahead, wrinkled her brow in a frown.

Kinbrace looked over at Lawrence. "As I told you yesterday, Mr. Carver, I'm certain that it's somehow all related to her 'friend' Adam. Since Krissie refuses to offer us much information in that regard, I'd like your permission to place her under hypnosis so that, with any luck, I'll be able to speak directly to this—other part of her."

Maureen asked warily, "Could there be any danger?"

"No," Kinbrace replied immediately. "And at this time I believe it's probably the best suggestion I could offer."

Lawrence said, "You mean now, right here?"

"Yes, if there are no objections."

Lawrence did have objections. Plenty of them. He was worried about Krissie, there was no question of that. And he wanted to do whatever was necessary to help her overcome these problems she was experiencing. But if there was one thing he distrusted more than psychiatrists it was hypnosis—the probing into another human being's subconscious. He had heard stories about what could be suggested to a vulnerable subject during one of these hypnotic episodes and how the process could lead to other difficulties, and that was something he was unwilling to risk.

Kinbrace said almost as an afterthought, "Oh, Mrs. Carver, I wanted to ask. Now you're sure that Krissie couldn't have known about what happened to her teacher?"

"What happened to her teacher?" Lawrence said, focusing on Maureen.

"She was murdered last night," Maureen answered lowly. "She was shot to death by her husband." Turning back to the doctor, she said, "Staying inside her room all day, I don't see how Krissie could know. Why?"

"When I was talking with Krissie she mentioned her teacher—and that she was dead."

Maureen tensed. "Oh God, I just got shivers all over. But that just doesn't make sense," she said incredulously. "How could she know?"

"If I could have your permission to put her under hypnosis I might find the answer."

Maureen looked over to the bar. "Lawrence?"

Lawrence's jaws tightened. "I don't like it."

"But why, Lawrence?" Maureen said. "Dr. Kinbrace said there's no danger involved."

"I know what he said, Maureen. But I'll tell you—I'm just not comfortable with the whole idea." Lawrence then spoke quickly. "Besides, how do you know Krissie would even go for it? Look how you both say she's been behaving."

"Then what would you suggest?" Maureen asked, stating her question almost like a challenge.

Lawrence had no answer to give her. He exhaled a frustrated breath.

"We don't have any other option at this time," Maureen said. "We've got to at least let him try."

Lawrence took a swig of his beer. "Look, you're gonna do what you want anyway," he said.

Maureen turned to the doctor and gave a slight nod. "Please, if you really feel it will help…"

Kinbrace glanced over at Lawrence whose head was turned, and rested his cup and saucer on the coffee table. He rose from the chesterfield.

"There is one thing, though," Maureen said. "I want to be there." She looked over at her ex. "Lawrence?"

He hesitated; then gave a slow rock of his head.

* * *

Surprisingly, Krissie offered no objection when her mother came into her room and asked if she would mind trying a little experiment. Probably because she didn't understand what was to happen, Krissie looked upon it as some kind of game.

Also, she appeared to be her usual self again. To the totally perplexed Maureen, it seemed that lately her daughter's moods shifted back and forth like a pendulum.

When Kinbrace came back into the room, Krissie behaved as though she was seeing him for the first time that day, seemingly confused as to why he was there.

Lawrence followed and closed the door behind him. He stood with Maureen off to the side, against the wall. Kinbrace again pulled out the tiny chair from the desk and slid it over to the bed.

Kinbrace smiled at Krissie. "How are you feeling now?" he asked.

"I feel okay," she answered slowly, shrugging, eyeing the psychiatrist curiously.

"When I was with you before you looked as if you might be getting a headache," he told her.

"Before?" Krissie seemed totally oblivious about talking to Kinbrace earlier. She paused before saying: "No, I'm okay."

"That's good."

The atmosphere in the room was perfect for the procedure. With the afternoon daylight beginning to fade and the bedroom curtains drawn together, it was dark enough in the room for one to become drowsily relaxed. Kinbrace undid the top buttons of his shirt and removed his gold Libra medallion. It was not exactly what he wanted to use as a focusing object, but he figured it would serve the purpose. He flicked on the bedside table lamp and a faint glow emanated from within the shade.

He said, "Krissie, I don't know if your mother explained to you what I'm going to do, but I want to place you under hypnosis. Do you know what hypnosis is?"

Krissie nodded. "I saw some people get hypnotized on TV once. They get them to do funny things."

"Well," Kinbrace smiled, "what I'm going to do is a little different. Krissie, you are going to become very relaxed, and I promise that when you awaken you are going to feel very refreshed." He started swinging his medallion back and forth, smoothly, back and forth…

In no time the little girl was under.

Kinbrace handed the medallion to Maureen. He shifted around in an attempt to get more comfortable.

"Krissie," he began, quietly, "what is the name of the school that you attend?"

"Reuben Willis Elementary," she replied in a slow whisper.

"And what grade are you in now?"

"Grade Three."

"Do you like school this year?"

"Sometimes."

"What is the name of your teacher?"

Krissie hesitated. And her expression grew taut.

"Krissie, what is the name of your teacher this year?" Kinbrace repeated.

"Mrs.—Rossen." Krissie barely mouthed the name.

"Do you like Mrs. Rossen?"

Krissie seemed to have a difficult time giving a reply. But finally:

"No."

"Krissie, did something happen to Mrs. Rossen?"

"I don't know," she answered through what sounded like a weak sob. "But she shouldn't have hit me."

Maureen turned to Lawrence with a troubled look. "Krissie never told me that Mrs. Rossen hit her," she said with a frown.

Lawrence gestured for her to be quiet.

Kinbrace: "When did Mrs. Rossen hit you, Krissie?"

"Yesterday. She hit me yesterday. She shouldn't have done that."

Again Kinbrace asked, "Krissie, did something happen to Mrs. Rossen?"

"Yes."

"What happened to her?"

"I can't tell you."

"Why can't you tell me?"

"I'm not supposed to."

"No?"

Krissie gave her head a weak shake.

Kinbrace spoke gently. "Krissie, I'm your friend. You *can* tell me."

"He'll be mad if I do."

"Who will be mad, Krissie? Adam?"

"Yes."

"No Krissie, I promise you he won't be mad."

"I…"

"Krissie, tell me about Mrs. Rossen."

Krissie went silent.

"Tell me, Krissie. You don't have to be afraid."

"Mrs. Rossen—is—dead."

"How do you know that?"

"Because—" She cut off. "I don't know."

"But you know that something bad happened to Mrs. Rossen."

"Yes."

"So how would you know?"

"I… just know that she is."

"Well, is it a feeling that you have? Or maybe did you dream something?"

"I don't know."

"Krissie," Kinbrace was speaking in a firmer tone of voice, "tell me how you know Mrs. Rossen is dead."

Silence.

Then Krissie's body started to tremble…

And: "I wished for her to die!"

Maureen let out a gasp and instinctively slipped her hand into Lawrence's.

"Kinbrace," Lawrence said heatedly, "I think that's enough."

The little girl appeared to be in a state somewhere between laughter and tears. Kinbrace uttered a few relaxing words, and Krissie drifted off deep into her trance. Her face took on a peaceful, serene look.

＊ ＊ ＊

Downstairs…

Maureen, her voice shrill and broken, said, "But Dr. Kinbrace, we still don't know how Krissie could have known."

Kinbrace turned toward the couple, both of whom were indulging in a strong drink. "Adam told her," he said straightly. "I'm practically certain of that."

"Come off it, Kinbrace," Lawrence said with annoyance. "How the hell could this… Adam know if Krissie didn't?"

"Oh, Krissie had to know. Somehow she did find out what happened. But as you told me, Mrs. Carver, she was fond of her teacher—but there was an incident between them."

"I honestly didn't know about that," Maureen said numbly. "Krissie never said a word about being hit by her teacher. Still, why would she say such a thing about wanting Mrs. Rossen dead?"

"Mrs. Carver, most children react strongly to discipline. They may think and sometimes speak in the extreme, but it's usually only a temporary reaction. Don't forget, one of the main characteristics in a child is resiliency."

Lawrence breathed. "That still doesn't explain how she knew about her teacher."

Kinbrace let out a thoughtful sigh and wore a puzzled expression. "No, it doesn't."

Maureen was confused. "Doctor, where does 'Adam' fit into this?"

"My guess is that when Krissie learned the news about her teacher's death—however that was—it was the kind of information that she couldn't process. It was probably put out of her thoughts until her next encounter with Adam. *He* had to be the one to tell her. Again, he comforts her."

"But… that means she would have had to know about Mrs. Rossen – *yesterday*."

"Yes. That's what baffles me. Perhaps a prescient knowledge."

"Prescient?" Maureen said, not understanding the term.

"Foresight. Knowing what will happen before it does," Kinbrace explained.

Lawrence was frustrated. He held up his glass of scotch in a mock salute. "I'll drink to that."

"She's also very protective of Adam," Kinbrace said. "Whenever I try to question her about him, she now avoids answering me."

Maureen considered. "What if you tried to reach Adam under hypnosis? Couldn't you maybe speak directly to him, through Krissie?"

Lawrence shot a look of disapproval at his ex-wife for what she was suggesting. But before he could interject Kinbrace spoke up.

"Possibly," the psychiatrist said, though his tone was dubious. "But it also seems apparent that Krissie may have created a block."

"A block?"

"Yes," Kinbrace responded, "one between her conscious and subconscious. I mentioned it to Mr. Carver yesterday; Krissie's defenses are switched on whenever a situation arises where Adam's existence is threatened. I'm sure this particular defense, this block, was created unconsciously by Krissie's intense—and I think intense is the important word—protection of her friend."

"So strong that even through hypnosis you couldn't break through?" Maureen queried.

"There's more to consider," Kinbrace said. "I'd like to offer a theory on these 'defenses' as they apply to certain incidents that have occurred. Mrs. Carver, when you say that Krissie threw you against the wall, without so much as touching you; or the phantom voice which I found on my tape, we're likely considering a specific area of parapsychology: psychokinesis, telekinesis. Despite skepticism regarding such subjects, when you consider that humans use only a minimal amount of our brain capabilities, the idea ceases to seem so fantastic. To illustrate another way, I'm sure you've heard accounts of ordinary people who, in situations of extreme urgency, have exhibited superhuman strength. I personally am familiar with the case of a middle-aged man suffering with a heart condition, who alone lifted an eight-hundred pound pipe off a little boy who was trapped underneath." He paused to take a breath. "The workings of the inner mind, of which we really know so little—why can't similar powers be unconsciously unleashed during situations of severe mental stress? There have been many claims—some scientifically verified— of individuals possessing the ability to move objects with just their thoughts, or communicating telepathically. When you think about it, is it really so impossible to believe that in one of these psychologically stressful situations one might tap into some unexplored recess of the mind and manifest these powers?"

"Which is what you're saying Krissie has done?" Maureen asked, intrigued.

"It's only a theory." But Kinbrace was quick to add: "But one that I subscribe to."

Lawrence sucked a tooth and said dryly, "Which is what the study and practice of psychology is based on." He paused; then spoke wearily. "Look Kinbrace, I won't dispute you're a well-studied man. I'll even be willing to validate certain aspects of the therapy you prescribe. But… this mind over matter stuff… that's circus sideshow."

Kinbrace chose not respond to Lawrence's remark. He understood that in certain matters Lawrence Carver was a dedicated skeptic. No argument would likely convince him. Instead he said to the couple, though speaking more to the woman: "With your permission I'll to attempt to get through to Adam. Because of the apparent strength of her resistance, however, I may not be able to succeed. Not yet."

Lawrence remained opposed to the idea. "Then why the hell even bother, Kinbrace? Why put her through any more?"

"Because the answers are there," Kinbrace answered simply.

Lawrence looked at Maureen, but he'd already determined he wouldn't get her support. While her willing attitude puzzled him, it was clear Maureen wanted the doctor to probe deeper. Lawrence glanced back at Kinbrace, sucked in a lungful of air, and settled back heavily in his seat.

Back upstairs, Kinbrace resumed speaking to Krissie. His first sentences were muted, and neither Lawrence nor Maureen could hear what he had said. Then, still quietly, but more audibly:

"I am now speaking to Adam… Adam, you hear my words and must answer my questions. Do you understand?"

No acknowledgement left Krissie's slightly parted lips; her expression remained placid.

Again: "Do you understand?"

Nothing.

Kinbrace attempted a different approach. He said, "Adam, my name is Dr. Kinbrace, and I am a friend of Krissie's. I'd like to be your friend, too… if you'd let me."

For a split second an eerie stillness hung in the air—

And then with startling suddenness Krissie began screaming— prolonged, piercing screams that seemed to reverberate off the walls of the small bedroom. Her hands shot up from her lap and squeezed tightly against her temples. The color draining from her complexion, the girl was in fierce agony. Lawrence and Maureen both quickly stepped over, but before anything could be done to comfort her, Krissie passed out cold.

"What the fuck did you do?" Lawrence raged at the doctor.

Kinbrace quickly examined the girl while Lawrence attempted to calm Maureen, who was trembling and sobbing while struggling to free herself from Lawrence's grip to go to her daughter.

Finally Kinbrace glanced over his shoulder at them.

"I think she'll be all right."

"What—what the hell happened?" Lawrence sputtered.

"More *intense* than I thought," the psychiatrist muttered, intrigued.

* * *

Kinbrace came downstairs fifteen minutes later to find Lawrence and Maureen sitting quietly at the bar.

Maureen looked over anxiously at him and started to rise. "Doctor…"

Kinbrace offered a reassuring smile. "She should sleep until morning."

"You want a drink?" Lawrence offered, getting up and going behind the bar to freshen his scotch.

"I really wouldn't mind a glass of wine," Kinbrace said.

"Everything but," Lawrence told him. "Beer and hard stuff."

"No, there's some wine in the fridge," Maureen said.

"You should consider something stronger, you probably could use it," Lawrence suggested.

Kinbrace declined. "No, a glass of wine will suffice."

Lawrence lifted a shoulder and poured himself a little more scotch, dropping in an ice cube from the ice bucket but not adding any mix.

"I just have red, will that do?" Maureen said from the kitchen.

"Red is fine," Kinbrace answered.

Kinbrace walked over to the bar, his expression thoughtful. "Mr. and Mrs. Carver," he said, "I'd like for you to consider having Krissie admitted to the Landsbrook Clinic for a thorough physical and psychological evaluation."

"Oh shit," Lawrence muttered, heaving a breath, and he turned away. Maureen regarded Kinbrace with curious concern. "Why a… clinic, Dr. Kinbrace? Do you suspect something that you're keeping from us?"

Kinbrace sighed. "I'm not sure. But there are professionals at the clinic who I know would be very interested in looking at Krissie."

"Why don't you exhibit her in a goddamned sideshow already?" Lawrence said irately.

"Lawrence!" Maureen was suffused with embarrassment. "Doctor, I'm sure that Lawrence—"

"I understand perfectly the reason for your husband's concerns, Mrs. Carver. It does seem as if negative developments keep occurring without our getting any clear answers."

"Damn right," Lawrence mumbled.

Kinbrace said, "And that is why I recommend Krissie's admittance to the Landsbrook Clinic. I'm sure that working together we can start to find some solutions to what you've been dealing with."

Lawrence frowned. "Yeah, but you're being evasive as to just what they're gonna do at this clinic—and what precisely they'd be looking to find."

"Study your daughter, Mr. Carver. Under controlled conditions. As I told you before, I've never run across a case like Krissie's. There are elements involved that are beyond conventional psychiatric therapy."

"Are you dropping that psycho-*whatever* line again, Kinbrace?"

"*Psychokinesis?* I certainly wouldn't be surprised, Mr. Carver." Kinbrace spoke his words with utter seriousness.

"Yep," Lawrence mocked.

"Lawrence," Maureen said, "I don't think you should so easily dismiss what Dr. Kinbrace is saying. How else can you explain what Krissie did to me yesterday?"

"Yeah, well, I'm not convinced of that either," Lawrence said in exasperation. "Maybe you tripped or lost your balance. Come on Maureen, can't you see you're becoming brainwashed by this guy? Sure, Krissie has a problem, but it has nothing whatsoever to do with 'out of this world' powers." He spoke directly to the psychiatrist. "Look Kinbrace, if you're gonna continue working with Krissie—and personally I don't think that's the best idea—stick with the reality of her situation. Knock off this horror movie investigating."

"Lawrence," Maureen said harshly, "he knows what he's doing."

"He's screwing up our lives, that's what he's doing."

"*Our* lives?"

"Christ, Maureen, don't start this crap again."

Maureen held her stance. "I will as long as you refuse to let him help us."

"You call having your daughter probed and gawked at by a bunch of voodoo doctors *help*?"

Kinbrace interceded. "Mr. Carver, I assure you that—"

Lawrence brushed him aside. "Forget it, Kinbrace." He looked solidly at his ex-wife. "Maureen, you don't want what you just saw up there to happen again, do you?"

"Lawrence, that's what we're trying to prevent."

"Exactly. And the best way to prevent it is to stop stirring it up. The only reason Krissie reacted that way was because of Kinbrace playing hypnotist. What do you think they'll be doing at that clinic? The same—only more of it, with a lot more of these quacks sticking needles into her."

Maureen didn't say anything for a moment. Then she looked at Kinbrace. "Doctor, could *that* happen again?"

Kinbrace answered truthfully. "Yes, Mrs. Carver, it could, of course. But keep in mind that until we discover what the problem is, there's no guarantee these incidents won't reoccur, at any time—without any type of provocation."

"I doubt it, Kinbrace," Lawrence said thickly. "It's just like these headaches you were telling me about. Why is it they never bother Krissie until she's with you. Well, maybe they are psychosomatic, but it's your damned brain probing that's the catalyst."

"Doctor," Maureen said, "I think I'm going to have to talk more with Lawrence about this. Of course I want you to help Krissie, but—well, maybe Lawrence is right about the clinic. I don't want her hurt anymore."

Kinbrace sighed and nodded resignedly. "The decision has to be yours."

22 Revelations

ERNEST PICKED UP the carving knife from the counter and began sawing through the loaf of bread sitting in front of him. After two thick pieces were cut, he paused. He pulled the knife back over his shoulder... and mimicking the headman with his axe, drove the gleaming blade down toward the center of the loaf. But it slipped in Ernest's uncertain grip, missing its mark and veering off to the side of the cutting board, slicing deeply into his middle three fingers, just below the knuckles.

He didn't flinch.

"Skin ripped real good," he observed without emotion.

He stared at his wound dumbly, uncaring; then he rubbed the thumb of his other hand under the coarse ridges until the pressure forced the blood to bead out of the gashes, soon coating the top halves of his fingers. He watched as droplets began falling onto the floor, like thick, red raindrops, splotching the tiles. Then, slowly, Ernest brought the fingers up to his thin, colorless lips and began sucking in the flow. It tasted warm and salty. Not only was he finding some sort of perverse satisfaction in the stinging pain, Ernest also found himself actually enjoying the taste of his own pulsing blood.

"Don't want to damn well bleed to death," he finally mumbled, and he trudged over to the toilet. He unrolled a long strand of toilet paper and wrapped it around the cuts until it resembled a thick, though sloppily-applied, bandage.

He returned to the counter where he took his bread and sat down at the kitchen table. He munched on his stale lunch absently, his eyes directed at the dusty old book perched on the opposite end of the table.

Origin of the Alpha Traveler was written in 1897 by Sir Ronald Hyatt, but not published until half a decade later, after the author had gained widespread notoriety in other endeavors outside of literature. The book was not a critical or commercial success, but the few people with whom the enigmatic Hyatt had associated believed that he had never intended it to be either.

They claimed it was a book that he had written specifically for himself.

Briefly, this massive tome dealt with the pre-historic colonization of the earth by a race of benevolent extraterrestrials whom Hyatt referred to collectively as the "Alpha Traveler." Under the leadership of *One-All-Powerful*, this civilization flourished, until revolution claimed the lives of almost half the population. Ernest found Chapter 29, with many of its passages underlined in red pencil, of particular interest. It told of a time when the rebel leader and two of his followers were captured by the Guard and brought before the Galactic Court. Although guilty of treason and responsible for many deaths, the three traitors were not executed. Instead, the penalty for their crimes was banishment. Hyatt wrote that the three were taken to the crest of a hill, swallowed up by a great cloud and removed to the land where "one lives an eternal existence in exile" to be guarded for eternity by exiled servants, who had conspired in an earlier revolt.

But it was prophesized that a future civilization would see the return of the three. According to the book, two would return first "through the mind of a dreamer," to prepare for "the child who shall bring Adamm." They would serve as the "protectors" of Adamm. The ultimate result of their return was not predicted, but the record of violence outlined in Chapter 29 promised that if such were to happen, the fate of the planet rested uncertainly.

There was more to the story of the Alpha Traveler, including a detailed description of the race's extinction following a plague of unexplained origin. But for Ernest, as apparently for Danny O'Ryan, the book had nothing more of interest after Chapter 29.

However, there was a postscript to the chapter, scribbled in almost illegible handwriting (Danny's?) on the flyleaf:

"Hyatt, said by intimates to possess remarkable powers, died in an English mental hospital in 1904, claiming to the last that his book was not mere fiction, but the final result of a lifetime of study...He died convinced that he had made contact with the exiled rebels and, through experimentation with the powers it was claimed he possessed, had fulfilled the first part of the prophecy by willing 'the protectors' into the world of the early twentieth century..."

Ernest now understood what Danny had meant when he lay dying. "It'll explain to you what I can't."

As incredible as it all sounded, Ernest could not dispute what he had read in those pages. In fact, it made too much sense. The message came through in Chapter 29, allowing its ultimate warning to sink deep into his thoughts. Danny O'Ryan had indeed sought him out for a purpose. Because he knew. He knew the importance of the book; he knew of his own power; and he knew of Ernest's shared secret.

Danny had sacrificed himself because he was too old and weary to prevent what was coming. Ernest had to take over the fight, since he also had the power. The power had compelled him to do terrible things and when he tried to resist against its force it would control him by inducing crippling headaches, great physical pain intended to display a force which a man broken in body and spirit like Ernest was not to challenge.

Yet all the time, during each of those periods of agony, surrendering to its will… Ernest had the ability to protect himself against its influence.

Ernest now understood that he had a mission.

He found it a terrifying and overwhelming responsibility.

And, because he knew who it was he must seek out, it was laced with irony.

Thinking back, it all fit into place. The schoolyard. The little girl he recognized without even knowing it was her. It could be no other. It had to be *her*. To quote the book: "The child who shall bring Adamm."

And somehow—

Ernest choked on his bread, even though the same thought had come to him many times before, though never with the same comprehension.

—he was the one responsible.

Oh holy Jesus, if only Danny had known. His own attempt to cheat the prophecy; turning his mission over to a man who, without realizing it, had been acting as an agent for the Alpha Traveler—or, as he interpreted it: *the voice.*

Ernest brushed the scattering of bread crumbs off the table; then he sat back and began rubbing his hand against the back of his neck. While he had so often tried to erase it from his memory... now he made himself remember the day when he was first drawn to the little white-haired girl. Two years ago.

He remembered the old empty house with the broken back lock (where the voice had led him) and the gentle words he'd used to encourage the girl to explore it with him.

And...

As it had done since the beginning—since the first day it had made its presence known—the voice urged him in its sinister purpose...

But even as he struggled to remember the details of that day, so Ernest was wrenching his brain to understand what had happened during those few minutes when he was alone with her. There was no direct physical contact... but a sort of energy transference.

What passed from his body into hers? From his soul into hers? To allow the being mentioned in the book to escape from its cosmic prison.

Now he knew.

Somehow he had passed into her his power.

For she had to be the one to fulfill the prophecy!

Ernest found himself standing by the counter, scouting the cupboards for... for what?

For a goddamn drink, what else!

Then he remembered he didn't stock this week. He stood, his body tense—experiencing the signs of a momentary mental withdrawal. He swallowed hard, dryly, as a sweaty heat rose out of nowhere, consuming him whole.

And then he exhaled, gradually relaxed and maintained control over his urge. Although the craving for liquor was strong, he realized that was one influence he could not succumb to at this time.

Ernest shut the cupboard door and went back to the table. If the time on the alarm clock was correct, it was now 1:15 p.m. He grabbed his sweater, which was lying on the floor amidst a heap of dirty underclothes, and headed for the door.

He had a bus to catch.

* * *

He had to hang around outside the school grounds for a while, and this made him uneasy. To avoid suspicion, he circled the block a few times, ducking into back alleys. This also gave him time to decide how he would handle this. What would he say to her? No matter how he rearranged his thoughts, it still all came out like ravings. There was no way a man could explain a situation as fantastic as this and have it make sense to a child…

As Ernest once more rounded the block, he found himself facing a new worry. One that, surprisingly, he hadn't considered before.

Would she remember him?

The thought occurred to him so suddenly that his heart skipped a beat.

And he slowed his step to a virtual crawl.

It had been two years; she was hardly more than a baby when it happened. But was it possible for his face to have stuck with her, in her memory? Even if she didn't recognize him outright, was it possibly she might associate his face with something bad?

Still walking in low gear, but nearing the school, Ernest engaged in a battle with his inner self. Although part of him yearned to turn away and forget the whole thing, there was no escaping the horrible reminder that this was his doing and that it had now been thrust upon him to prevent the possible outcome of his actions. He also could not forget that if the evil should return with consequences anywhere near the scale hinted at in the prophecy, his soul would surely be condemned to darkness. He recalled vividly what Danny had told him with his dying transference of thought:

(*But prepare for your soul to be eternally damned… as is mine. That… is the price we must…*)

Although he had never given much thought to God or the afterlife, this prospect genuinely terrified him.

He stepped up his pace.

While admitting that he could never *truly* take responsibility for what happened two years ago, the curse of that day had haunted him ever since. Maybe there might still be hope for him by preventing this sinister force from entering the world.

Damn, at least once in his life he might do something to justify his tragic and tortured existence!

He determined that the little girl recognizing him was a gamble he would have to take.

About a dozen yards from the wire mesh fence, apprehensive, but feeling a definite sense of purpose, he heard the recess buzzer sound. He halted just momentarily. Squinted in thought. Then he moved on.

By the time Ernest reached the outer fence, the hardtop and playing field were swarming with children, boys tossing balls and frisbees, girls lining up to jump rope.

Ernest bit down hard on his lower lip, almost drawing blood. He concentrated on the hardtop, where the girls were gathering. Within minutes it appeared as if the school had emptied itself of all its children... and a slightly plump, elderly woman who evidently was the teacher on recess duty. Twice, Ernest carefully scanned the hardtop, from the weathered wooden fence at the far left end to the gravel lot that bordered the playing field on the right. But the little white-haired girl was nowhere to be seen.

He waited for another couple of minutes; then he started back to the highway, moving slowly alongside the fence, still hoping that maybe he could notice her.

Suddenly he stopped. A rapid cold flash swept through him... and his eyes were drawn down to his side.

The little white-haired girl was standing directly beside him, on the other side of the wire mesh fence. She was looking up at him askance, an odd, telling smile on her lips.

Ernest's own lips parted just a crack. He shifted his body until he was looking straight down at her.

For a moment, nothing. Even the playful sounds of the other children went suddenly silent. But then a familiar burning ache began to develop inside Ernest's skull, intensifying. Still, he found that he couldn't release his eyes from the gaze of the little girl. With a sudden blaze of awareness, he remembered when he had experienced this specific agony before: the night... Danny... died...

Again, just before the pain could completely overwhelm, it vanished.

Ernest stepped back uncertainly. A few feet, but then he was drawn back to the fence. The girl's eyes, charged with flaming energy, never left his. And, as Danny had done, she spoke directly into his thoughts.

Her first words realized Ernest's fears.

(*I know who you are*)

Ernest felt something click in his throat. He was trembling in a chilled sweat. Then, in a few seconds, concentrating hard, he communicated back to her, without speaking.

(*You know me?*)

The girl responded:

(*Of course I remember you*)

There was a maturity to this young girl's communication that was both uncanny and frightening.

Ernest:

(*I never wanted to hurt you*)

(*I've seen you here before. Why do you come here?*)

Ernest felt his thoughts beginning to twist.

(*I don't know... I... But you gotta believe me; I didn't want to hurt you. It's just... I couldn't do nothing about it*)

For a moment a softness reflected in the girl's eyes.

(*I believe you*)

(*And you're not afraid?*)

(*Oh, I never have to be afraid. Not anymore*)

The girl's smile suddenly vanished as her next thought came through dramatically to Ernest.

(*But how come you want to do something bad?*)

Ernest stepped closer to the fence. He hooked the fingers of one tremulous hand around a link. He found them pumping.

(*Why do you think that?*)

(*My friend told me*)

(*No. Your 'friend' is wrong*)

(*I don't think so. My friend knows everything that you're thinking*)

(*No, if he knows that then he's got to know I only want to help you*)

(*He says I don't need your help*)

(*But you're in danger. No, not just you, but many others, too*)

Now the girl was frowning.

(*He said you'd try to stop me from helping him. First Dr. Kinbrace, now you. Dr. Kinbrace tricked me yesterday... but I won't let you. You're still a bad man*)

It started as a dull throbbing inside his forehead. Ernest gasped and his eyes started to bulge.

"No," he whimpered, now voicing his words. "No, don't... pl-please."

But the girl had closed off the communication between them. Her energies apparently were now channeled into shooting psychic fire bolts into the very depths of his brain.

To Ernest the pain was more severe than anything ever produced by the voice. The inside of his skull felt like a volcano on the verge of erupting.

And it was impossible to fight back. Her powers were incredibly tuned, as finely honed as the blade of a razor... only countless times more deadly.

Her eyes had rounded into spheres of red fury, blazing like miniature suns.

Ernest was forced to his knees—moaning, hitting his fists furiously against his forehead, as if trying to beat out the brain fire.

Then he felt some invisible energy thrust him to the ground and his body involuntarily rolled off the sidewalk onto the grass verge.

Another shove, and he rolled toward the curb... then over it.

The black Lincoln squealed onto the block!

Ernest lay a few feet into the road. Still twisting in agony, he tried to pull to his feet. His agony was such that he didn't see or hear the black beast jet toward him.

Then someone in the schoolyard screamed, and that was a sound Ernest did hear.

The little white-haired girl whipped around to the direction of the shout. Her concentration broke…

Suddenly free of the girl's energy, Ernest saw through a teary haze the Lincoln racing in his direction. His eyes and mouth widened in horror—

And at the last possible second, displaying an agility he never would have suspected, displaying almost a superhuman feat of survival, Ernest somersaulted back onto the grass… straining nearly every muscle in his body.

The Lincoln sped through the red light at the intersection, veering into a left turn where it came close to colliding with an oncoming vehicle; then it disappeared like a ghost down the highway.

When Ernest had finally regained his breath, he looked back at the school. A mass of wide-mouthed children were pressed against the fence. The teacher on recess duty was rushing toward him…

But the little white-haired girl was gone.

23 Mastery

THE WHEEL OF LIGHT was spinning furiously before them, sizzling and cracking; discharging a multicolored shower of whizzing sparks that lit up the blackening skies like distant falling comets. This impressive display of Krissie's psychic aptitude had been going on for an interminable length of time, and the little girl felt her strength ebbing.

The mind-created translucent flames began to die…

"Concentrate!" Adamm commanded.

The wheel again burst to brilliant life!

"Concentrate harder! Enlarge it! You can!"

The strain was evident on Krissie's face. An S-shaped vein protruded, pulsing, from her forehead.

Her eyes closed, Krissie envisioned the fire-wheel in her mind. She pictured the outer flames shooting ever higher with each rotation.

It reached its most glorious stage: A massive cosmic wonder. A mini-nova! For seconds it blazed boldly against the midnight sky…

Then it began to fade.

"Yes child." Adamm said with a subdued glee. "Your effort is allowing the sphere to pass through into the next dimension, where it too shall flourish."

An awe-inspiring vision, but the effort had taken a toll on Krissie. Her shoulders, tensed, raised up high, began to sag. The heavy dark lines of concentration around her eyes eased into marks of fatigue. The flush that had masked most of her face had now given way to a pale complexion.

Her breath came raggedly as she lowered her head, shook it vigorously and then looked up at Adamm.

He was smiling.

"You have achieved mastery over your gift," he said. "The power now belongs to you."

"What does that mean?" the breathless Krissie asked, though anticipating the answer.

"Simply, that there is nothing further for me to teach you. Your time has come."

"Really? Are you telling me the truth, Adamm?" Krissie asked excitedly.

"It is the truth. You have passed your most important test. For once you have begun the transfer, you must not surrender. If you do... if you should weaken and fail... there will be no second opportunity."

"When will I be able to bring you back with me?"

Adamm said: "It is not yet the time."

"But you said that once I learned how to use—"

"Yes, and as I have told you, you have learned well and rapidly. Your time has come. My time is near."

"But why do we have to wait?"

Adamm brought his hands up from his lap and crossed them in front of his chest. He then slowly separated the fingers and reached out, lowering his hands onto Krissie's arms. Her skin tingled at his touch.

He said: "The man to whom you spoke yesterday... he is an enemy. One who would prevent me from entering your world."

"Yes Adamm," Krissie said, nodding, her features taut, "you told me about what he *did* to me."

"Yes. And perhaps now is the time for you to be made aware that it is because of him you are with me now."

Krissie wrinkled her brow. "I don't know what you mean, Adamm."

Adamm rose up from the cool grass on the hill. "I suppose you could say he is... your 'father'. As it is through him that you developed the *ability*."

Krissie stood up next to Adamm. "He... gave it to me? How did he do that?"

"That day I had reminded you of... the day you had forgotten..."

"When he—hurt me?" Krissie said softly.

"No, child: The day of your 'birth'!" Adamm exclaimed: "Which shall lead to the glorious hour of my rebirth. He provided you with the seed... a seed which you have nurtured."

"But Adamm, tell me... I still don't understand. If he's done all this for me—and I really believed him when he told me he didn't want to hurt me—why did you have me try and hurt him yesterday?"

"Because he lied to you."

"Lied to me?" Krissie questioned.

"Yes. He intended to hurt you again."

Krissie fell silent and her expression became troubled.

Adamm said: "Do you recall the first time you exercised your power? The boy at your school? You were upset... you no longer appreciated your gift. Do you remember that I then made you a promise that you would never again use the *ability* to harm anyone?"

Krissie's eyes glistened. "Yes, I remember, Adamm. But I did get very mad at Mrs. Rossen, and I..." To herself she muttered: "But how come I don't really feel bad about it?"

"In that instance you lost control. A human weakness; but one that as you grow stronger and more confident in your *ability* a frailty *you* shall overcome."

"Why is all this happening, though?"

"Krissie, when one possesses a power as great as yours, one must expect opposition. If not directed at the power you have been given, then at the changes that power may bring about, such as your assisting me. Some people would harm you to prevent this. That I cannot permit."

Krissie shook her head. "Just because I'm trying to help you?"

"Have we not discussed this before? Your—Dr. Kinbrace?"

Krissie spoke hotly. "Yes, he tried to fool me into getting you to talk when you told me not to."

"Indeed, and you almost swayed, but out of necessity I took control."

"And the same thing with that—funny man at the school?" Krissie queried.

"Yes. He, too, would have you turn against me. He is particularly dangerous... both to you and to me."

"That would never happen, Adamm," Krissie said firmly. "You are my only real friend."

"Yes, child, I am your one friend. Others may pretend to be, but they are not to be trusted."

"You—you rescued me from those horrible monsters."

"True. But they are not the real threat," Adamm said.

Krissie cocked her head, quizzically.

Adamm took Krissie's hand and they strolled across the hill crest.

"Those people you mention—who exist in the world from which you come... *they* are the true enemies, Krissie," he said. "Enemies because it is they who deceive you, with their false promises of help. And they must be dealt with as such: for your own protection as much as to help me."

"They all... would hurt me?" Krissie said timidly.

"Yes," Adamm replied somberly.

Krissie thought for a moment; she then asked: "But I still don't understand why that man would stop me from bringing you back with me if he was the one who gave me the *ability* to help you."

Adamm smiled and turned the girl toward him. "You are so young... so inquisitive... and I fear, so trusting. How can you hope to understand the complexities of your people?"

"What are—*complexities?*"

"The common denominator of your kind," Adamm answered. "What unifies you as a species... yet sets each of you apart."

"But what is it?"

Adamm stepped quietly ahead; a few feet, but not far enough to vanish from the girl's sight. With his back now turned to her, he began his answer slowly, with a voice of calm, but speaking words that were somehow amplified.

"It is what allows you to think the way you do. To act as you do. It is the individuality each of you possesses. The perplexity that almost always accompanies that—privilege." He paused to momentarily gaze off far into the dark, as if in an attempt to reach communion with his cosmic soul.

When he resumed, it was with intensity. "Indeed, as a child you are perhaps fortunate not to recognize or comprehend that free will is the bane of human existence; the tragedy of the mortal experience. Individualism, within which are constituted these complexities... Is it any wonder your world exists as it does? Multitudes of people, and each with his own precious way of handling situations... many rising to positions of great responsibility..."

Krissie's brain was traveling in progressively larger circles. For the past several visits Adamm's behavior had become ever stranger to her; his attitude... growing more distant. He would break off on his own, seemingly obsessed with his mysterious discourses.

"...when that most frail of human components—the ego— is challenged it promotes conflict; it becomes threatened and retaliates through aggression leading to chaos and devastation— and inevitably to finality?

"Your world is as it is because man has been allowed to think for himself, and thus there has been no order. Has not your history proved this?"

Then, in a whispered but no less intense cadence:

"All this must change. And through a return to a state of order and obedience, it all *will* change."

Silence descended upon the hill.

Adamm walked off, slowly, rigidly, as if in a self-induced trance, until his form was swallowed up whole by the black. Krissie suddenly became aware of a slight trembling in her throat.

"Adamm?" she whispered.

She was answered only by the quiet.

Krissie felt herself tensing. She lowered herself back onto the grass. Again she whispered his name.

And waited.

She was puzzled and somewhat worried. Was Adamm just playing a game with her… or what was he doing? Whatever, she wasn't finding it very funny.

The blackness wrapped around her like a cold shroud. She suddenly realized she was very alone.

"Adamm!" she called out in a quivering voice. "Don't leave me here by myself!"

And then Adamm emerged from the dark, re-entering her sight with the same kind of gradual magic as someone walking through a solid wall.

Krissie felt a rush of relief. She scrambled to her feet and ran toward Adamm, her arms outstretched.

She embraced him.

"Adamm, you had me really scared!" she exclaimed.

"Indeed, child."

Adamm raised his arms in the air, revealing open palms streaked with blood.

Slowly he closed his arms around her.

He said: "The time is very near."

24
Ernest and Dr. Kinbrace

ERNEST FOUND SLEEP impossible to come by. No matter which direction he attempted to focus his thoughts, the events of the past day kept entering his consciousness with a relentless intensity, populating his brain with disturbing reminders and troubling images.

Yet there was something else, too. It was like a faint voice far back in his head, urging him to remember something specific. He struggled with that thought until it broke through that it was the name the little girl had mentioned at the schoolyard. It occurred to him that perhaps he was working with an ally and didn't know it. It might be imperative that he find that person. But all he could remember was that she had said *Doctor*.

It was a chilly morning, but Ernest lay sprawled atop the blankets, clad only in his undershorts. The room was painted with shadows... shifting, malignant images that took on an almost sentient existence in Ernest's unsettled brain. Quiet... with the only sound the gentle ticking of the alarm clock. He was subject to a paranoia that he struggled against, with little success. Any slight sound beyond what was intimate and familiar filled him with a dark and consuming dread.

Ernest got up from the bed. He stumbled over to the window and tore open the curtains, welcoming a gray, overcast morning, but the ill-defined shadows continued to dance on the walls, as if mocking him. Ernest stared out the window for a long while, watching thoughtfully as a few scattered lost souls walked aimlessly along the dirty and dusty street.

He could relate to them in their pathetic poverty—but unlike those who carried on in an aimless existence, he discovered he had a purpose. One he wished he could be spared. A responsibility thrust upon him that no one could imagine would be so vital.

His face contorted into a mask of rage; his hand balled into a fist. He struck it against the filmy glass, again and again, rattling it—finally shattering it; blood-tinged shards falling to the street below.

He stood oblivious to the seeping gashes in his hand, unmindful of the accompanying pain.

"It's not fair," he sobbed.

Damn   that   book!   Damn   Danny's   soul! *Damn... DAMN... DAMN*!!

* * *

"Mrs. Carver, good to hear from you," Kinbrace said into the receiver. "How is everything with Krissie today?"

"No real change, Dr. Kinbrace. I, uh, hope I'm not catching you at a bad time. I could call back later if you'd prefer."

"On the contrary, Mrs. Carver, you couldn't have called at a better time. I'm quite free for the next hour."

"Oh, that's good."

Silence.

The doctor quickly could detect her reluctance to speak.

"Is there something specific you'd like to talk to me about, Mrs. Carver?" Kinbrace asked gently.

"Doctor," Maureen said hesitantly, "you *do* feel it would be beneficial for Krissie to go to this clinic you mentioned? I mean, it *would* help her?"

"It would help us understand what is happening with your daughter, yes."

"How soon would she have to be admitted?"

Kinbrace answered immediately. "I could make the arrangements today. We could have her in possibly by the beginning of next week."

"Next week," Maureen mumbled, drawing a faint breath. "That soon?"

"Does that present a problem?"

"Uh, no," Maureen responded hastily. "But there is one thing. Would you be able to come over beforehand, to explain to Krissie why she has to go? It's just that she's—never been away from home before. And I don't know how she would take to being in such a strange environment."

"I understand, Mrs. Carver. Of course I'll be glad to speak to her."

Suddenly: "Dr. Kinbrace, what is happening to my little girl?" Pent-up desperation came pouring out in her voice.

"I promise you, that's what we're going to work to find out."

"I know," Maureen whispered, "I'm sorry. I..."

"Don't apologize." Kinbrace then asked, "How does Mr. Carver feel about this?"

There was a pause before Maureen said, "Lawrence has his own problems. I realize now they're beginning to get in the way of our helping Krissie. No, I have to be the one to make this decision."

"You're sure there'll be no difficulty?"

"I want you to make the arrangements, Dr. Kinbrace," Maureen said resolutely.

After he hung up, Kinbrace placed a call to the Landsbrook Clinic. He asked to speak to Dr. David Lindberg, Chief of Psychiatry, about special admitting arrangements, but was told that the doctor was out of town and wouldn't be back until the following morning. Kinbrace wanted to first speak with his colleague and so decided not to make firm arrangements until the doctor's return.

If this were a less complicated case, immediate admittance wouldn't pose a problem. However, if Kinbrace's theory proved correct, he would require full outside cooperation.

A theory? Perhaps. But a damned probable one, he was convinced, no matter how absurd it might sound.

His conclusion: Krissie Carver was *responsible* for two murders.

To Kinbrace, the evidence began with the Peter Grubbish killing: Krissie's strong dislike of the boy; her confession of having "bad thoughts" toward him right before the incident happened. And her dream that night in which Adam appeared to comfort her; reassuring her, easing her of whatever guilt she might have been feeling.

Krissie's relations with Janet Rossen before her death were somewhat more clouded. All that Kinbrace did know for certain was what he believed to be the most important link: Krissie's sudden and intense anger toward her teacher—to the point where, under hypnosis, she admitted to wanting her death. And then her knowing of the teacher's death without being told...

Leaning back in his chair, Kinbrace attempted a methodical explanation of his diagnosis:

Telepathic hypnosis.

He believed that Krissie telepathically implanted the suggestion of murder in the accused killers' minds. Again, he could relate it to the Peter Grubbish murder because the Gautron boy claimed to have no recollection of the bludgeoning. Kinbrace had been unable to learn much about the second murder, but he felt sure that Janet Rossen's husband would deny having any memory of pulling the trigger, firing the shots that ended her life.

But he was also convinced that Krissie was ignorant of her mental powers. She might have blindly wished the two dead in a momentary release of anger, but it seemed doubtful that she had actually put conscious effort into causing their deaths. It was more probable that her considerable energies became inadvertently channeled—as a result of her anger—into triggering these tragedies.

Kinbrace intended to further investigate this theory, though prudently keeping it from Krissie's parents until through further professional examination and testing it could be confirmed.

* * *

Ernest stumbled out of his hotel, and, grabbing the cast iron railing, slowly guided his footing down the six steep steps. He staggered along the sidewalk, repeatedly burping up the sour aftereffects of the day's activities; oblivious to the harsh autumn wind and the pounding sounds of street construction farther along.

Quite bluntly, he didn't give a shit. It had not been easy laying off the booze—if only for a few hours. But he was never going to suffer through a night like that again. At least with a couple of good belts he should be able to paralyze his brain to some extent.

Anyway, who really gave a damn?

And hell, who was he kidding?

He wasn't strong enough to fight this…*prophecy*. The incident at the schoolyard the other day sure as hell proved that. Also, now he knew how right Danny had been: *"Now they'll do whatever they can to stop you."*

They would. They had tried. Next time he might not be as lucky.

No way! he determined. He didn't have much of a life, but he wouldn't have it end the way it did for old Danny, bleeding to death on the cold, hard pavement of a city slum.

Ernest's decision provided a slight comfort: a contented, albeit inebriated lift, in fact. As far as he was concerned, his mind was made up.

He just wanted to forget.

His tongue crept out of his mouth and traced a dry curve along his leathery lips…

When of a sudden, much to his dismay, Ernest discovered that he wasn't meant to forget.

That he wasn't meant to abandon this mission.

It came to him in a flash, though not through a spark in his memory; rather, the name was somehow directly spoken to him:

Doctor…*Kinbrace*.

Yet despite this unexpected and "unwelcome" revelation he continued toward his destination, finally reaching the liquor store, placing his hands on the horizontal push bar across the glass door. But he found he couldn't press it to open. For close to a minute he stood with his palms firm against the aluminum bar, genuinely shocked at his inability to give in to that urge just to walk inside. He might have remained there longer if it weren't for the well-dressed young executive type who walked briskly up to him and bluntly told Ernest to get his butt out of the way. But his snotty words hardly sank in with Ernest, who stepped aside without so much as giving the man a glance.

His eyes were directed at a corner telephone booth.

Kinbrace, he thought to himself. Even the correct spelling was clear: K-I-N-B-R-A-C-E… *Doctor* Kinbrace.

Let it go, the alcohol-sodden side of reason begged.

"I—can't," Ernest mumbled aloud, his eyes beginning to glaze.

Still, he did have to push himself toward the booth, approaching it like a condemned man walking toward his execution chamber. Because Ernest knew that once he found the address he'd have no excuse for turning back. With what he would say he would be committing himself fully.

He slid open the folding glass door with his shoulder. He pulled one shaky hand from his sweater pocket and reached for the telephone book. Balancing it on the phone base, he flipped through the white pages, wetting his fingers periodically.

"Kinbrace," he muttered to himself, "Kinbrace…"

Page 317, midway down the last row: Kinbrace Warren Dr.—

But the address remained out of focus, blurred either by a hangover haze—or perhaps an intentional resistance. He closed one eye and lowered his head closer to the page.

—1407-181 Smithton Street

Ernest continued staring at the address, letting it penetrate deep into his brain. Then he slammed the book shut and slid out of the booth, still mouthing the two sets of numbers. From the side pocket of his trousers he removed a handful of silver and counted out transit fare.

The closest bus stop was less than a block away. He started toward it.

* * *

Kinbrace munched on his tuna-on-whole-wheat while sitting hunched over his desk, his eyes centered on the latest edition of *Psychology Today*. There was no telling how long he'd been gazing at the full-page ad for an expensive set of learning tapes, but he could not have been quizzed on what he'd read. Nor could he have named the composition of his sandwich.

He remained deeply preoccupied with his thoughts concerning Krissie Carver. He was so engrossed in mentally reviewing all that he had learned about the girl that he was startled by the sudden ringing of the telephone. His hand quickly clamped down on the receiver and he raised it to his ear.

The outer door to the waiting room slowly opened, and, from his office, Kinbrace saw a strange, disheveled individual step uncertainly inside. The doctor squinted curiously. A drunk maybe, who just wandered in? That seemed ridiculously unlikely. Who just wanders onto the 14th floor of a building? Kinbrace politely tried to hasten his telephone caller along.

Ernest stepped into the waiting room, sniffling uncomfortably. He moved to the low-backed couch and was about to sit down when his posture straightened abruptly and he walked over to the large picture window overlooking the west side of the city. It was an impressive view; the remaining foliage blazed with autumn color in the park next to the building. Ernest yanked a cigarette from his pack and checked all his pockets for matches.

Dammit, he didn't have any. He broke the cigarette in half and dropped it into the ashtray on the center table. He went back to the window and continued to gaze out on the miniature world spread beneath him. But soon he grew queasy and a little dizzy from the height and likely the booze he'd consumed earlier and he had to back away.

A throat clearing sound from behind caused Ernest to spin around and his hands instinctively tightened into fists.

"Can I help you?" It was a youngish-looking fellow with fuzzy hair.

Ernest took a tentative step toward him. "Yer Dr. Kinbrace?"

"Yes, and you're—"

Ernest flattened his hand and brought it up to chest level, waving it in a nervous gesture. "It—it don't matter who I am."

Kinbrace managed a nod. "Would you care to talk in my office?" he asked.

Ernest nodded and silently followed him inside. While the doctor walked behind his desk, Ernest glanced around uneasily, chewing on his bottom lip.

"Please, have a seat," Kinbrace said, suddenly aware of the overpowering smell of booze that emanated from the stranger.

Ernest turned to the two chairs against the wall and dragged one close to the desk. He sat down almost hesitantly, his eyes still darting about the office.

Kinbrace couldn't deny feeling somewhat cautious with this character; his appearance, unpleasant odor and obvious edginess. But he exercised his professional calm. He leaned back casually in his chair, with his hands folded loosely on his lap.

"So what can I do for you?" he asked.

Ernest's gaze shifted back to Kinbrace. He fidgeted in his chair, reaching for the cigarettes in his shirt pocket, but then drawing his hand away.

His eyes began to drift again. "I shoulda brought the book," he mumbled through drawn lips.

"I beg your pardon—book?"

"The book," Ernest repeated emphatically. "I shoulda brought with me the damn book."

"I don't understand."

"Yeah, the book that'll explain all 'bout that girl."

Kinbrace shook his head. "What girl?"

Ernest snorted. "Oh hell, you oughta know. She—she's a patient of yers…I think. Leastwise someone ya gotta know. 'Else I wouldn't be here."

"If this girl is a patient of mine, I can't discuss her," Kinbrace told him straightly.

"Yeah? Well ya'd better discuss this one," Ernest said with utter seriousness. "You don't know what she's capable of. She's evil." He paused to consider. "No, it ain't her really. It's that—*whatever* they talk about in the book."

"Look, you're speaking in riddles. I'm willing to listen to what you have to say, but you're going to make clear exactly what that is."

Ernest knew that his words weren't making any sense. He stood up from his chair and began to pace the office, trying hard to shake off the booze and arrange his thoughts into some cohesive order. Kinbrace's curiosity was piqued and so he remained patient.

Ernest finally sat back down and fixed his eyes on the doctor. Then he began. He went into detail about Danny and the old book, the prophecy outlined in Chapter 29, and the little girl with the power. When he finally finished he noticed that while there was no noticeable change in Kinbrace's expression, his complexion had paled.

Ernest said, "Yuh know this girl, don't ya?"

Kinbrace eyed him speculatively.

"Yeh, I can see yuh not believin' me; can't blame ya for that." Ernest's mouth twisted in a slight smile. "But ya recognize somethin' in what I told yuh."

"You speak of a *power*," Kinbrace said carefully. "A power that supposedly will bring this—'being' back into the world. How are you so certain that this girl you're talking about possesses it?"

Ernest hesitated with his answer.

"If you want me to even consider this a possibility," Kinbrace said, "I need to know."

After several uncertain moments, Ernest finally spat out: "Because I gave it to her."

"You?" Kinbrace said, a hint of disbelief in his voice.

Ernest could understand the doctor's skepticism. He was a lowlife and looked every bit the part. How could someone in his condition be in possession of such a "power"? He half-expected Kinbrace to order him out of his office. But before that could happen he had more to say.

"It gets crazier all the time, don't it?" Ernest said with a grim smile. "But every word I'm sayin' is true. An' yer gonna hear how serious I am. I'm gonna tell ya somethin' that—well, that I sure as hell wouldn't admit to normally." At this, his eyes narrowed into slits while his mouth worked around the first inaudible words. He coughed and tried again, stiffening noticeably. "Two years ago," he said, "I was... I was forced into *doing somethin'* to that little girl..."

All at once Kinbrace didn't have to hear the rest. Those words hit him with impact. It was difficult for him not to react, but he kept his composure.

Did something to the girl? *Two* years ago?

Ernest continued, having difficulty squeezing out his words. "For what it's worth, I tried to resist it. I thought I was too weak, but now I know that the power this thing has is too strong. It guided me along, an' every time I'd try to put up some kind of fight against it, it'd... well, all I can say is it's like havin' an inferno ragin' inside your skull."

Kinbrace was frowning, intently. He was a man of science, yet here he was listening to and not totally dismissing an outrageous story told to him by some stranger who in appearance looked to be a person of little credibility.

Ernest's eyes lowered to his restless hands. "I forgot what I was saying. Oh yeah, that little girl. Well, before I even knew anything had happened, it was over. Y'know, for two years I've had to live with this... been haunted by it, an' that ain't no lie; 'specially 'cause I couldn't ever figure out what had happened. I just couldn't see it. Unless maybe I'd gone nuts. An' then old Danny, as he lay on the road that night bleedin' to death—well, he told me about the book. An' inside the book it told about the girl, or 'the child.'" He paused and began to vigorously scratch his scalp. "I guess it kinda makes some sense when ya think about it," he then said. "Hell, a kid wouldn't know no better. Me? Even though I got this damn power, I woulda tried to fight it, even if it meant it had to kill me. But a little girl—hell, it could fool her easy enough."

"And how do I fit in?" Kinbrace wanted to know, though he'd already suspected.

Ernest looked up. "Well, that's why I came to see ya. If you know her, like I'm sure yuh do, then maybe workin' together we can do somethin' to stop this from happening. But I'll be damned twice if I know what."

"Why are you so sure I'm involved in this?" Kinbrace queried deeper.

"Oh, I ain't all that sure ya know about her power," Ernest answered quickly. "As a matter of fact, wouldn't surprise me to find out ya don't know. But yuh definitely gotta know this girl. She knows you; she mentioned yer name to me, an', after all, yer the only Kinbrace who's a doctor that I could find in the phonebook."

Kinbrace asked, "How exactly did she mention me?"

"Oh shit," Ernest muttered as he now scratched the back of his head. "I can't remember exactly... there was too much else goin' on. But I do remember this much, it weren't nothin' good." He suddenly snapped his fingers. "Wait a minute, come to think of it I do remember. Funny how I coulda forgot. In a way she sorta compared us —said we both was tryin' to stop her..."

"Stop her?"

"From bringin' this *thing* back with her. She said that you tricked her."

"Tricked her?" Kinbrace said with interest.

"But you gotta know now what she means. An' I'll tell ya this: she fights back. There are others, too. The two written about in the book... that came before this other one, the head honcho if you will, is supposed to arrive. To prepare the way for him, so that no one interferes. Yeh, I found that out yesterday. And they were the ones that took out old Danny."

"When is all this supposed to happen?" Kinbrace asked. "The arrival of this..."

"I dunno," Ernest shrugged. "The book don't say for sure. But if the girl is bein' used for that purpose, the time can't be far off."

Kinbrace glanced at his watch; then he stood up and walked over to the office window. He stood silently gazing outside, his hands clasped behind his back.

Why did he find himself not disbelieving this man? He had come across more plausible stories in the science fiction magazines he'd read as a kid. *Pre-civilization aliens to be willed into the world through the mind power of a little girl.* Yet somehow he accepted that this guy's story was not as farfetched as it sounded?

It was some of the specific details that were convincing him, definitely relating to Krissie Carver. He had thought of just one question. And he almost chilled at the thought of asking it. Because he was sure he knew the answer.

"Does it mention this creature's name anywhere in the book?"

Ernest slowly glanced over at the doctor.

"He's called the Alpha Traveler... but the name is Adamm."

* * *

Kinbrace left his office at 4:34, shortly after his meeting with the stranger whose name he had refused to provide. As Kinbrace took the empty elevator straight down to the parking garage, he struggled to compartmentalize his thoughts, which were whizzing through his head with erratic urgency. He was beginning to feel a slight pressure building inside his skull.

The floor indicator panel glowed *P*. The elevator stopped with a smooth landing and a moment later the doors slid open on their tracks. Kinbrace stepped out and started toward his car, parked at the far end of the row. He was walking slowly, massaging the side of his head, and unusually aware of the hollow echoing of his footfalls on the concrete. Suddenly he stopped, wanting to re-check something. From the inside pocket of his corduroy jacket he removed a thin, brown-covered notebook, turned through the pages, and glanced over an entry marked 3:00 p.m.

The stranger had suggested a second, more detailed meeting the following day, again at the office. This time he promised to bring the book.

Kinbrace had agreed to another visit, if surprising himself by his willingness—even though he now determined he had more to learn from the man.

… Adam…

Kinbrace felt strongly this was much more than a coincidence or some delusional drunken rambling.

He slid the notebook back into his pocket and moved on to his car.

A sudden engine rev, followed by the echoing, ear-splitting shriek of tires spinning on concrete. Kinbrace swung around to where the sound was coming from.

The black Lincoln had swerved around one of the end support pillars and was roaring down the corridor—

Heading right toward him!

Reacting swiftly, Kinbrace maneuvered his body between the back ends of two parked cars. His pulse was pounding.

The Lincoln raced forward several yards before squealing to a stop. The brake lights flashed red, and in an instant the car tires were again screeching as the vehicle now swerved wildly in reverse.

Kinbrace's face registered a look of panic as the shiny back end of the Lincoln bore down on him.

Pacing backward, his arms bent out gunfighter-style, he spun around to the Rambler on his left and completed a half-flip, half-roll over the hood, falling out of sight just as the Lincoln slammed into the back of the Rambler, skewing it 'round at an angle. Kinbrace had landed by the front tire, and at that crushing impact, he scrambled to his feet and moved cautiously, crouching breathlessly behind the parked cars.

At the next reverberating crash, he risked a glance over the hood of another car, parked a safe distance away. He watched numbly as the Lincoln was demolishing the Rambler with a violent fixity of purpose; repeatedly pulling forward, then screeching back, ramming by turns into the trunk and passenger side, like some black prehistoric monster attacking its prey with frightening, unexplained ferocity.

This mindless destruction continued for several long, resounding minutes, until finally the Lincoln screamed ahead, halted; then sped off down the corridor, disappearing up the curving ramp.

Kinbrace remained where he was until the roar of the engine had faded completely. Then, stepping back carefully into the corridor, he approached the Rambler—rather, what was left of it. The force of the assault had driven the vehicle out into the center of the wide passage, where it remained at a defeated sideways angle.

The air was thick with the acrid smell of exhaust fumes.

He circled the Rambler to the side of the repeated impact. He shook his head dazedly as he examined it. It resembled nothing more than a mass of twisted metal and broken glass. He moved a few steps closer, chips of glass crunching noisily under his feet. He peered inside… turned around…

The black Lincoln faced him, silently, not twenty feet away; the gleaming chrome grille resembling a fixed, sinister grin.

Kinbrace stumbled back against the side of the Rambler; his head felt as if it were ready to explode.

The Lincoln lurched forward.

Kinbrace never had a chance. With tremendous impact, the Lincoln again slammed into the side of the Rambler, only this time crushing the doctor in between the two vehicles. He cried out only once and an eruption of blood accompanied that scream, spurting from his mouth and splashing onto the windshield of the Lincoln.

The pressure eased, but Kinbrace was too broken inside to notice. The Lincoln was slowly backing away, stopping.

Kinbrace fought to hang onto consciousness… onto life! But he felt himself rapidly weakening; numbing from the neck down, his body sagged forward. He was bleeding profusely from the mouth.

He struggled to focus through the washes of color into the car… to see who was doing this horrible thing to him. But his vision grew dimmer—

The tires squealed as, again, the engine thundered to life. Once more the Lincoln plowed into Kinbrace's body…

His eyes popped out like champagne corks. Another gusher of blood burst from his throat. His body convulsed for an instant; then it went limp and dropped to the concrete floor.

For a moment the scene was still…

Before the Lincoln slowly backed away down the corridor.

25 Purdue's Gun

IT TROUBLED MORE than confused Ernest the next day when he found Kinbrace's office locked and there was no response to his knocking. After waiting impatiently for several minutes he rode the elevator down to the main floor and dialed Dr. Kinbrace's telephone number, only to receive the recorded message on the answering machine. He dug into the coin return slot and looked to retrieve his change, which, expectedly, was gone. Tightly grasping a shopping bag, which contained the Hyatt book, he trudged over to an unoccupied bench, sat down and tried to decide what to do next. Should he hang around for a while longer? Maybe Kinbrace had to rush out on an emergency call or something...

Ernest shook his head firmly. Hell, he couldn't make himself accept that.

For a brief instant he experienced a dark sensation of premonition... but he snapped himself free of such thoughts. He had to!

But it was late. Almost half an hour past the appointment time. And Kinbrace *had* shown an interest and promised to be in his office at three o'clock.

Ernest rose, carefully lifting his bag up with him, cradling it in his arms. Really, he had no other choice. He'd have to wait. Wander around the mall (sparsely populated, thank God. He felt nervous in crowds, especially of late), and perhaps check back upstairs in a little while.

At 3:45, Ernest took the elevator to the fourteenth floor, where he stepped out and once again proceeded down the narrow hallway to Suite 1407. He closed his hand around the knob, hoping that now it would—

Still locked.

Ernest thought angrily: *Damn Kinbrace, what are you doing to me?*

He raised a closed fist and drove it repeatedly against the door. For about a minute he continued hammering, releasing his frustration by hitting the door.

Finally a door down the hall opened and a heavyset woman stepped partly out into the corridor. After a moment Ernest heard a voice query: "Is that the doc's place you're at?"

Ernest completed a slow half-turn toward her, dragging his hand down the wood frame of the door.

"Doctor—Kinbrace," he replied, squinting.

"Oh dear," the woman breathed. "Are you one of his patients?"

Ernest responded with a noncommittal shrug.

"I suppose you didn't hear then."

Ernest straightened up and stepped down the hall toward her.

"It's been going all around the building," the woman continued. "Heard about it myself just this morning. But I guess you must be a patient of the doc's?"

"Uh, yeah, kinda," Ernest finally mumbled, squirming in his lie.

The woman sighed. "It's a tragedy, what happened to him," she said. "He was such a nice man. It's hard to believe that he's gone."

Ernest felt his stomach tense. "Gone?"

"Yes. It happened yesterday."

"What're ya talking about, lady?" Ernest demanded.

"Dr. Kinbrace was run over in the parking garage. He was killed."

Ernest stared at the woman, the color drained from his expression.

* * *

Much to her relief, Maureen found Krissie to be in an extra sunny mood all that Friday. And with a workman-like appetite! At dinner, she spooned up the soup with great relish, although it was cream of mushroom, never one of her particular favorites.

Maureen carried a coffee cup half-filled with vodka and orange juice over to the table and sat next to her daughter.

"Another five minutes for the chops," she said. Looking at the empty milk glass in front of Krissie, she asked, "Would you like some more, honey?"

Krissie glanced up from her bowl just long enough to give her head a fast shake.

Maureen was wishing there was some way she could now explain to Krissie about the clinic, and why it was important for her to go there. Worried as she was over how her daughter would take this news, she knew it would be a long weekend. It was unfair to spring it on her at the last moment, but she couldn't gamble on Krissie's reaction if she was told about it now. Her moods had simply become too unpredictable. And Maureen feared for her own wellbeing after her last episode with her daughter. God, how she wished she could count on Lawrence's support. But she knew that once he discovered she'd gone ahead and gave Dr. Kinbrace permission to book the appointment, he'd likely react worse than Krissie.

"Hey listen," Maureen said with a snap of her fingers. "What say we do something different this weekend? Maybe drive up to cousin Harold's trailer. Y'know, this'll probably be the last chance we'll have to visit him this year."

Krissie pushed her soup bowl to the center of the table and wiped around her mouth with her napkin.

She said, "You said that Daddy might be coming over this weekend."

Maureen sniffed. "Well, I really don't think you should count on that, sweetheart. I was speaking with Daddy this afternoon and he thinks he'll probably be working this weekend."

Two vertical lines deepened between Krissie's eyebrows.

"He always has to work," she said glumly.

Maureen wore a thin smile. "That's the kind of job Daddy has."

"Well, I'm not going to the lake!" Krissie flared—and at that moment, unassisted, the soup bowl flipped off the table and spun around crazily before smashing onto the floor.

Maureen froze at this, but she deliberately didn't react, not wanting to say or do anything that might further antagonize Krissie. Instead: "Okay Krissie. How about we do whatever you feel like?"

Krissie's eyes narrowed. She turned her head away and just stared ahead.

Maureen waited for another moment, then, glancing down at the shards of broken soup bowl around her feet, quietly asked: "Sweetheart, are you all right?"

Krissie remained silent and unmoving, her gaze distant.

"Krissie," Maureen whispered, rising tensely out of her chair, "are you okay?"

Krissie blinked quickly; then she looked back at her mother. Her gaze was steady and slightly malignant.

* * *

Ernest locked himself in his room.

He had all weekend to plan his next move, and that was good. He'd need every hour.

He was shocked, there could be no denying that, feeling an almost personal loss, but he also realized that he hadn't time to concern himself with Kinbrace's supposed "accident." Immediately after learning the news, he'd experienced twinges of doubt again. But he determined not to give in. With Kinbrace dead, his mission took on an even greater urgency. It had become a question of survival—not just conceivably for the existence of the human race, but also his own survival, though he had to realize there could be no guarantee of that. Ernest understood why Kinbrace had died and was sure that he would be next, no matter what direction he now chose. His only hope of staying alive lay in preventing the Alpha Traveler's return to physical existence.

Unfortunately, he hadn't any plan how to handle this. It was impossible to reason with the girl; she saw him as her enemy. And if she were able to read into his thoughts and know what he was intending, she'd likely use her power to kill him.

He would have to work against her.

But how?

He doubted his own power would be effective against her. Her "talent" was much stronger, more accelerated, and in any challenge he'd be sure to come out a *dead* second.

No, the only solution was one that he could barely bring himself to consider.

He would have to kill her. Quickly. Allowing her no advantage to defend herself.

But how could he manage that?

Not more than ten seconds later, as if directed by some influence outside himself, Ernest's rheumy eyes fell upon the answer, printed in dull gray shades on the picture atop the October calendar—

A gun.

But anything as awkward as a rifle, which was the image pictured on the calendar, wouldn't work. It would have to be some kind of handgun, which he could carry unnoticed to the school.

But where would *he* get a gun like that?

Ernest began pacing the floor, trying to think. One thing he knew for certain: he didn't have either the time or the money to purchase such a weapon... if he even knew where to obtain one.

Damn, it was frustrating. But Ernest knew he had come across his only answer. A gun would be fast; most importantly, she'd never have the chance to fight against him... if he could properly mark his aim and succeed with one shot.

The negative thoughts began flooding in: It was *murder*. Also, he had never handled a gun before. And... how could he pull the trigger in front of all the other children? Commit what would be determined as cold-blooded murder in front of their eyes...

"No!" Ernest shouted loudly.

He gradually calmed himself. "None of that's important," he whispered. "None of it."

A far worse fate possibly awaited the children if he didn't follow through, he reasoned. Yes, at first he would be remembered as a child murderer, his memory scorned; but perhaps history might remember him differently. A martyr. The cipher who took it upon himself to save humanity.

But none of that was important. He wasn't committing this unspeakable crime for future glory. In fact, no one would ever know of his sacrifice.

With that thought taking prominence in his brain, Ernest's determination was reinforced. He might continue to suffer moments of doubt and weakness before he met with the girl for that final time, but there would be no further indecision.

He prepared to meet destiny.

And that was when he thought of Purdue, two floors below. Ernest was sure he could remember hearing the old geezer bragging about some old model revolver that he claimed to own.

Sure, now Ernest was positive of it. He remembered Purdue called it his "Wild West Pistol."

The problem was how could he get the gun from old man Purdue? It was a prized possession, likely the only thing of value Purdue owned; not something he'd just hand over willingly. And even he did, what about the questions that would be sure to come up? What the hell could he tell him? *I'm going to use it to kill a little girl to save humanity from an evil space alien.*

No, that still sounded insane even to him.

As it stood, there looked to be only the one solution.

He'd simply have to take it.

* * *

Shortly after eight the following night, Ernest stood outside Purdue's ground floor room gripping a brown paper bag that contained a bottle of cheap rye whiskey. Purdue lived as virtually a hermit, but Ernest was hoping that he might not object to a little friendly drinking.

Surprisingly, Purdue seemed glad to see him, though Ernest was betting that the old codger—a step away from total senility—couldn't even remember who he was.

And for the next hour or so they drank, or at least Purdue did; Ernest needed to keep his wits about him, and though the temptation was there, he consumed only the soft drink mix. He struggled to make small talk, never mentioning the gun until after the telltale signs of inebriation had begun to manifest on his companion; the slurred speech, the obvious drowsiness. Even then, Ernest was cautious. He broached the subject of the gun subtly, in innocent conversation, nothing to stimulate Purdue's suspicion. Then, in passing comment, he asked the old man if he still owned the gun. Purdue nodded but didn't elaborate. Ernest could detect that even though he was pretty well intoxicated, Purdue seemed reluctant to talk about his weapon. The subject was dropped until Purdue was right on the verge of passing out for the night. Ernest quietly and casually asked him if he kept the gun safely hidden, since it obviously was a treasured possession, and where that might be. At first he was afraid he might not penetrate a rye-induced wall of forgetfulness. But after continued mild prodding, the hiding place was mumbled out in Purdue's drunken irritation:

The revolver was kept in a chest under the bed.

A minute later Purdue collapsed into slumber.

Ernest took his time finishing his fifth glass of ginger ale. When he was sure that Purdue was deep into unconsciousness, he rose and walked over to the chair his companion was slumped in. He sank to his haunches, and in a moderate tone, spoke his name.

Not so much as a twitch in response.

Ernest smiled and pulled to his full height. He quickly went into the next room and reached under the bed. His fingers groped around, but found nothing. He then stretched out on his belly and wriggled partway under the bed. He saw the chest, hidden in the shadows under the headboard, resting snugly against the wall. Squirming over to it, he clasped his hands on both ends of the wooden frame and see-sawed it out. Fortunately, it wasn't very heavy.

Ernest scrambled into a sitting position and hurriedly snapped up the brass lock cover. Then, after working up the two end fasteners, he tried to lift the lid.

It was locked.

Ernest bared his teeth and growled, "Damn!"

He knew there had to be a key somewhere. But where would Purdue keep it? Ernest stood up and his eyes scoured the room. No key or key set on either the dresser or the headboard. Ernest checked the two sliding end panels of the headboard. A few ancient paperbacks and a disemboweled transistor radio, but that was all. He moved over to the dresser and scavenged through all six drawers. Mismatched socks and dirty underwear!

Where would that old fool keep the key?

Shit-damn, Ernest thought, maybe it was somewhere on Purdue; maybe in one of his pockets.

Luckily, Purdue looked to be even deeper in his coma. Ernest released a slow, raspy breath, then leaned over Purdue's chair. Slowly… steadily, he slid his fingers into the shirt pocket. Carefully felt around. Empty.

He was going to have to check the pockets of his trousers… and hopefully do so without arousing the man from his slumber.

Ernest couldn't afford to take that chance, however. There was only one sure way to keep him from waking up.

Again he got up, this time going into the bathroom to hunt for a towel. He found a moderately thick one and wrapped it tightly around his beverage mug, sliding his fingers through the exposed handle. He stepped back over to Purdue; paused to wipe off the perspiration that had begun to bead on his brow. He then raised the mug up over his head… and brought it down squarely on Purdue's crew cut. It hit with a *thump*, and the old man sighed and slumped farther down into his chair.

Ernest muttered an apology, and after a quick check to make sure he hadn't hit him too hard and that Purdue was still breathing, he grabbed the old man by the shoulders and laid him out flat on the floor.

In the first pocket he checked—a ring containing four keys!

Ernest immediately recognized the room key, so he flipped that one over. The chest key would be a small one, and there was only one tiny key on the ring. Ernest crossed his fingers.

He scurried back into the bedroom and got down hard on his knees. He was nervous and fumbled getting the key inside the lock. But it fit! He turned it… and the lock opened with a satisfying click.

Ernest pushed up the lid.

Lying atop a collection of well-preserved smut magazines was the weapon: a .45 caliber Smith & Wesson revolver with a clean, high luster blue finish and a sturdy walnut grip. He gazed at the gun with awe—as if it were some priceless museum piece. A true cowboy pistol; John Wayne would be proud, Ernest thought with momentary levity. He lifted it gingerly from the chest, holding it with almost the delicacy a father would his newborn baby. He then hefted the gun in his hand; it was heavier than he would have imagined. The fingers of his left hand lightly skated over the barrel. Maybe it was odd but he couldn't deny feeling a sudden surge of power.

He continued to hold it until he was completely comfortable with its feel. Then he carefully placed the pistol beside him on the floor and hunted through the chest hoping to find ammunition.

As he did this, his body suddenly erupted in sweat.

No, it couldn't be happening. Not now… Not when he was so close!

The *thing* was there again, beginning to gnaw at the inside of his head.

Gritting his teeth, Ernest tried to fight it off—at least until he was finished with what he had to do. He couldn't afford to surrender to the pain. He shuffled the magazines and trinkets with greater urgency.

His vision started to blur from its growing intensity.

"Not yet, dammit" he said through clenched jaws. "Not yet!"

He found himself losing control of his hands. Fingers pulsing, he fumbled erratically through the chest.

His shaking hand jarred a small cardboard box and he heard a muffled rattle inside. Somehow he managed to grasp the box and withdraw it. He opened it—

It was filled with about a dozen .45 caliber bullets.

Ernest shook out five and dropped the box back into the chest. Slamming down the lid and relocking it, he kicked the chest back under the bed.

He pulled to his feet and staggered out, clutching his head in agony, dropping the key ring to the floor…

* * *

Two hours later, Ernest awoke to find himself stretched across the bed in his own room. His pain was gone.

But he had no memory of how he'd gotten there.

26 Waiting At the School

MONDAY.

Ernest was up before sunrise: 5:13 to be exact. It was going to be one of those cold pre-winter days. Cloudy. There was a good possibility of rain. Perhaps even an early snowfall.

On this late October morning Ernest did something unusual; he ate breakfast. And a fair-sized one at that. Starting with four slices of stove-burnt toast, he then wolfed down two fried-into-scrambled eggs and a couple of strips of rubbery bacon, washing his meal down with a cup of something tasting remotely like coffee.

For most of the morning Ernest wandered undirected around his hotel room, trying not to give thought to what lay ahead.

Soon it was noon. Then going on for one. Still a heavy, billowing overcast.

At one-thirty, Ernest reached into the cupboard and withdrew the revolver, already loaded with the five bullets. He carried it over to the bed and carefully concealed the weapon in his old yellow sweater. He wrapped his own frame in the only decent piece of clothing he owned, a khaki hunting coat; soiled, a touch too large, but warm for the day which awaited him. Ernest's last stop was at the toilet. He walked a straight line to it. Clutching at both sides of the sink, he gazed intensely at his reflection in the mirror. For minutes he remained like this, his expression firm, determined, never changing; his eyes never wandering.

And when he finally did turn away and start for the door, it was with quick, determined steps.

* * *

The bus glided effortlessly over the first of the two bridges that separated the pulse of the city from the northeastern residential area. Ernest sat where he usually did, in a bench seat at the back of the bus, on the same side as the driver, glancing out on his wide view of old Rivercrest Cemetery before quickly averting his eyes from the fence-enclosed burial grounds.

His 'package' remained on his knees, with both his hands folded protectively over it. His mind was placid; a kind of numbness had come with commitment. Even his previous night's slumber had been undisturbed. He had thought about his mission just once after bedding down, but as quickly as the visions of what might lay ahead flashed to life, they flickered out. Strangely, he remembered only one of the most relaxed sleeps he'd ever had.

The only real sign of any apprehension was a torturous cigarette craving. And he'd crushed one out just before stepping onto the bus not five minutes before boarding it.

He was nearing his stop. He reached up and tugged twice on the bell cord, got to his feet and moved the aisle to the side exit door. He stood with one hand hooked around the overhead bar as he waited for the bus to come to his stop; his other hand was pressing the sweater and its concealed contents tightly against his belly.

After he stepped off (a block and a half from the school, he was no stranger to the distance), Ernest found his way to an alley that opened across from the school's hardtop. A high, straight-boarded fence blocked any schoolyard view of him. At the same time, he would have to move out several exposing feet to get a clear view of the hardtop. And, for a man who had never held, let alone fired a gun before, this was a significant distance… especially considering all the other kids who would be swarming around outside, youthful bodies in motion: running, jumping, playing.

All at once, Ernest found his original plan fouling up, badly in need of an immediate overhaul. He didn't know the exact time, but recess, his planned *execution* time had to be nearing.

He had only two choices: either he'd have to chance taking a shot from where he was, risk hitting another child, or missing altogether; or he'd have to take an even greater gamble and position himself directly outside the wire fence, where hopefully he could get a direct bead on the girl, and then, in full view of witnesses, in a quick yet accurate move, pull out the gun and—

But he hadn't prepared for any action like that. He had planned on taking slow, careful aim, ensuring that his bullet would hit its mark. Of course chancing to be seen, perhaps later described…

He still hoped this move could be done from a concealed location.

A short time later, while Ernest was still struggling with his decision, the children of Reuben Willis Elementary were let out for afternoon recess.

* * *

Maureen found herself close to tears as she responded to Lawrence's voice on the other end of the telephone.

"Dead?" she said disbelievingly. "How can that be? He was supposed to come over this week and see Krissie."

Even Lawrence, usually cynical, sounded subdued. "Yeah, I know it's a hell of a shock. I've gotta admit I never much cared for the guy—well, more what he represented, the whole psychiatry business, I suppose. But when I overheard Bud Turner this morning—he lives in the building where Kinbrace had his office... Y'know, he tells me the police are saying it wasn't an accident; that it likely was deliberate."

"Are you saying it was murder?" Maureen said in a gasp. "But—who would want to kill Dr. Kinbrace?"

"I dunno," Lawrence sighed. "But I guess when you consider the types of people shrinks deal with it doesn't seem too surprising that some dislocated psyche might try to knock him off."

"I don't know what I'm gonna do now," Maureen said numbly. "I was depending on Dr. Kinbrace so much."

"Look," Lawrence said impatiently, "before you go taking the high dive, why don't you count on me a little more?"

Maureen went silent. Even though Lawrence had just provided her with the opportunity to unburden so much of what she had kept locked inside, she realized that—especially now with Dr. Kinbrace gone—she needed Lawrence to work with her—not against her.

"Just tell me what's been happening?" Lawrence said.

Maureen inhaled a rattled breath. "Lawrence," she said softly, "This—*thing* with Krissie... it's getting more out of control every day. This weekend was another bad experience with her..."

"Wait a minute," Lawrence snapped. "When I talked with you on Friday you said that she seemed to be doing better."

"Yes, it did seem that way…up until dinner," Maureen said. "But just like *that* she changed again. She spent most of the weekend up in her room. I guess that in itself really isn't so unusual—"

"Not unusual?" Lawrence interjected.

Maureen ignored his interruption and continued. "But what was frightening were all the noises I heard coming from in there. And…at times it was as if she was talking to someone."

"That's ridiculous."

Lawrence could hear Maureen match a cigarette on the other end.

"I know. It sounds crazy but it's what I heard. I didn't want to go into the room and I haven't really had the chance to talk to Krissie since. I'm…just glad I could get her to go to school today."

"Christ, that is just bloody great." The abrupt change in Lawrence's tone rendered Maureen speechless. "Your daughter shut up in her room and you just don't give a damn to check in on her."

Maureen pulled the receiver away from her ear. Her nerves already frayed, she was prepared to slam it down into its cradle. But she didn't. She waited until her own anger subsided and then brought the receiver back to her lips.

She spoke with forced calm. "She just wanted to be left alone. That's all she seems to want lately: to be by herself."

"Yeah." Lawrence's tone remained biting. "And that behavior sits well with you…"

"Behavior? You've only had a small dose of what it's been like with Krissie."

"You're the guardian," Lawrence said hotly. "I'm just the sometimes daddy."

Lawrence's words sparked a defensive reaction in Maureen. He was going for the easy way out again, not wanting to acknowledge the seriousness of the situation.

Why doesn't he try living with this for a while, see how much better he deals with it?

This time she did slam down the receiver.

* * *

The last of the children re-entered the school. Ernest remained at his vantage point, watching with inexpressive eyes. The double doors closed and classes resumed for the remainder of the afternoon.

It could have all been over now, but Ernest never saw the girl.

She might have been somewhere on the hardtop, playing among the other children, but Ernest's distance—plus the realization that his eyes were no longer as sharp as they once had been—had prevented him from picking her out.

This proved to him that, like it or not, he couldn't chance firing his weapon from any great distance. He would have to somehow be within mere feet from her when he pulled the trigger. He couldn't forget that he would only be given one chance... all or nothing.

There was plenty of time left before classes would be dismissed for the day. Ernest remembered a little coffee shop only a few blocks away. Although he couldn't deny craving something a bit more potent, coffee had to be all he could allow himself. He picked up his 'package' which was lying next to him on a grass patch beside the fence, and trudged off.

Coffee had never tasted so good to him. Certainly not anything he had ever brewed. Ernest was nursing his second cup, smoking about his fourth cigarette. He kept both eyes on the wall clock just above the grease-smudged window to the kitchen. It was now a quarter past three. He'd have to finish this cup and then start back to the school.

This little break had been beneficial. A whole new strategy had developed over the past thirty-five minutes. It was by no means flawless, but it was a plan with certain advantages.

* * *

Maureen's conversation with Lawrence had necessitated a few calming drinks. Anger, mixed with the realization that she was more helpless now than she'd been since this nightmare started, prompted another couple of quick shots. She didn't intend to get drunk that afternoon, but her mood sped up both the intake and the effects of the alcohol.

Helpless, maybe. But she knew she wasn't entirely without hope.

She sat in the living room eyeing the telephone, debating whether she should call the Landsbrook Clinic to confirm Dr. Kinbrace's arrangements. She knew she would have to; she didn't know the day Krissie was scheduled to go in for her examination.

But she was hesitant. Her doubts had started up again. Was this really the answer? Or was Lawrence right: Would they just subject Krissie to a series of possibly painful tests and release her, unable to offer any solutions, and maybe even worsening the situation?

Maureen knew what she must do, and also why she resisted.

She actually hated Kinbrace a little, for dying on her. She had relied on him, yes, but realized that her dependence went even deeper than she'd thought. At times it almost seemed as if she'd expected him to take charge of things she might at one time have asked Lawrence to handle. Now she was back to square one… with one disturbing difference: Her daughter had become dangerously unpredictable. The fact hadn't eluded Maureen that since all this trouble began three people close to Krissie had died unexpectedly and tragically. It was her daughter's reaction—and *how* she might respond—when she learned about going to the clinic that filled Maureen with such trepidation.

She was embarrassed to admit it… but she had become afraid of her own child.

Yet, fears aside, she knew it had to be done.

What other choice did she really have?

Maureen reached for the telephone book and flipped through the pages. Her finger traced the listings.

Langevin… Lane…

Landsbrook Clinic

Aware that she wasn't completely sober, Maureen hesitated before reaching for the receiver, trying to clear the haze from her brain to decide what she was going to say.

She dialed the number, slowly. A few rings before the line was answered.

"Landsbrook Clinic, one moment please."

"No, I've gotta talk to someone now," Maureen said with hurried impatience.

The receptionist, however, had already put her on hold.

A moment later: "Sorry to keep you waiting. May I help you?"

"Damn," Maureen mumbled. "You don't know how important this is…"

"Pardon me, ma'am?"

"I, uh—" Maureen found herself at a momentary loss.

"Yes, hello. Is there something I can help you with?" the receptionist said again.

"Dr. Kinbrace…I believe he called last week about having my daughter—admitted to the clinic."

"May I have your name please?"

"My—my daughter's name is Krissie Carver. She's supposed…"

"Just a minute please, ma'am, and I'll check."

"No," Maureen snapped, "I have to tell you now!"

Shortly, the receptionist came back on the line.

"I'm sorry, ma'am, but I can't find your daughter's name on my admitting list…or anything about arrangements being made by Dr. Kinbrace."

"He called last week!" Maureen practically shouted into the receiver. "He made all the arrangements."

"I'm sorry, but I have—"

"Don't be sorry, just check again. He said he'd call."

"I'll have to put you on hold again, ma'am."

Maureen's hand trembled as she clutched at her drink. She took a swallow, and then the glass slipped out of her hand and fell onto the carpet. She let it lay there, the liquor spreading and seeping into the fabric.

"Yes, may I help you?" This time it was a male voice on the other end.

"Who are you?" Maureen asked.

"I'm Dr. Bryant King. The receptionist tells me that there seems to be a bit of a mix-up."

"No, there's no mix-up," Maureen said with stubborn determination. "Dr. Kinbrace…he made arrangements last week for my daughter to be admitted to your clinic. Now they're trying to tell me they don't know anything about this."

Dr. King spoke gently. "Are you aware, ma'am, that Dr. Kinbrace died last week?"

"Of course I'm aware of... I..." Maureen's voice trailed off.

"Ma'am, are you still there?"

Maureen felt defeated. Everybody was working against her. She just couldn't do anymore.

"It doesn't matter," she mumbled into the receiver, and then she let it drop.

"Hello?"

"It doesn't matter..."

* * *

At three-thirty, just as the first throng of children spilled out of the school, Ernest returned to the tall fence across the street. He stepped out into the open, his 'package' held securely in both hands. He scanned the children carefully—this time he had to spot her! He wasn't even aware that, in trying to get a more exact view, he was steadily moving farther from his preferred position, beginning to inch across the road. By the time he finally realized what he was doing, he was already standing on the same side as the school. He was too close! If the little girl came out now and happened just to glance in his direction, she'd be sure to spot him. Recognize him. And that could have devastating consequences—for him.

Dammit Ernest, just what in hell are you thinking?

But rather than re-crossing the street, Ernest remained where he was, fighting to loosen up from the tenseness he was feeling.

And he kept watching.

The other children still in the schoolyard seemed to dissolve into the background as soon as Ernest saw (as clearly as if he were standing right beside her) the little white-haired girl come out onto the school steps. She was wearing a blue mohair sweater and a pleated skirt. Her hair, unusually snowy today, almost luminous (even in the dismal gray), cascaded delicately over her shoulders and flowed down her back. Such a pretty child, Ernest thought... and for that moment he had to push from his mind what he intended to do.

Instead, he wore a smile.

The girl never once looked in his direction. Her head was held upright, eyes riveted only on what was directly in front of her.

She walked out of the school grounds. Alone.

She turned onto the sidewalk.

Ernest shook a cigarette out of his pack and lit it. He waited until she was a good distance ahead, and then he followed after her.

It wasn't the easiest walk for him. The girl strolled at a frustratingly leisurely pace. It was difficult for Ernest to maintain an inconspicuous distance.

But she never once looked back to notice him. He couldn't help considering that maybe she did know she was being followed, but was waiting for the right moment to confront him.

On the last couple of blocks, Ernest crossed to the other side of the street. Since he figured the girl must soon turn up the walkway to one of these houses, she could easily pass a casual glance in his direction. Ernest wasn't so far behind that she wouldn't recognize him.

The girl finally followed a curving path onto the lawn of a corner duplex. Ernest kept a tight watch on her as she hopped up the steps to the front door.

He narrowed his eyes and saw a woman watching from the front window, looking to wear a strained smile at the little girl's approach.

Ernest studied the house, carefully.

He would be back.

27 The Alpha Traveler

"SIT WITH ME," Adamm commanded.

Krissie slid her arms into his open hands. He gripped them tightly at the elbows and leveled her down with him into their cross-legged sitting positions.

The skies around the hill were a swirling gray, with occasional deep crimson tendrils creeping upward—like slowly bleeding scratches—from just above the horizon. A sudden harsh wind cut a path through Krissie's hair, just as it brushed back the grass into sweeping waves. Krissie shivered from the uncommon cold. The unadorned Adamm seemed oblivious to the chill in the air.

"You are aware that my time has come?" Adamm said.

"Yes, I knew it would be tonight," Krissie answered.

"You are prepared?"

Krissie replied with a nod.

"You are prepared?" Adamm repeated, more severely.

"Yes." Krissie's hands closed around his forearms.

Adamm said: "Proceed."

* * *

With startling abruptness, the picture snapped to vivid life:

There stands the little white-haired girl, rigid in the corner of an unfurnished black room, staring with intense purpose at the opposite corner. Soon, a hazy shape begins to materialize in that corner—tiny cosmic molecules, emitting a brilliant red glow, slowly and evenly fusing together, gaining strength. The girl continues to use her energies to project this three-dimensional form, which is beginning to take on a semblance of... almost human shape! Deep runnels begin to etch into the girl's face. Physically she is emptying herself. This becomes even more horribly apparent when the flannel nightgown she has been wearing begins to fold in on itself, lazily falling into a creamy pool on the floor. Deep, echoing laughter emanates from the other side of the room...

Ernest couldn't even begin to imagine what horror now existed in that dark corner of the room...

But none of this had been real. It was only a bizarre phantasm that had swept through the desperate man's mind.

Or was it?

Maybe it was more. A terrifying premonition perhaps... of what was soon about to happen?

Ernest was still blocks from the house. Nightfall had arrived, the streets were dark and he was walking with brisk steps—only now hoping he wasn't too late.

Gradually he broke into a short run.

He was crossing an intersection, now not too far from his destination, when seemingly from out of nowhere appeared a tall man in a black business suit... his eyes hidden behind a large pair of sunglasses.

Ernest gazed at the man and was instantly receptive to a dark presence. He felt his nerves grow taut but tried to avoid exhibiting any fear.

"Hey, look," Ernest muttered, "I got somewhere I gotta get to."

The stranger remained directly in front of him, staring silently, no expression on his face.

"Look, now I—I don't want no trouble," Ernest sputtered, tightening his hold on the sweater concealing the gun.

At that moment the stranger's hands clamped around Ernest's arms.

"Hey, leggo!" Ernest shouted, and, maneuvering with all of his muscle, managed to wriggle free. He backed away, reaching inside his rolled-up sweater for the gun.

"You're crazy, you sonofabitch!"

The stranger lunged at him. Ernest, reacting instinctively, dropped his 'package' and swung his fist wildly. It connected with the man's face. The sunglasses fell to the cement, but the man remained standing, unaffected by the blow.

Ernest look up at the face—

"Oh holy God…"

The man who again grabbed Ernest by the arms had features that were normal—except for eyes that were a solid black, like coal embedded into the sockets.

Ernest stared terror-stricken into those eyes as he was lifted effortlessly off the ground by the stranger's powerful grip and carried onto the road.

"The book!" Ernest gasped with the horror of sudden realization. "The two who… The *protectors*…!"

And the black Lincoln sped forward, spewing blue clouds of exhaust. It had been lying in wait, shielded by the night, not many yards from Ernest, who was trapped in a vise-like grip, dead center in the intersection, perfectly illuminated in the white pool of light from the corner street lights.

Ernest, at once accepting that he was a dead man, just parted his lips and mouthed: "No."

The man, still void of expression, then effortlessly tossed Ernest straight into the path of the speeding car. From that second on, Ernest's thoughts tumbled hazily. He was only vaguely aware of the impact hurling his body over the roof of the Lincoln... of his body slamming onto the concrete.

The Lincoln, half a block away, worked on a tight U-turn. Ernest's thoughts cleared. At first he couldn't see the car, but his hearing, suddenly unnaturally acute, picked up the unmistakable sound of its motor. All at once he realized that the Lincoln was starting back toward him.

The gun...

Where was the gun?

Lying spread-eagled on the road, Ernest craned his neck to the left, then to the right. The revolver, exposed, was lying several feet from the curb. He could never reach it in time...

And the Lincoln was racing back in his direction, intending to finish the job!

Finish him!

Ernest knew he had only once chance—

He had to call upon his power.

Could he...

He closed his eyes and concentrated. Oblivious to the pain from his injury, he focused all his thoughts on the Lincoln almost upon him... he mentally envisioned the black-suited *thing* standing watchfully on the curb...

(*NOW!*)

FLEX...

And in that instant, the thing on the curb was suddenly thrust upward and somersaulted through the air... its body twisting toward the Lincoln... landing on the hood with impact, its head smashing bloodily through the windshield.

Then the car itself careened away from Ernest... speeding away from him... before suddenly erupting into flames, becoming a fireball, continuing its rolling descent into the hell from whence it came.

Ernest managed to crawl to the side of the road. He clutched at the curb with both hands and clambered to a standing position. For a moment he swayed; struggled to refocus his vision. He didn't know how badly he'd been hurt, but he couldn't deny that his injury was serious. With effort he managed to reach down for the revolver. He rewrapped it in his sweater and held the whole bundle against his belly.

Instinctively, he accepted that he was dying. But he also had a vague understanding of how that was how it had to be. There was no other way this could end... he only hoped that he had the strength to complete his mission; he was now working against time with a distinct disadvantage.

The activity had begun to draw people out of their homes.

Ernest slipped away toward the back lane.

* * *

Their arms remained locked together, their bodies convulsing with surges of violent energy.

"Concentrate!" Adamm's resounding voice commanded the girl.

His fingers pressed deeply into Krissie's forearms. Unknown to the girl, claws had started to emerge from where his fingernails grew.

"Bring me with you!" he howled.

Krissie focused her will yet harder… despite the pain he was inflicting upon her. She could feel deep wounds opening and warm trickles start to run down her arms to her hands.

Adamm laughed manically as he watched the blood streak her arms.

The swirling gray skies had deepened to charcoal black. They thundered.

"The moment is at hand!" Adamm shouted…

* * *

Ernest had to push himself up the walkway to the duplex, coughing as he breathed, each time nearly doubling over from the pain in his gut. He noticed that the sweater he'd held against his belly was bloody; there was a gaping tear in his stomach. Before he started up the steps to the house, he threw the sweater into the shrubbery and struggled off with his coat. He draped it over his arm to conceal both his wound and the gun gripped in his hand. Painfully, he worked his way up each of the steps. Only several step, but he might have been climbing a hill.

Once at the door, he forced himself to regain his posture and stand upright. He tried to erase all signs of anguish from his face. He rapped his knuckles on the glass of the outer door.

Shortly, the porch light flashed on, giving him a momentary start. He quickly wiped his eyes with the back of his hand.

Seconds later, the inside door snapped open and Maureen Carver peered out.

"Yes?" she asked, cautiously.

Ernest inched closer to the door, his hand stealthily sliding over to the outer handle. He cleared his throat; he could taste blood. He swallowed, grimaced.

"Uh, I—I hope ya'll forgive me for callin' so late, missus," he rasped, swallowing again. "But is yer husband home?"

Maureen immediately responded with suspicion. She started to shut the door—

When Ernest instantly pulled open the outer door and charged inside. Before Maureen could react, Ernest reversed the gun and clubbed her twice over the back of the head with the butt. She tumbled limply into the open coat closet.

Ernest closed the inside door and fell back heavily against it. His coat slipped from his weakening grip and landed at his feet. He kicked it aside.

He looked down regretfully at the woman lying sprawled on the floor. He had hit her harder than he'd intended—her head lay in a widening pool of blood. Ernest couldn't tell whether or not she was still breathing, and there wasn't time to check.

Blood was again rising up in his throat. This time Ernest didn't bother swallowing it down. He opened his mouth and released it, letting it sluice down his chin, droplets falling onto the carpet. His eyes were beginning to roll back. He felt he was about to pass out…

"No!" He pushed away from the wall and, reeling, moved deeper into the house.

He quickly glanced about… but he followed his instinct and headed straight up the stairs, grasping the banister for needed support.

He reached the second floor. The door on the left was closed. But Ernest knew this was *her* room.

He staggered down the hallway and halted outside the door. Then—he turned the knob and stumbled into the room, bracing his body against the door.

The bedside lamp was on, casting the only light in an otherwise darkened room. But this faint yellow glow only added to the overall horror of the scene he soon was to discover.

The little white-haired girl, naked, sat cross-legged on her bed, facing away from the door.

Ernest stepped over to the opposite side of the bed—and his eyes widened in disbelief.

The girl's cranium was swelling!

Like some kind of grotesque balloon: slowly and rhythmically expanding… then contracting… expanding… contracting…

Ernest could not suppress his cry of revulsion.

* * *

"It is time!" Adamm thundered triumphantly.

Krissie felt an enormous flow of energy pass from her body. Excited, she popped open her eyes… and caught full view of the *horror* she was willing back with her.

The creature sitting in front of her, still grasping her arms, no longer resembled Adamm. It was more hideous than any of the monsters trapped outside the *wall*. The smooth body had become scaly and slime coated, a sickening grayish-green color from which its exposed circulatory system protruded, with the veins and arteries pulsing spasmodically. Its head had become drawn, with the eyes shrinking into reptilian slits—no longer that warm blue that Krissie had found so comforting, but an intense fiery red. Where the nose had been there was now only a mucous-discharging snout. The tongue that lashed out of its fanged mouth was long and bifurcated. From its cavernous mouth was discharged a prolonged hissing.

Krissie's bulging eyes traveled down to her outstretched arms. Adamm's hands had become thick, lizard-like claws, and she saw with horror that her flesh had been ripped to bloody tatters.

Krissie wanted to get away. This... *thing* wasn't her friend. She began to struggle, but it was impossible to get free of its grip. She felt that if she could just pull herself free it would all be over.

She wanted to go home.

Suddenly, inexplicably, the air was filled with the mournful howling of the creatures in the mist.

Krissie glanced up at the Adamm-*thing* with eyes that were pleading.

"You feared the guardians," it hissed, its serpent tongue lashing out at her. "Indeed, they would never have harmed you... they served only one purpose... to keep you away from me... They knew what you could do for me... Your innocence convinced you that you were willing back a companion... Instead you have released the greatest threat mankind has ever known!... So trusting, child... so... so..."

As the fiend before Krissie began to fade, it laughed demoniacally...

* * *

Krissie's eyes flashed open: they had become like flaming coals. Blazing! Ernest watched with incredulity as they flared just briefly before both eyeballs liquefied out of their sockets, leaving only two black hollows.

A slow vertical fissure opened in Krissie's forehead, making soft snapping noises as it cracked the skull. It lengthened, zig-zagging down the bridge of her nose... to her upper jaw. The torn skin separated and twisted, folding over to each side, slowly, like wax melting in the hot afternoon sun. The neck snapped and the broken skull sagged forward…

A pulsating gray sack erupted, out of which a thick, clear fluid pumped and flowed… soon masking the skull in a syrupy veil.

And from this sac emerged a tiny hand. A tiny clawed hand, its fingers flexing before gripping one side of the skull for leverage. Then the other hand surfaced and it raised half of its body out of the cavity. Its chest was heaving erratically, the breaths that escaped little more than gurgles, as if emanating from water congested lungs. Its bottom jaw hung open lazily, releasing milky saliva. Its reptilian bifurcated tongue lashed about wildly.

The foul-smelling fluid mostly obscured its form, but Ernest could still determine its horrendous appearance. He was braced against the bedroom wall. The gun was clasped between both hands. Slowly, he raised his arms in front of him, until they were at chest level. The barrel of the revolver was trained on the creature's midsection.

Suddenly, he felt a strong suffocating tug against his throat and he was thrust backward. Someone was grabbing him from behind.

"You sonofobitch!" a voice he did not recognize screamed at him.

The stranglehold was tightening. Ernest was unable to turn his head to see who was attacking him with such violent force. He twisted and struggled against the suffocating grasp but was unable to put up much resistance.

"You killed Maureen… and now you want to kill my daughter!"

Daughter…

And in the next instant, Ernest heard a gasp… the arm locked around his neck relaxed its tension.

Ernest didn't wait. He took advantage of the moment. He swung around, stared only briefly into the horror-struck features, and instinctively pulled the trigger of the revolver.

A single shot—and Lawrence Carver, who'd had just a second to connect with the horrible transformation that was occurring to his daughter Krissie, crumpled to the floor with a bullet in his chest, the fatal wound blossoming red.

Ernest didn't have time to consider what he'd done. Almost immediately, before he could again take aim on the abomination that was emerging from the shell of the little girl, he felt his arms turn traitor. They were twisting, turning the barrel back toward him. Ernest tensed his wrists, tried to struggle, but the deep black hole kept turning implacably toward his face. He lifted his eyes until his gaze connected with the cold, penetrating stare of that hideous thing. Eyes that attempted to bore into his very being, to one final time exert its otherworldly influence over him.

Ernest struggled against its control, forcing his will to become stronger than that of this supernatural entity. This hideous *freak*! He made himself remember how he had been the pawn of this monster, its psychic will compelling him to do its evil bidding. How his life had been destroyed by its influence…

It now had to end!

"No!" The panic was alive in Ernest's sweaty face; not the fear that comes with approaching death—that was inevitable; he had already accepted his fate. What filled him with such dread was coming this close, sacrificing all, just to lose.

Ernest determined he wasn't going to lose. He thought about Danny, and of something the old man had said just before he died:

That the voice had spoken to him… *but that he had defeated it*!

Danny had managed to overcome its power. He'd conquered its manipulation…

Ernest found his opening. He channeled all of his remaining and now intensified mental energies into redirecting his aim.

"Fuck you, you ugly bastard!" he exploded… and the gun was working its way back toward the creature!

The *thing* howled, exerting more of its sinister will.

Ernest could feel its psychic claws ripping away chunks of his brain.

But by this time the pistol was aimed dead-on at the creature.

And he fired!

The bullet's impact was powerful and the creature was literally blown in half. An almost unbearable squealing filled the room as its viscera-spewing torso flew onto the floor and scattered onto the other side of the bed.

Then there was only quiet.

With a look of pity, Ernest gazed at the broken shell that was all that remained of the little girl. Her body was seated upright on the bed, still cross-legged, rigid. Fluid continued to trickle out of the sac.

But was it really over? The years of physical and mental torture; the brutal acts he had been made to do; the tragedy brought to this family? At that, he turned and gazed at the dead man lying on the floor, glazed eyes still wide, a reflection of that final moment of life when his last vision was of the horror that had overtaken his daughter.

Her father, Ernest thought with sorrow and regret…

He determined to destroy every last vestige of the monster's existence. Finding his last ounces of strength, he pushed his way across the room.

The creature's torso, barely visible in the shadows, was lying face up in a widening pool of its escaping life fluid. Both arms were raised, wide-spread fingers locked in an empty grasp.

The face was twisted, frozen in a rictus of defeated hate.

In the few brief seconds Ernest stared at it, a thousand thoughts—a thousand remembrances—passed through his mind.

And then he squeezed the trigger, releasing the remaining three bullets, watching with vindictive satisfaction as the physical remains of the creature dissolved into a pile of gore.

After the last shot had been fired, Ernest let the gun drop from his fingers.

He smiled once, before he collapsed to the floor.

He had done it.

His last moments were neither painful nor troubled by fear of what awaited him on the Other Side. They were filled with a glow; a warmth, a peace he could never before have imagined.

A peace born of accomplishment.

Through the vastness of the cosmos spoke a disembodied voice:

Fools, dare you hope to have destroyed that which is the essence? I have lived throughout eternity. I have waited through the earth centuries… and once more I will wait… for the next arrival of the child of light. My time shall come again. My wrath will be terrible to behold. The prophecy of my re-birth has yet to be fulfilled…

Yet, soon shall be the hour…

THE END

www.ingramcontent.com/pod-product-compliance
Lightning Source LLC
Chambersburg PA
CBHW050125030726
47505CB00007B/2043